DRAGGING IT OUT

The First Book In The Drag Queen Detective Series

By
Brian Johnson

Published in the United Kingdom by
Brian Johnson 2018

Copyright © Brian Johnson 2018

All rights reserved. No part of this publication may
be reproduced in any form or by any means - graphic,
electronic, mechanical, photocopying, recording, taping
or information storage and retrieval systems - without the
prior permission in writing of the publishers

Brian Johnson has asserted his right under the Copyright,
Designs and Patents Act, 1988 to be identified as the
author of this work.

The publishers make no representation, express or implied,
with regard to the accuracy of the information contained
in this book and cannot accept any legal responsibility for
any errors or omissions that may take place.

ISBN: 978-1-907900-04-4

For my husband Mark

One

'An envelope with a black border? I wonder what that could be,' asked Peter as he peeled off one of his big curly eyelashes and plopped it into a small tray on his dressing table.

'I don't know but you'd better get home as soon as you can. It looks important,' said Bill as Peter removed the other eyelash and lined it up next to the first one and then snapped closed the little case.

'Barry's just stripping me down now. I'll be as quick as I can dear. Love you.'

Peter flipped the top half of his mobile phone down and it snapped closed with a clunk. He squinted as he looked in the mirror above the dressing table.

Its surface was littered with makeup, eyebrow pencils and little bottles of glitter. Some gold, some silver and some green – Peter's favourite colour. He looked at the figure before him, with its long, flowing white wig and enormous bosom. He chuckled to himself and leant closer to the mirror so he could see what he was doing. He wiped away the thick makeup that made him who he was on stage and slowly revealed the man beneath the dress.

He could hear the voice of the singer now on stage. She was singing one of Tammy Wynette's songs, Stand by Your Man. Peter listened for a moment and hummed along to the song and swung his head from side to side as he undid the clips that held his wig in place. Behind him he heard a knock at the door and then it opened ajar slightly.

'Great performance, Peter, Great!' said Barry as he slipped in through the small gap left by the poster-covered door. 'The audience loved you tonight,' he said, helping Peter off with his dress and putting it onto a wide coat hanger before slipping a plastic cover over it and hanging it on the back of the door.

'Ah, my adoring fans,' said Peter as he cocked his leg up onto the dresser and undid the clips of his suspenders, rolling the stockings along his hairy legs. Barry collected them as they were peeled away and carefully folded them and packed them away.

'Give us a hand to get me tits off dear,' said Peter as he undid the hook on the back of the prosthetic bosom he was wearing.

Barry, without thinking twice about it, cupped a hand under each of the heavy rubber breasts and supported them as Peter lifted it clear of his hairy shoulders and packed it away in its case.

Barry fingered the imitation diamond necklace Peter had put into its box and spread it out straight as he admired it. 'If this was real, it would be worth a fortune,' said Barry. Peter, tying the bootlaces of his Doc Martins', looked up and smiled.

'If they were real, my dear, I wouldn't be playing in a shit-hole like this!' Barry grinned and continued to pack away Peter's things and made sure the room was ready for the next act. 'Right my darling. I think we're all done,' said Peter, giving the room the once-over to make sure nothing had been overlooked. 'Best get home or hubby will be worried.'

They pulled the stiff door behind them and Barry, remembering something, turned and trotted back down the filthy corridor and unstuck the paper sign that had been taped on the front of the door. He read it: 'Dolly Parton'. Barry scrunched up the paper and threw it in the corner where he was sure it wouldn't be noticed amongst the other rubbish piled up there. He sang the words to Peter's last song, Jolene, as he rushed to catch up with his uncle Peter.

It was a narrow corridor and Peter went first. At the end, by the fire exit were a couple of young men. One was kneeling in front of the other and Peter knew what they were up to. They didn't stop as Peter approached but the man on his knees continued with his task. The man standing noticed Peter getting closer but simply smiled.

Peter pushed on the heavy fire door and manhandled his baggage past the two men. He couldn't help himself; he just had to look down as he passed. 'My. That looks like a mouthful,' he said just as Barry arrived and pushed him through the door and out into the car park.

***

Bill was in the kitchen when Peter and Barry returned. He was expecting them and he had already got their tea ready. He stood in front of the cooker, wearing his little piny, stretched across his wide belly and when he heard the door he knew that was his cue to take the plates out of the oven. He bent over and, using a terry-towelling tea cloth, he retrieved the hot plates from the warm oven and placed them on the table he had prepared for their return.

Barry swung his bags down on to the sofa and came thorough to the kitchen. He noticed the fish and chips Bill had laid out for them. Barry licked his lips and looked in the kitchen cupboard for some tomato ketchup. Bill noticed and told him it was on the table already.

Peter kissed Bill and hugged him gently. 'It's nice to be home dear,' he said as he hugged Bill closer and rubbed his back. Bill pulled away and, indicating at the table, told Peter to sit. He poured him out some strong tea – just the way he liked it and Peter looked at the portion of chips on his plate.

It was the size of a small hillock, thought Peter. 'My god!' he said, 'Are you trying to get me fat?' Barry looked at them greedily and Peter spotted his attention. He scraped some of the chips onto Barry's plate and it made him grin.

'Cheers uncle Peter,' he said as he squirted extra ketchup over the new addition to his plate.

'So how was the venue tonight?' asked Bill as he pulled off his piny and joined them at the table. Peter rolled his eyes dramatically and Bill knew what that meant.

'The crowd was good but the facilities...Puh!' sputtered Peter. 'I wouldn't let a dog use their gents and the dressing room...' Peter pointed to Barry with his knife. 'You saw it Barry. You can tell him, it wasn't fit for a star of my stature.' He spread out his arms like Marilyn Monroe and they all laughed.

Bill remembered something and he suddenly stood up and retrieved an envelope from the sideboard. 'Here,' he said placing it gently by Peter's plate, as if able to sense it wasn't something good. 'It was put through the door when you were out.' Peter looked at the envelope.

It was thick and quite square, with a solid black border around its four edges. It looked like a card of some sort. Peter was bemused. It wasn't anyone's birthday or anniversary and he was curious why someone had sent him a card. On the front of the envelope was the single word, Peter, written in blue ink in a nervous hand.

Peter wiped his knife on the side of his plate and used it to slice along the edge of the stiff paper envelope. You could tell it was quality paper by the crisp sound it made as the knife cut through it. He slid out the card, expecting some garish, colourful scene but no; the card was a simple design with a black border. The cover simply said Joe Trolley 1944-2010. Peter looked at the words and he recognised the name. He looked across at Bill who was curious to know what the card was for. Bill could see that Peter was upset.

Peter opened the card and read the contents: Joe Trolley died on the 17th of October 2010. He will be missed by all. His funeral will be held on the 25th of October at 11:30AM at St Andrew's Church, Lowfield. As a good friend of Joe, you are invited to attend.

It was signed by Agnes. Peter placed the card down on the table and stared at it in disbelief. Bill could sense something was wrong and he squeezed Peter's hand and waited for him to tell him in his own time. Peter sensed the squeeze and it brought him round and he turned and looked at Bill. 'Joe's dead,' he said.

Barry stopped eating mid chip and placed his knife and fork down, not sure what he was meant to do in this sort of situation. He had never experienced a death before and decided it would be best if he just sat and listened quietly.

Bill stood up and placed his arm around Peter's shoulder. He nuzzled into his neck and said, 'Sorry... I'll get you a drink.' He went to the kitchen and came back with a small tray with a bottle of Peter's favourite tipple and three glasses.

Barry looked confused. He didn't know who Joe was and couldn't recall there being a Joe in the family. He looked at Peter. He hadn't seen him look so out of sorts like this before. He wondered if he should get up and give him a hug. After all, he was his uncle Pete and if he was feeling sad at the loss of someone he loved then it was his duty to be there for him and comfort him. He was just about to get up and go over to kiss his uncle when Peter took in a big, dramatic deep breath and said, 'Ah! Life's a bitch... and then you die, as they say.'

Peter folded the card and pushed it under his plate. He looked up at Barry and noticed the concern on his face and he thought his puzzled expression deserved a response. 'Joe was my ex,' he said as Bill poured him a drink into the small tumbler sitting on the tray. 'We were together for almost ten years, before...' Peter took Bill's arm and rubbed his elbow. 'Before Joe decided he needed a younger model.' He smiled at his Bill and he smiled back in his gentle, cuddly way.

Barry sat and listened. He had always known his uncle was gay. He had lived with his aunty Bill for all of Barry's life and they were like his parents now. His own mum and dad found it difficult to deal with the fact that Barry was also gay and it was agreed in the family that it would be best if he lived with his uncle and his partner; to be brought up in an understanding and accepting environment. Barry didn't mind. He loved his uncle and aunty and he couldn't think of a better place to be brought up in.

Bill sat back in his seat and squeezed Peter's hand again. 'I wonder what he died of. He wasn't that old, was he?' Peter shook his head.

'No... He must have been about 66, I think.' He paused and a smile came to his face. 'Eeeh! I remember how Joe had an eye for the younger ones. He would always point them out in the crowd, saying things like, 'Oooh! Isn't he gorgeous!' and 'Oooh! Look at the arse on him!' Peter rolled backwards in his seat, laughing. 'He never had the decorum to lower his voice or keep it to himself – he was bold as brass.' Peter saddened and his head dropped.

Bill knew they were very close and he knew how distraught Peter was when he found out that Joe had been seeing a younger man behind his back for over a year. That was it for Peter and he left him. He just packed up his things and left.

Bill nodded, 'Yes. That was his Achilles Heel.' He noticed Barry's bemused expression and clarified. 'He liked younger men and once they were no longer young, he replaced them with someone younger.' He put his hand on Peter's again and said, 'No offence, dear.'

Peter tapped his hand and kissed Bill on the cheek. 'Don't be daft. I know where I'm better off and that's here, with you my dear.' He kissed him again and Barry grinned. He was pleased to see his uncle Peter feeling back to his old self. He liked the loving, gentle relationship his adopted parents had and he hoped, one day he could find a similar relationship of his own.

Peter helped Barry clear away the tea things and Barry filled the sink with hot, soapy water. 'I wonder what he died of,' pondered Peter as he wiped the dishes passed to him by Barry. 'He always kept himself fit and trim – He knew he had to if he was going to interest younger men.' He flicked the switch to the kettle and finished the last plate as he waited for it to boil. 'And poor Agnes, she must be devastated. They were very close, you know,' he said, stirring the tea bags in the big white pot. He looked at Barry. 'She was his sister and a good friend of mine too... I wonder if I should give her a call.' He raised his hand to his chin and leant slightly to one side in his usual camp posture.

Bill took the tray with the tea and said, 'You'll be seeing her at the funeral on Friday. You can speak to her then.' Peter nodded, still lost in memories of his time with Joe. He folded the tea towel and hung it over the oven door to dry.

They settled in the living room and Peter put his feet up on the big padded footrest and slumped dramatically into the sofa. Bill sat next to him and poured his tea. Barry always sat in the same seat. He liked it because it gave him the best view of the TV and TV was a big part of his life.

He loved watching his soaps. He knew all of the characters and often wished that he could be an actor on TV or a performer on stage, like his uncle Peter. He loved the idea of standing in front of a crowd of fans, all loving him and watching him perform. He attended all of his uncle's performances and he always sat in the audience and watched the crowd's reaction. He thought his uncle looked so glamorous in his Dolly Parton dress and wig. He wanted to be up there on that stage, with his fans, cheering as he sung the, now memorised, songs of Dolly.

Peter slumped back into his seat. Bill read his paper and Barry watched his TV. Peter wasn't aware of what was on; his mind was still thinking about the loss of his friend.

He had spoken to Agnes about a month ago, when he had bumped in to her at the library. He was returning his Agatha Christy and picking up the next on his list when he spotted her getting her books stamped. He had chatted to her in the cafe and caught up with what was going on in each of their lives. She had told him that Joe had been seeing a new man; a much younger man this time. She said he was in his early twenties and she thought it a bit sad that her older brother should be messing about with youngsters at his time of life and she wished he'd settle down and find a partner his own age.

Bill thought back to his time with Joe. They had been happy at first. Peter was still young and fresh when he met Joe. Their first few years were full of passion and love and Peter thought he had found the man he would spend the rest of his life with. But as things went on, Peter noticed the passion faded and Joe's interest in other, younger, fresher men developed. It was just the odd comment at first; just the odd look but it soon became an obsession with Joe. He eyed every young man he met and Peter often felt uncomfortable being around him when there was a young, pretty boy he could see or talk to.

In the end, it became too much for Peter. He wanted a long term, loving relationship and he needed security. He needed someone he could trust and love him for the rest of his life.

When he was a young man, he had many boyfriends. He experimented with sex and alcohol, trying the many experiences of live available to a young, free gay man. But he soon became disillusioned with the gay scene, the empty promises and the bitchiness, which was part of that lifestyle. He wanted to settle down.

He looked over at Bill reading his newspaper. His balding crown glowed in the dim light of the room and his greying hair hung around this circle of skin like a Franciscan monk's. He didn't care. He loved Bill. He was the kindest, gentlest man he had ever met and above all else he trusted him with his life. They had been together for nearly twenty five years and he knew he had found the man he would spend the rest of his life with. He leant over and kissed him on the cheek.

Bill, deep in the article he was reading, looked up. He smiled, 'What was that for?' he asked.

'Because I love you,' said Peter.

Two

Barry looked smart in his suit. He wasn't used to wearing such formal clothing and he had never been to a funeral before, so he just did as he was told and kept in the background. Peter looked in the mirror as he tied his black tie. He hated ties and never normally wore them. Bill saw him struggle and he stood behind him and did the tie up for Peter. Sensing Peter's nervousness, he squeezed his shoulders and told him it would be okay.

Peter raised his foot and stood on one leg as he ran his finger around the top of his socks, ensuring they were straight. He had chosen to wear his shocking pink socks today – his lucky socks he thought. Bill noticed and thought about whether he should mention that they may be a little bit camp for a funeral. Peter knew what Bill was thinking, he knew him so well.

'I think Joe would appreciate it,' he said as he balanced on one leg. 'I'm sure everyone there will be dressed in drab colours so, if Joe's up there watching, he'll see my socks and have a giggle to himself.' Bill knew that Joe was once part of the drag queen circuit and he was almost as flamboyant as Peter, so he saw Peter's point.

Barry paused, wondering if he needed to use the loo before they left but seeing his uncle and aunt in their formal attire ready to leave he decided he could wait. He smiled and held the door open for them.

***

It was a cold morning and the autumn wind had a definite chill to it. The funeral procession arrived at the graveside just as the leaves that had been piled up to one side decided to find a new home for themselves. They blew in swirls and Peter covered his face, now wishing he had brought a scarf.

The priest, in his long, flowing robes looked cold and hurriedly began his speech. His long gown fluttered in the breeze and Peter could see he was an old man and suffering in the autumn air.

Peter looked at the small crowd that gathered around the grave. He knew a few of them. There was Agnes, Joe's sister and her husband. A couple of their children and several of Joe's friends Peter knew from the bars. They looked odd. Peter knew that a couple of them were transvestites and he could see how uncomfortable they looked in their suits and shirts.

To the left of Agnes stood a tall, thin and extremely handsome young man; his dark hair hung in a heavy bow across his perfect brow and his slender cheeks were flushed with the coolness of the breeze. Peter admired his figure. This must be the boyfriend, he thought as he watched the young man throw his handful of dirt in to the grave and walk away.

Barry shuffled in his new shoes, bought especially for the occasion. He needed to pee and wished he had gone before they had left. He looked at his uncle, knowing that he had no choice but to hold it and he hoped that was the end of the funeral. As people began to walk away from the grave, he felt relieved that it was over and looked to his uncle for advice. 'I need to go,' he said, shuffling in his stance again. Peter knew what he wanted and pointed him to the door to the side of the church, where he knew Barry would find a gents' toilet.

Barry was just finishing up when he heard a voice of someone talking on a mobile phone. He flushed the toilet and hesitated as the voice grew louder.

'Yeah. That's the old bugger put to bed now.' The voice said as Barry was about to unlock the door. He heard the man laugh and respond to a question the caller asked, 'That's right. We should get the money by the end of the week and once the house is sold, we'll be sorted.'

Barry opened the door and headed for the exit. He turned to see who the man on the phone was and recognised him from the funeral guests. It was the tall handsome young man, that he had noticed Peter watching.

***

The reception was a small affair. Agnes had booked the church hall, so they didn't have far to go. Peter took a drink from the table, laden with all manner of bottles. He passed one to Bill and noticed Barry returning so he asked him what he wanted.

Barry didn't drink, so he pulled a can of coke from a six pack at the back of the table and flicked its ring. Peter heard the pop and sizzle as the fizzy gas escaped and thought the can, with its garish branding, looked disrespectful, so he handed Barry a glass and told him to empty his can into it.

Peter looked around the room. He was surprised that there were so few people there. He looked but he couldn't see the young man anywhere. He knew that Joe was a popular man and had many fans in his hay-day on the stage. Peter thought it was a shame that such a colourful life should end in such a drab church hall. He was now glad that he had worn his pink socks.

Agnes came over and Peter hugged her, giving her a soft kiss on her cheek. 'Really sorry for you loss, my dear' he said and Bill touched her on the arm and nodded in agreement. She nodded. She was becoming used to the words.

'Thanks,' she said as she sipped her sherry. Peter could sense she was more than just upset at the loss of her brother; he could tell there was something else. He touched her arm and asked her if she was okay. He watched as her eyes filled with tears and he pulled her close, giving her the support she needed. She stepped back a little and said, 'Peter. I really need to talk with you.' She looked around the room, nervous about what she was about to say. She pulled Peter into a corner, next to the table where Barry and Bill were picking at the buffet, deciding which quiche looked the best. Bill noticed Agnes's move and came over to join the conversation.

'I don't know what to do,' said Agnes. She looked over her shoulder and checked before she continued. 'I think that Greg character may have murdered Joe!' Peter stepped back, not believing what he was hearing. He looked around the room to see if anyone else had heard the statement but no one seemed to have. He looked into Agnes's eyes. They were full of grief and at the same time, full of determination. Peter held her by the elbow,

'What on earth do you mean,' he said, hushing his voice in

the echoing chamber of the room. Bill stood aghast, his mouth dropped, filled with quiche. Peter noticed and gently pushed closed his chin before resuming his conversation. 'Agnes. What makes you think such a thing?'

She sipped on her sherry and began her tale. 'Joe met this Greg character about two months ago. I never liked him from the start. He was just a kid of twenty or something but... you know Joe, he always went for the young and pretty ones.' She checked around the room again. 'Well,' she said. 'I've been doing a bit of cleaning for Joe these last few years and I've seen what's been going on. That young Greg fellow started flirting with Joe and promising him all sorts of things. And of course, Joe loved it. He loved all the attention this pretty young thing was giving him so he started buying him expensive presents.' She went on to tell Peter about the new car, the expensive watch and other barbells he had bestowed on his young lover.

'I tried to talk to Joe and to tell him he was being a fool and this young thug was using him. Of course, he wouldn't have any of it. He told me to go and he didn't want me to do any more cleaning for him. I was very worried about him. I know he's a bit of a sad old queen but he was my little brother and I didn't want to see him get hurt.'

Peter pulled her towards him and hugged her. He knew she was very fond of her brother and she had put up with his lustful antics for many years. He knew that she had a heart of gold and didn't like to see all those young men take advantage of Joe. He held her by the shoulders and asked her,

'Yes. We all know Joe was a bit of a tart but what makes you think this Greg killed him?' He waited as she gathered her thoughts, being careful to recount them as accurately as she could.

'I got a letter a few days ago from Joe's solicitor. It said that Joe had made a new will and that she was no longer the sole beneficiary of his estate.' She relaxed a little and Peter could feel her shoulders slump. 'I don't care about the money,' she said. 'But it's not like Joe to go and do something like that. That house was passed on to him when our mother died and we had always agreed that it would go on to me in the event of Joe's death. Joe wanted it to stay in the family and, not having any kids of his own, he wanted our Shane and Lucy to inherit it after he'd gone.'

Peter listened quietly and nodded. He remembered the agreement. He remembered Joe talking to him about it when Peter had raised the subject of making a will. He knew that Joe was adamant about his house going to his niece and nephew. So he understood why Agnes was so confused. He noticed Barry out of the corner of his eye. He was trying to get his attention but didn't feel confident enough to make his presence known.

'Peter,' said Barry, spotting a gap in their conversation and nodding him over to his side. 'I've got something to tell you.' Peter nodded and waited but Barry thought he best to tell him in private, not knowing how it might affect the old lady, Agnes. He pulled Peter by the arm, who thought it was rather rude to leave Agnes mid conversation.

'Watch the suit!' said Peter as he brushed back the weave of the fabric on the sleeve of his only suite. 'What is it?'

'That man,' said Barry excitedly. 'The twink at the funeral... you know Joe's boyfriend?' Peter nodded, still not sure if this conversation was worth his best suit being tugged at. 'I overheard him on the phone in the gents. I heard him talking about how Joe's been put to bed and they should be getting the money soon and something about selling a house.' Barry panted, his chest rising and falling as he tried to calm himself down.

Peter looked at him in awe. 'Are you sure?' he said, rubbing his chin like he always did when he was thinking about something. Peter pulled Barry to one side, not caring if he tugged on his sleeve. 'Here,' he said, 'Now tell me, word-for-word, what the man said.' Barry looked at his own sleeve and frowned but then composed himself and thought about the conversation he had overheard.

'I was just about to leave when I heard this man come in talking on his mobile.' He said, Barry paused and slowed down. 'That's the old bugger put to bed now and we should get the money by the end of the week, and once the house is sold, we'll be sorted.'

Peter looked at him and rubbed his chin some more. 'And do you know who he was talking to?' Barry shook his head and said,

'I think they were friends. They were joking and the twink seemed in a very good mood.' Peter thought it rather odd to be in such a good mood at your partner's funeral.

Peter and Barry returned to the buffet to find Bill spooning himself a portion of cheesecake. Peter knew Bill loved cheesecake and he was famous for making his own. Bill noticed their return and quickly came over to see what the fuss was about. Agnes, also noticing the three men congregating, joined them to find out if the interruption to her story was justified.

She looked at Peter and she could see something was up. Peter noticed her concern and said, 'Agnes, I don't know if your suspicions are justified but I think they might need to be looked into by the police.' Agnes raised her hand as if to stop his train of thought.

'I've already told them but they say I'm just being paranoid.' She looked over her shoulder again and noticed the young man, Greg, had come in to the room and was, half-heartedly, trying to mix with the strangers there. 'They said that Greg was on holiday in Brighton when Joe died, so he obviously had nothing to do with it. Anyway, they said, the family GP was there at the time of death and it was recorded on the death certificate as natural causes, so that was the end of it.'

'What about the will being changed?' asked Bill, gently pressing into the slice of cheesecake with his plastic fork. 'They must have thought that suspicious.' Agnes nodded and continued,

'They said it was unusual but they had spoken to the solicitor and he confirmed it was a genuine, legal will and they had to accept that.' Bill nodded, his mouth still full of cheesecake. Agnes pulled on Peter's arm,

'Please Peter. You have to help me prove that I'm right. I won't be able to settle until I know what's what.' Peter took her hand and smiled at her. What could he do? He thought. He wasn't the police; he didn't know how to go about finding out things like this.

Three

Bill was sleeping next to him and Peter could hear his contented purr. Peter, wearing his full-length flannel nightie, tried to read his book but he just couldn't get the day's events out of his head. He looked down at the cover of the book and ran his fingers across the gold-foiled letters. He wondered how Poirot would deal with such a mystery.

He had read a lot of the Poirot stories and liked the little Belgium character. He liked how his mind worked; He liked how the smallest of details is all it took him to figure out who the murderer was. I'm not Poirot, thought Peter as he put the paperback onto his bedside table. He was about to settle down and turn off the bedside light when he thought about it for a second.

First he would have to establish the facts that he already knew. Peter sat up, being careful not to wake Bill and he pulled out a spiral-topped notepad he used for working out his crosswords on and he flipped over the cover and found a new clean page.

He thought about what Agnes had said and he made a list: 1. Joe's dead. Peter looked at what he had written and quickly scratched it out. It was obvious that Joe was dead, he thought. He needed facts relevant to the crime. Peter thought about the word crime and he smirked. He was actually sitting in bed, trying to figure out a murder?

Joe died of 'natural causes'

What happened?

Will changed before his death.

Everything now goes to Greg.

Greg away on holiday at time of death.

Where was he?

Peter's mind was blank. He couldn't remember what else was there was. He put his pad down and sighed. Maybe he was not to be the next great detective. He giggled and imagined himself on the Orient Express, gathering the characters of the story into the dining cart, ready to unfold his convoluted findings and finally reveal the murderer. He would, of course be in full drag, with his Dolly Parton wig and prosthetic bosom swinging before him. He laughed and Bill stirred but did not wake. Peter put away the pad, turned off his light and lay in the dark. He giggled some more at the scene playing through in his head and then put his arm around Bill and snuggled in.

***

Barry was ironing one of Peter's dresses when he came down the next morning and Bill was sitting at the dining table writing out Christmas cards.

'Oh, you are a dear,' said Peter, smiling at Barry and giving Bill a kiss on the crown of his head, as he headed for the front door. He wrapped his nightie around himself tighter, feeling the draft from under the front door as he picked up the paper from the mat.

Barry was wearing nothing more than a pair of boxer shorts and a vest. 'You must be freezing,' said Peter as he looked at the thermostat on the wall and turned it up a notch.

'Not really,' said Barry, swinging out the newly-ironed dress and holding it up against his thin and wiry frame. 'Do you think I'd look good in this?'

Peter looked at the skinny, pale boy and then at the dress, made especially for him by his friend Philippe. The dress was at least two sizes too big for Barry but Peter knew he wanted to follow his uncle into the glamorous world of show business, so he just said. 'Maybe that style isn't quite right for you. And maybe you need something more your size.'

Barry looked at the dress and agreed. He held it up against himself one more time and then hooked the clothes hanger on the back of the door whilst he ironed himself a clean T-shirt and pair of jeans.

Bill sealed another envelope. 'We're going to need more stamps. I didn't know we knew that many people. Ah well! The price I have to pay for being married to a celebrity.'

Peter looked over his paper and blew Bill a kiss. He looked at the local paper. There was nothing in it of interest but then he thought for a moment. He wondered if there might have been something in about Joe's death, with him being a local celebrity. Bill and he were away at Blackpool on the week that Joe was supposed to have died, so if there was any mention in the local press, they wouldn't have seen it.

Peter looked over at Barry as he pulled on his jeans. 'How would we get to see papers for during the time of Joe's death,' he asked and Barry looked up at such a strange question. He hesitated and then said,

'We could try the newspaper office – they might keep back issues, or you could do a search online.' Peter hadn't thought about using the Internet. He wasn't very techno-with-it, as he called it and the Internet was just one of those things that he didn't have much interest in. Barry noticed his bemusement at the suggestion and he offered to look it up for him.

Peter had forgotten the date that Joe had actually died but then he remembered the card on the sideboard and quickly checked it. 'He died on the seventeenth of October but you had better look for a week after that.' Barry nodded and scooted off up to his room.

Bill came in from the back garden. He had some washing in a basket and complained that he'd forgotten about it and had left it on the line overnight. It was stiff with the cold and he carefully laid it out on the wooden clothes horse which stood permanently in the corner of the warm kitchen, shaking his head at his poor memory. Peter thought about going upstairs and getting ready when Barry returned with a piece of paper in his hand.

Peter looked at him, surprised that he was able to find out anything in such a small amount of time.

'Anything?' asked Peter, expecting nothing. Barry handed him a printout of an article written about Joe. Peter's face lit up as he read the article. It was nice that someone had done this. The piece had the title: 'Joe, Dragged it out until the end' It detailed his career, his success on the stage and his later success on local TV as a comedy drag queen with his own talk show. 'Ah! That's nice.' He said, 'Although it doesn't help us much does it?'

Bill looked confused and Barry shared his expression. 'I've been thinking about what Agnes said to us and I think, as his friend, I owe it to him to find out if this Greg guy really did take him for a ride and kill him for his money.' The two onlookers sat and stared at Peter. They could see the determination in Peter's eyes and they knew from experience that when he got something in his head like this, there was no stopping him.

Bill and Barry came and sat at the table with Peter. 'What can we do about it?' said Bill, straightening the tablecloth and ironing it flat with the palm of his hand. 'I mean... the police have looked into it and they came up with nothing, so what more can we do?' Barry shuffled in his seat. He was excited at the thought of working alongside his uncle to solve a mystery.

Peter sat back in his chair, played with the frilly collar of his nightie and stroked his whiskered chin as he thought. He really didn't have a clue where to start but then it hit him. 'I suppose the obvious place to start is to see if Joe left anything that might give us more information.' He looked at the other two and at their vacant expressions. 'Maybe we should see if we can have a look around Joe's place and see if there is anything that might give a clue as to where to start.'

Barry smiled and said, 'Like a blood stain on the carpet or a footprint in the flower beds?' Peter looked at him. He was excited, like a small child looking forward to a trip to the pantomime. Bill stood up and started clearing away the cups.

'Well I think we should just leave it. We haven't got a clue what we are doing and it's just silly to think that we could find out something that the police couldn't,' he said, placing three fingers into three cups and lifting them onto his small tray. Peter stood up and wrapped his nightie tight across his hairy chest and said,

'Well, if not for Joe's sake then at least let's do it for Agnes.' He watched as Bill put the cups on the counter and paused as he remembered the tears in Agnes's eyes and her distress at the thought of what this young man may have done. Bill dropped his head and turned back to Peter.

'Yes, your right. We have to at least try and put poor Agnes's mind to rest.'

***

Agnes seemed more cheery. She was pleased that Peter had decided to help her. She put her key in the lock of the big white panelled door and she ushered Peter and Barry in. They felt nervous being in someone else's house after they had died. 'What about the boyfriend?' asked Peter as he closed the door behind him. Agnes slipped her set of keys back into her long coat's pocket and replied with a sweep of her hand,

'Oh! He works at the estate agents on Osborne Road. I saw him in there when I passed on the bus, so I know he won't be back until gone six.' She patted her pocket and continued, 'I'm pleased I kept a set of keys.'

She showed them around the large Victorian house. Peter remembered living there for several years and he remembered the convenience of being able to walk into town when he wanted but at the same time being far enough away from the city and sheltered by the mature trees that dominated this part of Jesmond, to feel he was safe. He remembered the snobby neighbours, the stuck-up students and the arrogance of the Mercedes drivers. He didn't miss it. He liked his simply but homely life with Bill.

'Where do you want to start?' asked Agnes as she noticed how untidy the place was and how dirty the marble floor was in the hall. She tutted as she ran her finger along the dado rail that ran the length of the hallway. Peter didn't really know where to start but he new Joe had a study and that is where he was most likely to leave anything important. He suggested this to Agnes and she agreed.

The wide, heavy door of the study was locked and Agnes didn't have a key. Damn, thought Peter and he was about to leave it and go upstairs when Barry slipped in between them and opened his wallet. 'What you doing?' asked Peter, keen to look around before the boyfriend got back. Barry pulled out his library card and slipped it in between the door and its frame. He wiggled it and slid it down and to Peter's amazement, the door popped open, silently and without force.

Barry turned and grinned, carefully slipping his card back into his wallet. 'I saw it done in a film once and I've always wanted to try it.' He pushed open the door and stepped aside to let his uncle enter. Peter grinned at his little cat-burglar nephew and entered the room.

It was just as Peter had remembered it. The walls were littered with photos of Joe in drag, shaking hands with celebrities and images of him on stage. There was a big open fire place, with a real marble surround and to either side of that where rows of costumes and a whole shelf devoted to nothing but wigs. Peter felt faint. To be in the presence of such beautiful dresses and ooh the wigs, he thought. Peter hovered over in the corner looking at the dresses and stroking the roughness of the wiry wigs. He wanted to try them on. He knew Joe was about the same build as him, so he knew they should fit. He picked up a long, following ball gown and held it against his chest. He looked in the full-length mirror Joe had positioned in the corner of the room and he swished the dress to and fro against his legs, admiring himself.

He looked in the mirror and noticed the two standing behind him. Barry's face was alight with joy and Peter could sense he too wanted him to try on the dresses but he noticed Agnes's expression and then he remembered why he was there.

'I had planned to give you all of Joe's dresses and wigs,' said Agnes. Peter froze, as if startled by some headlights and then jumped with an excited camp leap and clasped the dress he was still holding to his chest and hugged it, giving out a squeak of anticipation. 'But, as they now belong to Greg, I can't do that, I'm afraid.' Peter's heart sank. He looked at the beautiful, sequin-covered dress he was holding and sighed. If there was ever a bigger incentive to solve this puzzle, then Peter couldn't think of one. He stared at the dresses, mesmerised by their lure and then, reluctantly, hung it back on its rack and turned to look at the big wooden desk that sat by the French windows.

The sun was gleaming through them and the desk looked as it must have done on the day of Joe's death. It looked like nothing had been touched. There was still a coffee cup, a quarter full, sitting there. The pen Joe always wrote with lay on its side with its gold nib exposed to the air.

Peter knew that Joe had a habit of always putting the cap back on his pen when he'd finished using it, so Peter thought it odd that it had been left like this, knowing the tip would dry out. Peter fingered the papers on the desk. It looked like Joe was in the middle of writing a letter to someone. Peter had always had problems reading Joe's handwriting and as he had got older his writing had deteriorated along with his body.

Peter skimmed the letter but didn't think it relevant. He sat in Joe's seat. It was a big, warm leather chair with comfortable arm rests and castors that allowed him to glide around easily under the desk. He pulled open some of the drawers, not really knowing what he was looking for and he flicked through books and files.

In the top drawer there was an almost full sheet of crisp, new first class stamps, some letter-headed stationary and a bundle of envelopes with Joe's address professionally printed on the back flap. He remembered how Joe loved writing letters and he was always very conscientious about writing to thank people when they did something for him. He was a bit behind the times and still preferred a simply thank you letter to a phone call – he felt it was more personal.

Peter looked in the second drawer and he recognised the logo of Joe's bank and pulled out a pile of bank statements, loosely held together by a tired-looking paper clip.

Peter glanced down the columns of figures. He had no idea that Joe was so well off. He knew he had done well on the drag circuit and he knew how to market himself well but looking at the strings of large figures on the statement, he was surprised. He looked at the dates and noticed that his balance had steadily reduced over the period of the last few months. There had been regular withdrawals in cash almost on a daily basis. Peter wondered if that was the work of the boyfriend, Greg.

He had forgotten that Agnes and Barry were still there and he told Barry to have a quick look around the house and see if anything looks out of place or unusual. Barry nodded and left Agnes watching Peter as he sat at her brother's desk and rubbed his chin. 'What do you think?' asked Agnes, realising that Peter hadn't seemed to find anything of importance.

Peter looked up, not really knowing what to say to her. 'Well, looking at his bank statements, I can see that someone has made regular cash withdrawals everyday for the last couple of months.'

Agnes butted in,

'That'll be that Greg... Thieving Bas...' Peter stopped her mid curse. He didn't like swearing and thought it even worse when coming from the mouth of such a sweet old lady as Agnes.

He was about to leave when he remembered the pile of Christmas cards Bill was busy getting ready to send. He quickly opened up the top drawer and slipped the sheet of postage stamps into his pocket. After all, Joe had no further use for them, he thought.

He decided that there was nothing more the room had to offer so he headed for the door and gripped its big brass door knob. He wondered if Greg would notice that it had been opened and he was relieved to hear the lock click as it closed and he tried the knob again just to be sure it was locked.

They heard Barry upstairs. He popped his head over the polished banister and asked them to come up. He'd found something. Peter offered his hand to Agnes and helped her to climb the long, winding staircase, with its black, cast-iron railings and its quality carpet, held snugly in place by strong brass grippers at each side.

'Here,' said Barry as he handed Peter a crumpled padded envelope he had retrieved from the waste paper basket by the side of Joe's grand bed. Peter wondered why Barry was giving him rubbish and he peeled the packaging open and spread it out so he could read the writing on its front.

It was written in blue ink, probably a biro, thought Peter. He stopped and thought for a moment. He was getting good at this detective malarkey – being able to recognise it was a biro that wrote the script was pretty smart of him, he thought. He grinned and looked at the words.

It was simply Joe's address and the envelope had a stamp in it top right corner. Peter looked at Barry as if to say, so? Barry recognised his uncle's confusion and he tapped the franking mark that obliterated the stamp.

Peter looked more closely. It was faint but the black smudge that covered the stamp said 'Brighton'. Peter couldn't see what was so important about it and he returned his gaze to Barry's excited face. 'I don't get it. It says Brighton, so what?' Barry jumped up and down on the spot and excitedly said,

'Don't you remember? That's where Greg was supposed to be on holiday!' Peter thought about it and couldn't quite see what Barry was getting at. He looked at the padded envelope again, hoping what Barry had recognised as being important would suddenly make itself clear to him as well.

Barry, frustrated with Peter's slow thinking, said. 'Don't you think it strange that Greg should send Joe a package from where he was on holiday? Wouldn't it just be easier to bring it back with him and give it to him in person?' Peter thought about it and Barry was right. Agnes butted in and said,

'What's any of this got to do with Joe being murdered?' Barry and Peter stopped in their thinking and looked at Agnes. She was finding the whole situation quite difficult and she was obviously getting frustrated at their lack of any real evidence to put Greg behind bars, where he belonged. Seeing that Peter hadn't made the connection yet, Barry thought he'd better take the stand.

'Don't you see? If Greg wanted to make sure he was miles away at the time Joe died, giving himself the perfect alibi, he'd have to think of some way of killing Joe by... sort of remote control!' Peter looked at Agnes and then at Barry. What on earth was he talking about, he thought.

Barry, gleaming with enthusiasm for his new role of sleuth continued. 'What if Greg planned it so that once he was firmly planted in his holiday resort and had got enough witnesses to confirm he was there, he sent Joe something in the post – maybe something he knew he liked and would eat – like a box of chocolates or something.'

Peter smiled at Barry. He felt proud of his nephew. He was a lot brighter than he had thought and he obviously took to this detective stuff a lot easier than Peter did. 'That's true,' said Peter, looking at the envelope once more. He held it up to the light and he could see the faint outline of where the package had been brushed against other things during its journey up north. The clear dirty mark of a box was visible and he showed it to Barry and Agnes against the light of the sash window that spread across the enormous bedroom.

'Look for something about the size of that and we might have found the murder weapon,' said Peter. All three of them searched the room, looking in drawers and in the many wardrobes and cupboards that lined the perimeter of the room. Peter heard Barry shout from the adjoining en-suite bathroom and Agnes and him rushed in to see what he had found.

Barry stood grinning, knowing his deductions had been confirmed and he pointed to a small box, which sat on the edge of the big, palatial bathtub. Peter stood behind Barry and gripped his shoulders, as if to say clever lad and looked over in awe at the box.

It was a rectangular, purple box the size of a paperback book and it was covered in gold-coloured writing. 'Turkish Delight' it said across the top and Peter looked at it, frightened, as if would explode if he touched it. Barry pulled out a pencil from his jacket and lifted the flap of the box. 'Fingerprints,' said Barry, as he raised the cover to reveal the half-eaten contents.

Peter counted twelve compartments and only five of them still contained the powder-covered jelly-like sweets. They looked tempting but he knew they were probably deadly. Barry pulled out a clear plastic bag and Peter wondered why he had brought such a thing.

Barry grinned and said he'd seen how the police bag up evidence on TV and he's thought it wise to bring a few just in case they needed it. Peter looked at Barry again and grinned at his clever nephew. He watched as Barry carefully manipulated the box and slid it into the plastic bag with the pencil. He zipped up the end of the bag and proudly handed it to Peter, 'Here, try it in the envelope.'

Peter did as he was told and slid the plastic-covered box inside the padded envelope. The dirty outline lined up exactly with the shape of the box and they all nodded and agreed that this was what Greg had sent Joe.

They retreated back to the bedroom and Peter looked at Joe's bedside table. On it he saw a neatly folded piece of paper. He read the contents and then realised that he might have destroyed further evidence by handling the piece of paper. He really wasn't used to this sort of thing and he wondered if he was cut out for such activities. He dropped it onto the bed and it lay there, open.

It was a letter from Greg, obviously sent with the box of sweets and it read: 'Just a little something I hope you will enjoy. I really miss you and hope you'll write and tell me if you liked my gift. Love and cuddles, Greg. xxx'

Peter pointed to Barry and said, 'Bag it up.' Barry grinned, nodded and proceeded to transfer the note into another bag. He looked at Agnes who was smiling and pleased that they had managed to find such damming evidence.

Agnes heard a noise and stepped towards the door. She listened and heard the front door open and two voices talking. She looked at Peter and he froze, hearing the voices getting louder as they came up the stairs. Peter panicked. What were they going to do? They were in somebody else's house without permission, rifling through their possessions. He looked around the room and noticed the large white wardrobes that were fitted along the full length of one of the walls. He quickly opened the two centre doors and waved Barry and Agnes across as the voices got closer. He pushed Agnes into the corner and Barry tripped and landed on his knees at the bottom of the walk-in wardrobe. Peter pulled the door behind him just as the two men came into the bedroom.

Peter held his breath. He could smell the clothes that hung around his neck and a hairy jacket tickled his cheek as he tried to remain calm and still. He sensed Barry kneeling between his feet and he gently held him on the shoulder, prompting him to remain as still as he could. He could see Agnes's eyes in the dim light of the wardrobe and he could sense her fear. He winked at her and he felt her terror soften.

'Oh! I see what you mean,' said one of the men. 'This must be one of our best yet.' Peter looked through the narrow gap between the doors and could make out two men in suits; both slim and trendy-looking. The other man, whose voice Peter now recognised as that of Greg said,

'Yeah! This was an easy one. We should easily get 400 thousand for this and that's not to mention what's in the bank.' Peter shuffled, feeling Barry trying to balance on his ankles beneath him. He felt Barry tumble and grab a hold of Peter's leg for support. 'Sorry,' he heard him whisper.

One of the men looked towards the wardrobe and Peter froze, fearing that he had heard Barry. He turned back to Greg and asked him about how the current client was coming along. 'Oh, this old bugger might be a tricky one. I'm just about at the stage of getting him to trust me but I think it might be another few months before he ready for taking.'

'Well, keep at it,' replied the second man. 'I've got to go. I've got another mark lined up just in case this one falls through and he's due at the surgery at three.'

'Oh! What's the score?' asked Greg, interested to know what his next job might be. The other man replied as he headed down the stairs,

'I think you like this one. He's in his eighties and he's loaded...'

Peter listened as they walked down the stairs together and laughed, slamming the big heavy door behind them. He now knew what they were up to and he felt sick to his stomach that they had done this to his friend Joe.

He opened the wardrobe doors and he felt Barry stumble out on to his knees. 'Sorry Uncle Peter,' he said as he stood up and straightened his jeans. Peter helped Agnes out and he could see that she was in shock. He hugged her and felt her frail body quiver against his. He pushed her away and looked into her eyes.

'We'll tell the police. That's it. We'll let them deal with those bast...' He realised what he was about to say and he checked himself. He hated swearing but he felt this was a time that it was justified. How could these men do what they were doing? How could such people sleep at night? He shook his head and sat on the edge of the bed.

'I'll take that box and the envelope and I'll tell them what we've just heard. Surely that is enough for them to open up the case again for further investigation.' Barry nodded and he held Agnes by the arm, giving her the support she needed.

Peter could see Agnes was still in shock and he agreed to take her home. He picked up the envelope containing the box and Barry indicated that he had the letter, in its plastic bag and they left.

Four

'But wouldn't it show up in the post-mortem?' asked Bill as he dished out a big ladle of homemade soup into each of their bowls. Peter looked across at Barry who slapped his forehead as he, like Peter, had forgotten the most obvious point. If Greg had poisoned Joe, it would have been detected when the post-mortem was carried out.

Barry looked depressed, annoyed that he hadn't thought about that; annoyed that he was not the expert sleuth he thought he was. Peter put his hand up to his chin and thought for a moment. He had read many detective stories where the murder had used some sort of chemical to poison his victim, knowing that it wouldn't be detected in the bloodstream later. He couldn't remember what the poison was and he had forgotten the gist of the story anyway.

'Umh!' said Peter, 'Probably. Although I do know there are some poisons that can't be detected in a standard autopsy.' Bill looked at him, surprised. He knew Peter liked to read Agatha Christie's and watch Colombo on TV but he had never realised that he had taken that much of it in.

Barry dipped his slice of bread into the soup and blew on it to let it cool. He looked up and asked Peter what they should do. 'Well, I think we don't know what we are really talking about, so I think we should still take it along to the police and let them check it out. At the very least I'm sure they will want to know what those two men are doing and maybe we can prevent some other poor soul being ripped off and, god knows what else!'

Barry cheered up. At the very least the work they had done that day would hopefully put two criminals behind bars. Something he was proud to be part of, he thought.

***

Peter straightened his jacket as he sat on the hard, plastic chair in the waiting room. He wondered whether the green fluorescent shirt and pink jacket he had decided to wear were quite right for this environment but he thought it was too late now.

He had been there almost half an hour and he was getting impatient. He had told the man on the desk that he needed to speak to the person in charge of the Joe Trolley case. At first he didn't know what he was talking about and when Peter explained about the death of his friend, the man typed something into his computer and said, 'Inspector McGarry,' was the name of the person who ran the initial investigation but he didn't know if he would see him as the case was closed.

Peter didn't want to reveal too much to the man on the counter, he wanted to make sure the right man got the message. Peter said he would wait and he plonked himself down on the chair, where he had been ever since.

It was an awful place, he thought. He had never been in a police station before and it wasn't a location he wanted to frequent on a regular basis. There was a definite smell in the air. Peter couldn't quite make it out but he knew it wasn't a good smell. In one corner sat a young boy, about seventeen with his mother. The boy looked like so many of his age. He wore the stereotypical stripped jumper and tracksuit bottoms with their ankles tucked into his white sports socks. His hat was perched on his skinny head, backwards of course and his shaven neck carried a multitude of tattoos.

Peter watched as his mother berated him, telling him he was an idiot and she expected he would be back in prison again if he didn't change his ways. Peter looked at the posters on the walls again. He had read them several times now but there was nothing else to look at. During his time there he had seen men being dragged in by police officers and taken through to the back and he had watched as people came and went but the time seemed to drag.

He looked at his nails. He knew he needed a manicure and he held out his hands so he could see his nails in the light better. He twisted his head and tried to imaging his nails with a nice shade of pink. He didn't notice the man standing opposite him looking at him with his mouth open. Peter dropped his hand and looked at the man.

'Mr Grills?' he asked, looking at a piece of paper the constable on the desk had given him. Peter nodded and stood up. The man looked him up and down, noticing his camp stance and his bright shirt and jacket. He indicated for Peter to come around the desk and to follow him into his office. The officer on the desk raised his eyes as Peter was ushered into the back office and the inspector smiled at the officer in acknowledgment.

Peter sat in the chair opposite Inspector McGarry and watched him as he looked for a folder on his desk. He was a strange looking man; the armpits of his shirt were damp and stained and his fingers were yellow with years of smoking. Peter looked at his face. It was broad and square-like. He balanced a bushy moustache across his top lip and his face carried at least a day's growth of beard.

'Right, hear it is,' said the man as he pulled out a buff folder from under some other papers. He flipped over the stiff cover and read out what it said, 'Joe Trolley, natural death 17th September 2010.' He looked up at Peter and said, 'So,' he looked at the piece of paper again to prompt his memory, 'Mr Grills, What's this all about. My desk sergeant tells me you need to discuss this man's death?' He flicked through the folder as he waited for Peter to respond.

Peter was nervous. He had never spoken to a police inspector before and he felt a bit of a fool now. He straightened his jacket and held his head up high. 'I have reason to believe that Joe Trolley was murdered.' He blurted it out and was relieved that it was now over.

The inspector looked at the file again and looked up at Peter, along his nose. 'It says on the death certificate, signed by his GP, who was present when the gentleman died, that it was death by natural causes.' He closed the file as if to indicate that was the end of it. Peter breathed in deeply and replied,

'Yes, I know but...' he couldn't think how to put it but he struggled on, 'Joe's sister, Agnes, asked me to looked into it for her.' The inspector sat up, interested,

'Ah! You in the same line of work? A private investigator?' He smiled a condescending smile and Peter frowned.

'Not really...Just a concerned friend.' He said, realising he was out of his depth and wished he hadn't come. 'No. Agnes said her brother was being conned out of his money and his house by this Greg character,' The inspector flipped open the file again and said,

'Greg Wilkes... his lover?' Peter nodded and continued,

'Well, when we were looking through Joe's things we found a note and a package', Peter rummaged in his big floppy bag and retrieved the parcel. He put it on the desk and the inspector went to pick it up. 'Careful,' said Peter, 'We think it might be poison.' The inspector paused and took the parcel carefully from Peters grip.

Peter went on to tell him how they had found the envelope and then the box of Turkish Delight and then the note and how they had arrived at the conclusion they had. Peter was out of breath and he needed a drink. The inspector offered him a glass of water and he gratefully accepted.

'Well,' said the inspector, 'It seems a bit unlikely.' Peter knew this was coming but he persevered.

'But aren't there some poisons that wouldn't show up in a post-mortem?' asked Peter, trying to behave as professionally as he could. He wafted his face with his hand to cool himself in the hot and sticky office. He realised he was being camp, so he restrained himself as the inspector noticed him doing it.

The inspector stood up and pointed Peter towards the door, 'There wasn't a post mortem. Not necessary when the person dies under the medical care of their own GP. He was with him when he died, so no suspicious circumstances, so no post-mortem.' He looked at Peter's blank expression and continued. 'I'll have the lab boys take a look at it anyway.' He indicated to the door and smiled at Peter. Peter wasn't finished, so he sat down and said,

'Wait. There's more.' The inspector raised his eyebrows and reluctantly resumed his seat. 'I haven't told you about the con men yet.' The inspector dropped the folder on to his desk, pushed his chair back against the wall and raised his hands behind his head.

'Con men?' he said, raising his eyebrows. Peter noticed the sweat stains of his shirt even more and the distinct smell of perspiration smacked him in the face. The inspector noticed him cover his mouth and he dropped his arms. 'Sorry, the heating is on the blink in this office and I can't get it to turn off.'

Peter told him about the conversation they had overhead whilst they hid in the wardrobe and the inspector listened carefully. Peter was pleased to finally get the whole story out and off his mind. Now he could rest and let the police take over. He grinned and slumped back in his chair.

'Well, yes, I suppose it could be interpreted that way... On the other hand, taking it out of context, they could have been talking about something completely different – maybe a property deal,' he flicked through the folder again and confirmed his memory was correct, 'After all Mr Wilkes is an estate agent I believe.'

Peter was confused. Had he not given the fellow enough evidence to at least drag them in for questioning? He watched as the inspector mulled over the statement and he waited for his findings.

'I'll look into it, Mr Grills. Is there a number I can contact you on if I need to speak to you again?' Peter, deflated and tired, wrote his home number on a piece of paper and passed it to the inspector.

Peter sat in his car and wondered if that was the end of it. Could he have got it wrong? Could they have been talking about a property deal? He didn't know. He had done what he could and it was up to the police now to follow up on his statement. He started the engine and thought about it some more. He couldn't let it go. He knew he was right and he knew he had to get justice for Agnes.

***

When he returned home, Barry was already laying out his kit for the evening. Peter had completely forgotten that he was performing tonight. He had just been too caught up in this investigation thingy, he thought. Barry looked up at him as he came in. He hadn't noticed Peter's tired demeanour; he was absorbed in his own work of preparing his uncle's costumes for the gig. 'Is it going to be Dolly or Karen, tonight?' asked Barry as he held up two different outfits.

Peter was too tired to care. He waved his hand and said, 'Whatever.' Barry looked at him, concerned for his uncle. He had never talked about his profession in such a casual way before. Barry laid the heavy dresses across the back of the sofa and pulled Peter in by the arm.

'Are you okay?' he asked in his gentle, caring voice. 'Hear, sit yourself down and I'll put the kettle on.' He lowered Peter down by the elbow, like he was an old man in his eighties and left him for the kitchen.

'How did it go with the police?' asked Barry from the kitchen. Peter wasn't sure how things had gone so he said nothing. Barry popped his head around the door, curious why there was no answer. Peter, exhausted, realising he needed to say something said,

'Oh. Not brilliantly.' Barry lowered the cup he was wiping with a tea-towel and waited for the next instalment. Peter continued, 'I don't think the inspector believed me and I don't think he'll do anything about it.'

Barry was surprised. 'What about the poisoned sweets – he must have taken that seriously?' said Barry as he returned to the kitchen and came out with a tray. Peter watched him as he placed two mugs and a small tea plate with a selection of biscuits on it in the middle of the coffee table.

He was a kind boy and Peter was very fond of him. He had his father's eyes and his mother's wiry frame. He often wished he had been able to have kids of his own but being gay and a drag queen, he didn't think his chances of adopting a child were very good. Anyway, he was too old now, he thought. He didn't have the energy to bring up a child. No, in many ways, he thought of Barry as his son and for now, he was happy with that.

'He said he 'Would have the lab boys take a look'', said Peter, mimicking the inspector's deep voice as he reached over in his tight pink jacket and picked up a custard cream. Barry grinned. He liked the sound of that – just the sort of thing the characters in his TV police dramas would say.

'So, they'll let us know what they find?' asked Barry, sipping on his mug of tea. Peter shrugged. He didn't know if he'd here anything more from the inspector. He was tired and he knew he needed to rest, otherwise he'd be no good for his performance later that night. He wondered if he was getting too old to be singing in gay clubs and dragging it out across the North East.

***

The Boulevard was one of Newcastle's quality gay cabaret clubs and Peter always enjoyed performing there. The staff were friendly and the crowds were always well behaved. He'd had his share of working men's clubs and the other cesspits he had worked in over the years. As he got older he felt he deserved better venues and Bill did his best to check out any new place before he accepted a booking with them.

Bill was his manager and he looked after the business side of things for Peter, leaving him free to concentrate on the creative stuff. Barry worked as part of the family business, taking care of Peter's many costumes and wigs and generally doing any running around that was required.

Peter was due on at eight and Barry had already got him dressed and was pinning his big white wig in place, as Peter did the last of his makeup. 'It's a full house,' said Barry, standing in front of Peter and checking the wig was sitting properly. Peter tapped his bottom and pushed him out of the way.

'Out of the way... I can't see the mirror,' said Peter. 'Really?' he continued as he drew on his eyebrows with his tick pencil. He knew that his performances were always popular with the local gay crowd and he was proud to have built up such a following. He smiled and Barry grinned, proud of his super-star uncle.

They heard a tap on the door. It was Bill. 'You're on in five minutes,' he said as he held the door open as wide as he could to allow Peter to get past the narrow doorway with his big dress. 'Good luck,' he said as Peter swished his skirts through the door and kissed Bill on the cheek.

'Thanks darlin'' he said and looked back at Barry as he picked up the tail-end of his dress and followed Peter to the stage wings. He listed to the announcer talking to the audience and warming them up for Peter's entrance. Barry was always nervous and he watched as Peter went through his pre-performance warm up, which consisted of him stretching the muscles in his face. With his heavily-made up face and enormous wig it could be quite scary when you saw him yawning and growling like a lion just before he stepped out in front of his fans.

'Tonight gentlemen, we are proud to welcome back one of Newcastle's most successful artists. With a career spanning over twenty years and a name you will all recognise, please welcome Peter Grills as, Dolly Parton!' The crowd all stood up and roared with excitement. Barry jumped up and down on his toes and absorbed the atmosphere as the music began and he watched Peter step out on to the stage and swing his arms open wide and blow kisses to all of his adoring fans.

Peter began with one of the audience's favourites, Jolene. He held the microphone close to his mouth and sang the words in perfect sync with the music. Barry watched him from the side and dreamed of the day when he could be up there in his place.

Bill had already taken his place at the front and when Barry spotted him in the audience, he came around the back and sat next to him. 'He's really on form tonight,' said Barry, mesmerised by his uncle in his big pink and white dress. Bill nodded and said,

'Yes, even though I know he's tired and a bit out of sorts about this Joe business, he still always manages to put business first and put on a smashing show for the boys.' Barry grinned and resumed watching his uncle.

He wafted back and forth across the stage, singing into his microphone and tipping his head sideways as he went from: 'I Will Always Love You' to 'Islands in the Stream' and worked his way through her hits in chronological order.' The young and old men in the crowds, leaped and jumped with each popular tune and shouts of 'We love you Peter,' were heard from the back of the bar.

Barry looked around to see who it was and he noticed a couple of men at the bar who stood out as not being comfortable in their surroundings. One was a middle-aged man in a cheap grey suit, talking to the bartender. The other was a younger man, also in a suit but looking terrified as men looked at him and gave him the once-over. Barry watched as the older man tried to make himself heard over the noise and then he saw the bartender point towards Peter on the stage. The man in the cheap suit looked at Peter, with his enormous wig, his gold eye shadow and his garish pink dress and his jaw dropped. He pointed at Peter and then checked with the bartender to make sure he hadn't made a mistake.

Barry returned to the show and watched Peter take a bow. The music began again and off he went into his next number. Barry felt a hand on his shoulder and turned, surprised. It was the old man he had seen at the bar. He didn't recognise him and he wondered if he was trying to pick him up.

As a young gay man, Barry was used to being propositioned by men in the bars he worked in with his uncle. But Barry was a professional and always stood his ground and told any admirers he was here to work not play. Barry took his job very seriously and anyway. He didn't think he was ready for casual sex just yet. He wanted more than that.

The man nodded to Bill and Barry. 'Can I have a word?' he shouted, trying to make himself heard over Peter's singing. Bill didn't know who he was and couldn't quite make out what he was saying. The man, realising it was impossible to get his message across slipped his hand into his inside jacket pocket and pulled out a small, black leather, folded case. He flipped it open with his finger and showed Bill and Barry the police badge it contained. He nodded towards the door and Bill got the message.

They opened the heavy fire door and all four of them stepped out of the din of the club into the coolness of the service area. The man in the cheap suit introduced himself and his partner. 'I'm inspector McGarry and this is sergeant Finkle.' Barry looked at the scrawny young policeman. He couldn't have been much older than him and he looked like he was fresh out of police school or wherever it is these people go to get trained, he thought. He thought he looked quite cute and he had nice eyes.

The young officer noticed him looking at him and he whipped his gaze away and focused on his boss. 'I really need to speak to Mr Grills... But I see he's rather pre-occupied at the moment.' They listened to the muffled sound of Peter singing, 'Because I Love You' and Barry watched the young policeman. He wasn't sure but he thought he saw him wiggle his hips a little to the music. The young man noticed Barry watching and he straightened his stance.

Bill wondered how they knew they would be here and then the inspector answered then question before he time to ask it. 'We called at your home address but there was no answer. Your neighbour told us Peter worked here on a Friday night, so we thought we'd pop in and have a word.'

Barry, still watching the nervous-looking young man butted in and asked, 'Was the box of sweets poisoned then?' expecting his deductions to be confirmed. The inspector looked at the boy and twisted the corner of his mouth.

'Er. No. We haven't got the results back from the lab – that'll take a few days.' He returned his gaze to Bill and asked him when Peter would be finished. Bill looked at his watch and said he was due a break after the next song. The inspector nodded and asked if it would be alright to have a quick word during his break. Bill agreed and suggested they wait in the dressing room and he would let Peter know they were here.

***

Bill stood in the wings and watched Peter take a bow as the crowds roared and yelped. He wafted off stage. 'You were brilliant,' said Bill as Peter mopped his brow with a towel Bill had ready for him.

'It isn't over yet! ', said Peter, looking at Bill surprised. 'There's still the second half.' Bill nodded and pulled Peter into the plain corridor, where his bright and garish costume really stood out against the magnolia-painted walls.

'Inspector McGarry is here to see you,' said Bill as he puckered up Peter's dress and followed him back to the dressing room.

'Here!' said Peter, drinking on a glass of water filled with ice. Bill nodded as they approached the door to the room.

Inspector McGarry stood up as Peter flounced past them in his dress and the young sergeant Finkle retracted himself and clung to the wall. Peter sat in his seat, the beads of sweat clinging to his foundation and the whiskers on his chin breaking through the thick layer of makeup. Inspector McGarry looked at him and tried to keep a straight face as he spoke about the events mentioned in his statement.

Peter sat, his tall white wig balanced precariously on his hot head and his eyes encircled with big flushes of gold eye makeup. His lips were bright red and his enormous bosom wrested on his pot belly as he enjoyed the cooling effect created by Bill wafting him with a small towel.

'Can you give me a description of the man that Greg was talking to in the bedroom when you were hiding in the wardrobe?' said the inspector. The young Finkle got out a small notebook and flipped its cover, poised for the information Peter was about to furnish. Peter held his hand up to stop Bill and he thought about it for a second.

'Well, the door was closed... I could only see a little bit, through the gap and that wasn't much.'

'Anything about him would be useful,' said the inspector. Peter stroked his chin as he thought.

'He was thin... I'm fairly sure of that. And tall, about the same height as Greg and he talked with a professional's voice – you know, like a solicitor or,' The inspector butted in,

'A doctor?'

Peter nodded, surprised that the inspector knew what he was about to say. He pulled out a small photo and passed it to Peter. 'Is this the man you saw?' Peter looked at the picture.

'Well, like I say, I couldn't see much of him... He's about the same sort of build, the same shaped head and,' Peter looked closer at the image and noticed something on the man's left hand. 'Yes. That's him,' he continued. The inspector was curious what he had seen that now made him certain it was the same man.

'I recognised the ring on his finger. I spotted it through the gap and I remember thinking, ooh, that's nice. That would go nice with my purple and orange sweater. Bill leant over and looked at the photo. He nodded and said it would.

Barry popped his head around the door and noticed the young officer standing against the wall with his foot supporting him. He looked at Peter and Bill and said, 'Five minutes.' Peter nodded and pulled out his compact and dusted his face with a fresh layer of makeup.

'So what does this mean,' asked Peter, checking his bosom in the mirror and lifting it up back into position. 'Are you looking into the case again, or not?' The inspector stood up as Peter rose from his seat and turned toward him waiting for his answer.

'If the results come back positive, then we'll definitely open the case back up but for now we are investigating the character you recognised.

'Oh?' said Peter.

'That's all I can say for now...I'll let you know when we get the results from the lab.' With that he pulled the young Finkle from his propped position and tugged him out of the door. Barry smiled at Finkle and he thought he smiled back but he wasn't sure.

Five

Barry looked at the dress in the window and wondered what he might look like wearing it. It was a long, flowing wedding dress, with little cream flowers stitched into the arms and a traditional, bunched-up bustle at the back. It was the sort of dress he dreamed of wearing one day – if he ever found Mr Right.

Barry stood back a little and noticed the clock above the jeweller's door in the reflection of the glass and he remembered why he had come out. Bill had asked him to pick up some Vaseline for Peter's feet. Barry knew how Peter's feet suffered wearing the tight, pointed-toed shoes which formed part of the Dolly Parton costume. Just like a marathon runner, he would put Vaseline between his toes when he wore those shoes. It prevented them rubbing and making his toes sore.

Barry thought about the things professional female impersonators had to do for their craft and felt proud that Peter was one of the best in the business. He pulled himself away from the window, knowing he had to get on.

The chemist shop was on Blackett Street and was one of the larger Boots stores. It was very modern and clinical, with its large prescription counter and massive array of perfumes and cure-alls. Barry often bought his uncle's cosmetics there. He liked the store and often forgot the time as he looked at all of the different shades of lipstick and eye shadow.

'Barry Sidewick...Is that Barry?' he heard a voice say behind him as he read the small print on the side of a bottle of peppermint foot lotion. He turned, not recognising the owner of the voice and he grinned. It was his friend Beth from school. He hadn't seen her for years and apart from being older, she looked just the same as he remembered her.

She was a tall, thin girl with big, purple, spiky hair; made to stick out as far from her head as she could possibly get it (within the confines of the laws of hair). Her face was pale, covered with an almost white foundation and her eyes had enormous black rings of eye shadow encircling them. Her lips were thin and covered with a light coat of black lipstick. In her nose was a stainless steel ring, the size of a pound coin and around her neck was a studded dog collar.

She really was a sight to be seen and Barry had quite forgotten what a character she had been at school. She was well known for being a Goth and famous for hanging around the local cemeteries and for floating around school in her black cape and pounding up and down the corridors with her big, studded boots.

There was no cape today. She hid her extrovert black uniform under a plain white doctor's-style, full length lab coat and on its breast pocket was a Boots employee badge with her name, Beth Morgan printed in bold characters.

She smiled. She had always liked Barry. Everyone knew he was gay at school but she liked the fact that he didn't care. She admired his ability to mince into a class full of straight boys and confidently sit right amongst them. She said, 'Wow! You look good,' as she looked him up and down. Barry grinned.

'You too,' he said, admiring a small tattoo on the side of her neck and generally pleased to have met up with her again after all of these years. 'So, what's with the coat and badge,' he said, tapping the small plastic insignia on her top pocket.

She shied away; embarrassed that she had come to working in a chemist. 'Oh! It's just a job... Listen,' she looked at her big, bold watch and said, 'I'm finished here in five minutes. Do you want to go for a coke and catch up?' Barry nodded and watched her scurry off and deposited her white coat behind the counter. She slipped on a long black coat in its place and swished back to meet him, waiting by the door. She grinned, slid her arm through his and they headed for the Tyneside Tea Rooms across the road.

The tearooms were directly above the Tyneside Cinema – an old, art deco building which showed cult and arty movies to minority audiences. The cafe was on the top floor and it was a place that Barry and his uncle and aunty often frequented. Barry liked the old decor and the friendly staff. The cafe often had out-of-work actors and other creative types in and it had a welcoming, homely feel to it.

Beth brought two cans and two glasses back to the table and laid them out on the table in front of Barry. 'Cheers, Beth' he said as she pulled off her enormous coat. Beneath it Barry could see how thin she was and he noticed the stud in her belly button as she tugged the coat over her shirt.

'So, are you still 'Dragging it out' with your uncle Pete?' asked Beth as she popped the ring on the can and tried to catch the inevitable froth as it forced its way up, out of the can. Barry, not taking her comments the way it sounded – he knew Beth and he liked the way she spoke her mind – confirmed that he was working as his uncle's assistant.

'I'm in training myself now,' he said, taking a drink from his glass. 'Peter's going to get me fitted out for my first costume soon and I can't wait to get on stage.' Beth watched him over the top of her glass and smiled.

'So what's it going to be..? Another, ubiquitous country-and-western singer?' Barry shook his head.

'No. I want to be Liza Minnelli... I just love her!' Beth grinned, using her glass to cover her smirk and she nodded and said,

'Well, you've certainly got the figure for it.' Barry looked down at his young, boyish torso and said,

'Do you think so...I think I'm getting too fat?'

'Don't be daft...Anyway, how's Uncle Peter?' she asked settling down for a chinwag.

'Oh! He's fine... Well apart for the murder thing.' Beth's eyes widened like a horny pander when it's spotted its mate. She took her boots off the table and leant forward and stared Barry in the face. Barry was a little taken aback and wondered what he had said to justify such a response. He realised and then continued,

'Peter's friend died recently and it looks like he may have been killed by a gang of con men, trying to get hold of his money and his house.' He casually sipped on his coke and watched Beth's eyes widen and her lip tremble with excitement.

'Go on!' she said, eager to get the full story. Barry sat back, recognising that he had an audience and he slipped into stage mode. He looked either side of him and then continued to tell Beth about the funeral and the Greg man, who he didn't like the look of. He told her about Agnes and her suspicions and how they had to hide in the wardrobe when the murders came in. He told her about the box of sweets and how he had deduced that they must be poisoned.

Beth sat in silence, occasionally sipping on her drink, to

moisten the increasingly dry lips that were a result of her jaw being in a permanent state of dropped. 'We're just waiting for the results from the lab boys before we go any further with the case,' said Barry as he sat up and looked over at the cake display by the till. He looked down at his torso again, deciding to forgo the cake. If only Liza had done the same later in her career, he thought.

'Wow!' said Beth, leaning back against her stiff plastic chair. 'So are you two like... private investigators... when you're not dressing up like women, I mean?' Barry smiled at the idea.

'Umh,' he said, 'Not really. We just wanted to help out Joe's sister and get to the bottom of the mystery. The police closed the case, saying it was death by natural causes. But they will have to re-open it now, once they test the sweets and find they're poisoned. Beth looked at him and thought about it for a moment.

'But... If they were poisoned, wouldn't that have shown up in the post-mortem?' she said putting her boots back on the table. A waiter noticed her doing it and stared at her until she removed them. Barry looked irritated, tired of everyone asking the same question. He looked at her big, pander-like eyes and said,

'You of all people should know,' he said gathering his things together and folding the big flap of his bag over. 'There are some poisons that can't be detected in the system after death.' He stood up and checked himself in the mirrored wall, which surrounded the cafe.

'How would I know about such things,' she asked.

'Well, you work in a chemist. You must know about poisons and things.' Beth laughed and stood up.

'I fill the shelves and help old grannies decide which laxative to buy.'

***

Peter's feet were sore and he hoped that Barry hadn't forgotten his Vaseline. Bill put a bowel of warm water under his feet and gently eased them into it. 'Ah. That feels better. Thank you dear,' said Peter as he relaxed in his chair and watched Bill rub his weary feet.

'Maybe we should have a new pair made. These are obviously too small for you now,' said Bill paying particular attention to Peter's sore toes.

'Oh, they'll have to do. We can't afford to splash out on a hand-made pair of shoes just now.'

The front door slammed and in came Barry with his friend Beth. Peter looked at the creature before him and she smiled. He looked at her big, black, strap-covered boots, with their silver studs and toe cap. He had never seen boots like them before. His gaze followed up her legs, which were shrouded in black trousers, again with straps and silver chains hanging from the pockets. He looked at her face and the sudden shock of seeing her big black eyes made him sit back in his chair and squeak. He didn't know what to make of her but he could see Barry was proud of his find so he tried to think of something to say.

'Oh, I like your hair,' he said, noticing how it's purple and black streaks spat out stiff strands into all directions as it made its statement. He wasn't lying. He was sure he had a dress in that colour and he had always liked it, he thought.

'Cheers Pete,' said Beth as Barry pulled her into the middle of the room. He noticed Peter's feet in the bowel of water and he suddenly remembered he had forgotten his Vaseline.

'Damn,' he said, 'Sorry Uncle Pete, I forgot the Vaseline for your feet.' Beth looked at the man with his feet in water and smiled.

'The hell of womanhood,' she said, pointing to his feet. Peter nodded. He liked her, even though she looked like something out of a cartoon, that toddlers might watch, he felt a connection with her almost immediately.

'Oh! You'll have to excuse me dear,' he said, lifting his feet out of the bowel and shaking of the water droplets, 'Look at me in this state when we have visitors.' Beth watched as he started to get up.

'Chill man,' she said and indicated for him to stay seated by waving her ring-covered hand.

'We used to go to school together,' said Barry as he plonked himself down on the sofa and pulled Beth down next to him. 'We used to be mates.' He looked at her. Beth butted in,

'Not that there's much chance of us mating, by the way,' she said laughing and they all giggled with her.

'Do you want to come up to my bedroom?' said Barry as he started to get up. Beth looked at him and smiled, saying,

'Woooh boy! I'm not that kind of girl!' as she grinned at Barry. Barry laughed and replied,

'Don't worry; I'm not that sort of boy either, so you're in safe hands with me.' They all laughed and Barry pulled Beth up the stairs by the hand. Bill looked at Peter and said,

'She's an interesting character.' Peter just nodded and rubbed his sore toes with his foot, sucking in air as he cursed his beautiful shoes.

The phone rang just as Bill was empting the bowel into the sink. He popped his head around the door and indicated to Peter that he had his hands full. Peter leapt up, barefoot and headed into the hall. The phone stopped as he lifted the received and said hello. 'Oh!' said Peter. 'Umh... right.' Bill came through and waited for the call to end. He could tell by Peter's expression that it wasn't good news. He hung up and turned to Bill. 'You'd better get Barry – he'll want to hear this. Bill looked worried but followed his instructions and called Barry down from his room.

Peter was sitting in the living room again when Barry and Beth came springing down the stairs like a couple of young Giselle. Barry looked at Peter and knew something was up. Peter looked at Barry and said, 'They've got the results back from the lab and they're negative – no poison.' Barry's face dropped and he looked at Bill and Beth.

'But...'said Barry. 'How can that be?' Peter shrugged his shoulders and continued.

'Inspector McGarry said as there was no poison, there was no case, so they're closing the file on it.' Bill lowered his head and said,

'Poor Agnes, she'll be devastated.' Peter looked at Bill with his head bowed and Barry with his expression of disbelief and he pulled back his shoulders and took in a deep breath.

'No! They might have given up on Joe but I haven't!' The others raised their heads and stared at him. They could tell he was about to go in to one of his theatrical performances and they waited, ready for the show to begin. 'We all know that those two men we saw in Joe's bedroom are up to no good and if they're going out to con old and vulnerable gay men out of their life's savings, then we have to do something about it!'

Barry nodded excitedly and sat on the edge of his seat, gripping Beth's hand. 'When we last heard from Inspector McGarry he said he was investigating the other man – I want to know why and I want to know what came of that.' Bill looked up, aware that Peter was nearing the end of his rant and he asked,

'Do you think he will tell you? Isn't that sort of thing confidential – for police only, I mean?' Peter looked flustered and didn't like his flow being interrupted. He glared at Bill and he got the message and said under his breath, 'Sorry.'

Peter took another deep breath and continued, 'I'm going to go around to the station and find out what's going on.' He pointed at Barry and gave his orders. 'Barry, you take Beth and go round to Agnes's. I want to know about that will. Find out what you can.' Barry nodded excitedly and squeezed Beth's hand harder. She pulled it out from his grip and said,

'Owh. Let go, princess!' Peter grinned at Beth's confidence and he asked Bill to go to the registrar's office and ask to see the death certificate – he wanted to know exactly what Joe died of. The collective looked at each other and then Peter waved his arm, indicating for them to get out and bring him back his data. Bill pushed his arm through his coat and looked over at Peter.

'And what are you going to do now?' he asked curiously. Peter swung his feet up on to the sofa, clicked on the TV and said, 'I'm going to watch the Coronation Street omnibus I taped last night.'

Six

'Like I said on the phone, the file is closed on this one,' said Inspector McGarry as he slammed the drawer of the filing cabinet closed. 'There was no poison found in the Turkish delight and nothing else suspicious about the packet. Peter looked at his eyes. He could see he was determined that that was the end of it.

'But you must have something. It's obvious that these men are criminals. It's obvious that they are seeking out wealthy old gay men, and using young gigolos to lure them in and then getting them to change their wills before knocking them off!' The inspector sighed and sat behind his desk. He pointed to the chair next to Peter and told him to sit. Peter shuffled in his seat, waiting for a reply.

'We had hoped your idea was right, as we've been after one of the characters involved for some time. We just haven't had any evidence to get him. When you came in with the box of sweets, I thought that this might be it. But when it turned out not to be poisoned, that was it for us – no evidence.' Peter looked confused and butted in.

'Who were you after and what for?' asked Peter as he crossed his legs and straightened his yellow socks. The inspector noticed the socks and rolled his eyes.

'Well, that's strictly police business,' said the inspector. He noticed Peter's face darken with frustration and his brow crease. He stood up and closed the door to the office. Peter watched him as he returned to his seat.

'But, I suppose there's no harm in telling you.' He pulled out the file again and opened it in front of him on his desk. 'The other man that you described as having seen from the wardrobe?' Peter leant forward, intrigued by what was to come. 'Well his name is Dr Edward Collins. We questioned him about a similar case six months ago. A gay man was found dead soon after changing his will and leaving everything to a much younger man. We had our suspicions he was involved somehow and because he is a toxicologist, we assumed he might have poisoned the victim.'

The inspector flipped the file closed and sat back in his seat, being careful not to raise his arms. Peter was bemused. His head was beginning to hurt and he had trouble working it all out in his mind. 'But, couldn't the poison have been in something else?' asked Peter.

The inspector looked at the clock above the door and suggested that they leave things there. Peter had a lot to take in but wasn't sure if he had anything else he needed to know. The inspector stood up and pointed towards the door. 'I'm going to look into this myself,' said Peter and the inspector frowned at him.

'Really, Mr Grills. We've done everything we can and without further evidence, we can't proceed any more. Best just let it drop, eh?'

***

Barry and Beth were sitting at the kitchen table when Peter returned. He heard Barry talking about the dress he had seen in the shop window and how he wished he could try it on. They looked up as Peter came in and Barry asked, 'Any news?' Peter, still heavily laden with shopping bags looked at him and he knew what that meant. Barry helped him with the bags and sat Peter down in one of the chairs.

'Well,' he said. 'Did you find out anything?' Peter nodded.

'I think so... Apparently the other man we saw was suspected of being involved in a similar case six months ago...' Peter continued to relay the information that the inspector had given him and he watched as Barry's face glowed and grinned.

'What's a toxicologist?' asked Barry and Peter was about to explain when Beth butted in.

'It's an expert in poisonous substances,' she said and sat back in her chair, waiting for praise. Barry looked at her in amazement but said nothing. Peter continued to tell them everything that he could remember about the conversation with the inspector. Beth sat and listened and Barry put the kettle on.

Beth looked at the table and stroked the colourful tablecloth. 'Hang on,' she said, 'If the police found no evidence of poison in either case why are we still assuming Joe was poisoned? Just because that bloke was a toxicologist, doesn't mean he poisoned them. If he had been a fish monger, should we assume that he beat his victims to death with a kipper?'

Peter laughed. He was beginning to really like Barry's new friend and he liked the way she used the words we and us. It was nice to know his team of helpers was growing with his own confidence. 'We just thought it odd that Greg would go to all the bother of posting Joe a box of sweets when he was away on holiday. We thought it was the ideal way for him to give himself an alibi.' Barry poured the tea and said,

'To kill him by remote control.' Beth thought about it and nodded.

'I suppose so,' she said, eyeing the hot tea that Barry placed before her. 'But as the sweets didn't contain any poison – what was the point?'

Barry sat back at the table and looked at Peter. They hadn't thought about that.

'Anyway,' said Peter, taking his jacket off to reveal a bright orange shirt. Beth noticed the garish shirt and commented on it. 'Ooh! Barry got me this for Christmas. Isn't it lovely?' Beth just nodded, scared to reveal her true thoughts. 'Anyway, I was about to ask how you two got on?'

Barry pulled out a small notebook and flipped over the stiff cover. He read out what he had written down: 'The solicitor, a Mr Goldfish,' Peter sniggered and almost sprayed his shirt with tea. Barry grinned and continued, 'Mr Goldfish said the will was not drawn up by him. It was typed up by someone else. The wording was legally correct and the signature was witnessed by two independent witnesses. He had no reason to believe it was anything other than a genuine and legal last will and testament.'

Peter rubbed his chin and thought for a moment. 'I suppose they could have drawn up the will and forged Joe's signature, getting two people to act as witnesses... Do we know who the witnesses were?' Barry grinned and flicked over the page of his notebook.

'Yes. Mr William Goody and Ms Julie Jacob.' He smiled and put the notebook away. Peter grinned at him.

'Well let's hope that Mr Goody isn't a Baddy.' They all laughed and didn't notice Bill coming in the front door. His face was pale with the autumn air but he had a smile on his face. Barry got up and fetched another cup, pouring Bill as cup as he sat with them at the table. Peter could tell Bill was bursting to tell them his news. He took a sip of hit hot tea and thanked Barry as he pushed the biscuit barrel towards him.

'Well,' said Bill, dunking his digestive into his cup, 'At first they told me to go away and the person on the desk was very unhelpful. Then, just I was about to give up and come home, who do you think I saw working in the back office?' Peter looked at him blankly. 'Trevor!' said Bill, searching Peter's face for a reaction. Peter still looked blank. 'Trevor Thompson... You know, Catherine Carpenter for many years.' Peter's face lit up.

'Trevor Thompson! I thought he'd went off to the states?'

'He did,' said Bill, 'But he's back and now he's working as a civil servant at the registrar's office.' Peter smiled and said,

'Ah! From drag to dreary... What a waste!'

'Anyway,' continued Bill. 'When he saw me at the front desk, shouting at the poor receptionist he came over. It turns out he's settled down with a nice man from Hartlepool and they now live in Gosforth.' Peter nudged him in the arm and told him to get to the news.

'Well I told him about Joe and he was shocked. He was horrified to hear about our suspicions and he offered to help me find out what we could. He was very nice. He sat me in his office and showed me the file on Joe.' Bill took another sip and continued whilst the three onlookers waited in anticipation.

'Did you copy out as much as you could?' asked Peter, hopeful for as much information as he could get. Bill grinned and leant over to his bag.

'Better than that,' he said, pulling out some lose leaves of paper. Trevor photocopied the whole thing for me. He said he wasn't meant to but Joe was a good friend and if he thought it would find his killer, then it was worth it.'

Peter put his arm around Bill, kissed him on the cheek and patted him on the back. 'Brilliant, brilliant,' he said, tapping the pile of papers into a neat stack and laying it out on the table to read.

He lifted the pair of big reading glasses that hung on a lanyard around his neck and slipped them onto his nose. He struggled to read the technical words and everyone looked at him. He held his finger on the paper, so as not to lose his place. He read out the important bits.

'Cause of death: Myocardial Infarction.' Peter looked up puzzled and Bill said,

'Heart attack.'

Peter nodded and read on. 'Usual General Practitioner was present before and during death... Deceased had a history of heart condition... No suspicious circumstances.'

Peter put his glasses down and said into his chest. 'Poor Joe.'

Barry cleared away the tea mugs and Beth helped him in the kitchen whilst Bill and Peter talked. The news of how Joe actually died made them feel sad and they mourned the loss of their friend again.

Peter thought back to his time in Joe's office and of all those wonderful dresses. He remembered the big fireplace. It was one of the old Victorian types that stood almost at eye level and had a big mantle edge that stuck out about twelve inches. If you tripped and banged your head against that, it would surely do you a serious injury, he thought. But he also remembered that Joe was fastidiously tidy. He didn't like anything out of place and hated to see things lying on the floor that weren't meant to be there. So what could he have tripped over, he wondered? Maybe the police had taken it away during their investigation or just moved it.

Barry and Beth came back through and sat on the sofa. Bill pulled Peter by the hand and sat facing them. 'So what do we do now?' asked Barry, looking at Peter. Everyone turned and looked at Peter as if he had all of the answers. Peter, recognising his new role as group leader, said, 'Well, we know that this Dr Collin's fella is a specialist in poisons... but we now know that this has got nothing to do with the case, so we can forget that. We know that Joe died by tripping over and banging his head,' He squeezed Bill's hand. 'And we now know that the solicitor says the will was legal.' Peter looked confused and didn't know what to say next.

Barry butted in and saved Peter's embarrassment. 'So we need to find out who forged the will, who this Dr character is and what part he plays in all of this and find out how they killed Joe and made it look like a natural death?' Peter sat back astonished at Barry's quick thinking and said,

'Yes. That was just what I was about to say.'

Bill raised his hand as if he was at a board meeting and was asking permission of the chairman to raise a point. Peter nodded and Bill said, 'Well I don't really see that we are any further forward than we were yesterday. We still can't prove that Joe was killed or even than he was conned out of his money.' They all listened and realised that Bill was right.

Beth, being the new member of the team, stood up and waited until the others all noticed she was about to speak and then said, as she straightened out one of the long spikes of hair that stuck out in front of her face, 'Well, isn't it obvious?' she looked around the table at the bemused faces, 'We obviously can't prove they did this to Joe but didn't you say you overheard them talking about their current,' she raised her hands either side of her and wiggled each pair of forefingers to indicate quotation marks, ''Mark'. Isn't that what con men call their victims?' She looked again at the faces around her and she noticed the content of her speech beginning to sink in and she recognised it first in their eyes and then in their smiles.

'So, they must be in the middle of another scam and I think the best way to get them is to catch them in the act before they kill another innocent old man.' Barry grinned at her, excited at the prospect of being a detective again and Peter smiled, realising what an asset she could be to his little team of sleuths.

Barry put both hands on the table and started to stand up. He said, 'We need to follow them and find out what they're up to!' Peter waved him down, back into his seat.

'Hang on a minute,' he said, rubbing his chin. 'From the way the two were talking in Joe's bedroom, it sounds like the Dr is the ring leader and Greg is just the gigolo. So who do we follow?' Peter rubbed his chin again and sat back in his seat, wondering if they needed more tea.

Barry looked up from the notepad he had been scribbling in, grinned and said, 'We follow them both!' Peter nodded,

'I suppose that makes sense.' He stopped rubbing his chin and looked in the tea pot to see if there was enough for another cup. 'If we split into two pairs, that way we can watch them both and report back at the end of the day.' Bill nudged him in the arm and reminded him that they had the man coming to fix the boiler tomorrow and they needed to be in for that. Peter frowned but agreed having a warm house was just as important as solving this case.

'You stay in and deal with the plumber dear. I'll scout out this Greg fella. I know he works in the estate agency on Osborne Road.' He looked over at Beth and Barry. 'Beth. I know you work at the chemist so if you don't have the time I Underst...' Beth stopped him mid word and, excited to be part of the team, said she only worked part-time and she wasn't due back in until next week. Peter smiled and nodded.

She looped her arm through Barry's and stood up with him, ready to receive orders. Peter grinned. They looked such an odd couple, he thought; Beth, with her massive purple hair and her stomping boots; Barry with his skinny, boyish-body and his beautiful blue eyes, highlighted with just a hint of eye shadow.

Beth's expression changed as she realised something. 'Hang on. We don't know where to find the doctor. We don't know where he lives or works.' Barry released himself from her grip and disappeared into the hall. They watched him leave and wondered what he was up to as they listened to him flicking through pages. He came back in to the room carrying the Yellow Pages and he was fingering something he had found.

'Dr Edward Collins, The Gosforth Surgery,' he said as he let the book slap closed. Beth looked up at Barry smiled at him, saying,

'Smart arse!'

Seven

Peter sat in his car opposite the estate agency. He had a clear view in through the window and he could see the different people sitting behind their desks talking to customers and showing them details of different properties. He watched as people came and went but there was no sign of Greg. Maybe it was his day off, thought Peter. Maybe he was away and he'd be sitting there all day for nothing. Peter tapped the steering while as he listened to Dolly sing 'Before the Next Tear Drop Falls' on his CD player. He liked the song and he hummed it as he sat and waited. He wondered if he should add it to his repertoire.

He thought about the number of Dolly's songs he had performed over the years; the number of sleazy men's clubs he had worked in and the awful crowds and pub owners he'd had to deal with. Peter sighed. He realised he was getting older. He looked at his hands on the steering wheel. The skin was wrinkled and loose. He remembered when his skin was firm and tight, not like now, with its blotches and dark lines.

He flipped down the sun visor and looked in its mirror. He looked at his face and checked his eyes for sleep. He had to get up earlier than he normally chose to. He didn't know what time Greg started work, so he made sure he was there in plenty of time. Peter closed the mirror, agreeing that he was still as gorgeous as ever and looked at his watch. It was only nine twenty and he was bored already.

The CD changed tracks and Dolly started to sing '9 to 5'. Peter's mood lifted as he sang along to the lyrics. He danced in his seat and swung his arms out, as he did when he was performing this piece on stage. He was lost in his own world and loving it. An old lady stopped as she walked past his car, pulling her shopping trolley behind her. She looked in his window to see if he was okay, concerned that he may be having a heart attack. Peter turned as he started to sing the next line and he saw the face pressed up against the glass. He jumped and squeaked as he suddenly noticed the wrinkled old face. He stopped singing and smiled at the lady who, realising that he was not dying, continued on her way, dragging the tired old cart behind her.

He reminded himself why he was here. He tried to focus on the job at hand and looked in the window of the estate agents again. Nothing seemed to have changed. The lady sitting at the desk in the window was still talking to a young couple, showing them photos of houses and trying to convince them that the rooms are bigger than they look.

There was still no sign of Greg. Peter didn't know what his job was there. He didn't know whether he was management or just the young office boy, who was sent out showing prospective buyers around properties. Peter looked at the sky above. It was beginning to cloud over and he knew it was going to rain. Peter didn't like the rain. He knew if he was caught in the rain without an umbrella, he would end up looking like a washed-out pander.

He tapped the steering wheel again and looked at his watch. Well, if this is what's like to be a detective, then sod this for a lark, he thought. He sighed and glanced back towards the window. He sat up as he noticed a character in the back of the office. It was Greg. Peter swung around in his seat so he could watch more comfortably and he observed Greg pulling down a bunch of keys from a rack on the wall behind a desk and then shaking hands with the young couple he had seen previously. He guided them towards the door and pointed down the street. Peter watched as they headed off down Osborne Road, towards the church.

Peter wasn't quite sure what he should do. Should he follow them or just wait for them to return, he wondered. He watched as they got further away and he decided it better that he get out at go after them. At least, that way, he wouldn't be stuck in the car all day.

He felt his knicker elastic cut in to him as he trotted along, trying to catch up with the young people in front. He passed a shop with a mannequin wearing a sparkly, sequinned dress and he stopped for a second to admire it. He saw out of the corner of his eye that the young people were getting further away and he had to drag himself away from the window and force himself to catch up with them.

He was quite out of breath when he noticed them come to a stop. Peter held on to the wall as he panted and got his breath back. He looked up at the avenue of trees and he recognised where he now was. This is Joe's street, he thought as he watched Greg unlock the big heavy white front door and allow the young couple to enter before him.

There was a for sale sign at the entrance to the long gravelled path, which Peter never noticed when he was last there. He stood and waited, not really sure what he was meant to be doing while they were looking around Joe's house. Peter noticed a phone box across the road and he thought he would look less obvious if he stood in there and pretended to be on the phone.

He looked up at the sky and it threatened rain. Damn, thought Peter. He had left his umbrella in the car. He pulled open the heavy aluminium door of the phone box and slipped in behind it as it swung closed. The place was surprisingly clean and didn't have the usual graffiti, so common in such locations. Peter stood, holding the receiver and watched as the locals walked by, walking their dogs and carrying their M&S bags. He noted what a different sort of area this was. There were no rough-looking kids in baseball caps hanging around; there were no boarded-up properties and the street was clean and free of litter. He watched as an old couple walked by. She wore a smart tweed suite and matching pearls and he strode proudly, with his cane, holding her on his arm. Ex-army, thought Peter as he pretended to talk to someone on the phone.

Peter stared across at Joe's door but there was still no sign of them. Peter wondered if it was doing any good watching Greg like this. What was it going to prove, he thought. His gaze wandered and he looked at the notice board over the phone. In the corner was a small card, someone had slid in between the rim and the glass. Peter pulled it out and read it.

'Private Lessons Given For Naughty Schoolboys. All tastes catered for. Call...' Peter laughed and thought the posh people who lived here weren't quite as proper as they made out. He slid the card back into its home, not wanting to deprive any naughty schoolboys of their lessons, and turned to see Greg locking the door and talking to the couple.

Greg looked at his watch and waved off the couple. Peter got ready to follow him back to the office but was surprised when he headed in the opposite direction up the street towards an outside bar. Peter kept to the sides of the street, just like he had seen in countless spy films, as he followed Greg up the street and watched him take a seat at one of the tables that sat outside the restaurant. He ordered a drink and Peter decided to slip in to a seat behind Greg, where he wouldn't be noticed and could watch under the protection under the umbrella.

'What can I get you sir,' asked a voice over Peter's shoulder. Peter looked at the young waiter, with his slim waist and white teeth. He looked like a student, working his way through university and he smiled at Peter. Peter thought he was a pretty young thing and was a little flattered at his attention.

'Er,' said Peter, quickly looking at the menu on the rickety table. 'I'll have a coffee,' The waiter grinned and was about to leave when Peter added, 'And an éclair, please.'

'No problem,' said the handsome young waiter and he winked at Peter as he went off to the bar.   Peter wasn't sure if he was being given the eye by the pretty young waiter but it felt good to believe it. He looked over at Greg. He could only see the back of his head and he watched him as he flicked through some papers. The waiter came and deposited Peter's coffee in front of him. He then slid the small plate containing the éclair to one side and asked him if there was anything else he needed. Peter dismissed the images that flashed before his mind of licking the cream off this young man's chest and said no, that was all.

He licked the cream along the side of the éclair and relished in its taste. Just then another man approached Greg's table and Greg stood up to greet him. Greg kissed him on the lips and hugged him. He obviously knew the man and he sat with him and ordered a coffee. Peter couldn't hear what they were saying but he tried to make a mental note of the man's features, in case he needed to describe him at a later time. He wished he had thought to bring a notebook with him, like his more expert nephew, Barry.

Peter felt a sudden grip on his shoulder and he was startled, letting out a squeak as he turned and saw Barry and Beth standing behind him. He looked up at their grinning faces and said, 'What are you doing here? You're supposed to be following Dr Collins.' Beth swung down and sat on the seat opposite and Barry pulled out another chair next to Peter.

'We are,' they nodded over to Greg and his companion and

said, 'He's sitting over there with Greg.' Peter said,

'Ahh,' and he looked at the man again. He watched as he raised a cup to his lips and Peter spotted his ring. 'Yes, I see.' He turned back to the others and smiled at them.

'So what's Greg been up to, then?' asked Barry, eyeing up the remainder of his uncle's éclair. Peter spotted him looking at it and picked it up, and swallowed it in one mouthful. Barry's eyes dropped. Peter felt guilty; fist for having an éclair in the first place and second for depriving his nephew of it. He waved the young waiter over and asked him to bring two more. He nodded and Peter watched him as he went back into the restaurant, admiring his little bottom as it wiggled in his tight, black trousers. Barry noticed his uncle and slapped his arm.

'Uncle Peter! What would Aunty Bill think if he saw you doing that?' Peter grinned and replied,

'He'd probably tell me to act my age and get a stair lift fitted.' Barry grinned and watched as the waiter returned and leant across him to deliver his plates. Barry watched his uncle, making sure his gaze did not wander where it shouldn't. Peter was about to say something about the waiter's bottom when he remembered Barry's question. 'Oh not much of interest has happened. I followed him to Joe's house,' Beth sat up and paid more attention, taking the ear buds from her ears and turning off her iPod. 'He showed a young couple around and then came here. Nothing much to report really. How about you two?'

He watched as Barry poked his thin tongue into the éclair and licked it clean of cream before biting it in half and swallowing it. He had his mouth full so Beth stepped in and filled Peter in on their adventure so far. 'Well we first saw him at the surgery but it must have been his day for house calls because he didn't stay there long. He got into his flash Mercedes and went off. We knew we couldn't follow him, so we decided to head over to here and meet up with you. We were just getting off the bus at the end of the road there,' She pointed up the street,' when we saw him coming out of a big house on the corner. We watched him as the old man he had been visiting waved him off.'

Peter listened, intrigued. 'And was it a big house, like the others in this area?' he asked. Beth nodded and bit straight into her éclair, not bothering to lick around the edges first. The cream squeezed out as she bit in to it and she scooped it up with her little finger and licked it off. 'Yeah! I suspect you could fit my whole flat into his kitchen.'

Peter rubbed his chin and wondered if this could be the Mark they had talked about. 'Did the old man look gay?' asked Peter. Beth looked at him and smiled.

'If you mean, did he go around wearing women's clothes and made up like Dolly Parton, then no.' She smirked at Peter and he got the message. Peter spread out his arms and said,

'Well. If you've got, flaunt it, I say.' Barry grinned and finished off his chocolate éclair.

'No. I don't know. He might have been... I just don't know.' Peter put his hand on hers.

'It doesn't matter,' he said. 'It would just rule it out if we knew for sure.' Barry stood up and told them to wait a minute. He jumped over the little chain-link fence that surrounded the seating area and we wandered off in the direction of the old man's house. Peter watched him as he minced up the street in his cut off T-shirt and white sandals.

'Where's he going?' he said, looking at Beth. She stared at Barry, not knowing what he was doing either.

Barry looked at the large, brass doorbell to the side of the grand entrance. Beneath it was a small white plaque that read ' Prof. Gerald Winslock'. Barry rang the door bell and he waited for what seemed to be a long time. He straightened his top and adjusted his shiny silver belt buckle, pushing it down, so it emphasised his crotch. The old man opened the door and Barry stood before him, trying to look innocent and boyish.

'Hello,' said the old man as he looked Barry up and down and smiled. 'What can I do for you,' he said in a posh, sophisticated voice, looking Barry in the eyes with a gentle, caring smile. Barry noticed him glance down at his crotch and he knew he had already answered the question.

'Hello Sir. I'm doing a door-to-door survey of the area, trying to find out people's views about the proposed opening of a gay night club on the corner of Osborne Road. I just wondered if you had any views on the matter.' The old man, who looked in his eighties and wore a deep red cardigan, smiled and looked at the pretty young man before him. Barry noticed him eyeing his crotch again and he smiled, saying,

'Oh that'll be nice for the young ones. You know in my day it was illegal to go into such places but now young men have it so much easier.' He smiled at Barry again and invited him in for a cup of tea. Barry declined but thanked him for his time, saying he had a lot of other doors to knock on. The old man watched him as he scurried off down the road back to his curious audience.

'So, where' you've been?' asked Beth, watching as he helped himself to his uncle's coffee and took a drink. He had a big grin across his face and he said,

'Well, that's confirmed he's definitely gay.' Peter held his hand to his mouth, worried that Barry had prostituted himself for his work. 'I could tell, just by speaking to him.' He told them about his ruse and how the man reacted to his belt buckle trick. Beth looked down at his crotch and said,

'Well I can't see what he was looking at. Pass me a magnifying glass someone.' Barry slapped her on the shoulder with all his might and said, '

Bitch!'

Peter watched as the two young people slapped each other and giggled. He finished off the coffee Barry had left in his cup and noticed Dr Collins standing up, about to leave. Peter slapped Barry and told them to look.

The man was wearing an expensive-looking suite and he was laughing with Greg, who hugged him as he departed. They watched as he got into his expensive car and drove off, leaving Gregg to pay the bill. He turned and looked in their direction as he downed the last of his coffee. The three of them turned quickly, pretending to look at something behind them but it was no good, Gregg had recognised Peter and he came over to their table.

'Hello Peter, fancy seeing you here.' Peter pretended as if he didn't recognise Gregg at first and then said hello, nodding and grinning like an idiot. Greg waved as he walked off, not staying to make polite conversation. Peter felt bad. He's not much of a detective if he can't even follow someone without being seen by his prey, he thought.

He heard the drip as the rain began to fall on the big umbrella above their heads and the heavens began to open in a torrential downpour. Peter wished he'd brought his umbrella and knew his hair would be ruined if he went out it this. Barry rummaged around in his big bag and pulled out a small pop-up umbrella and offered it to Peter. Peter grinned. Once again his nephew had saved the day.

Eight

'Just because he's gay and the fact that the doctor called on him isn't proof that he is their next victim,' said Bill as he massaged Peter's feet. Peter wasn't listening. He lay back on the sofa with his head resting on the flowery pillow and enjoyed the feet rub Bill was giving him. He had his eyes closed and was smiling to himself as Bill worked his magic on his sore feet. Bill noticed he wasn't paying attention, so he stopped and waited to see if Peter would notice.

Peter opened his eyes, realising the pleasurable sensation had stopped. He propped his chin on his chest and looked along his body to see why Bill had stopped. 'What's up dear?' he asked. Bill frowned and replied,

'I was saying about the old man... How can we be sure he's the mark?' Peter stayed where he was and rubbed his chin. Bill smiled. He knew, if Peter was rubbing his chin, he was thinking and that was good. Bill took one of Peter's toes and began to massage it. Peter let out one of his squeaks and giggled, quickly withdrawing his foot from Bill's grasp.

'Hey. That tickles,' he said, gingerly returning his foot to Bill's soft and loving hands. 'True,' he said. 'Barry seems to think he fulfils the criteria. He's obviously loaded, living in a big house like that. He's obviously gay – Barry made sure of that one.' He giggled remembering the tale Barry had told them. 'And he's obviously an old man – probably living on his own.'

Bill twirled each of Peter's toes in a circular motion and stretched the ligaments back and forth. He had done a reflexology class at the local school in the evenings, so he knew a little bit about foot massage and enjoyed giving his husband a foot rub that he knew he loved so much. Bill nodded and agreed. 'But that isn't definite proof that he's their mark. The doctor might just have been calling on him as one of his regular patients.'

Peter sat up, frustrated with Bill's negativity. 'Let's just assume he is for now. The odds are stacked in his favour and rather than make this bloody case any more complicated, let's just take it that he's their mark!'

Bill sat back, surprised that Peter had sworn. He looked at him and he could see he was weary. Maybe this detective malarkey was going to be too much for him, he thought. He sat and watched his husband, sitting with his legs crossed in the flowery skirt that he liked to wear around the house and his cosy cardigan, wrapped tightly around his bosom. Bill loved him so much and he wanted to be there to support him in whatever madcap things he got involved in.

Bill moved along the sofa, sat next to Peter and wrapped his hand around his. 'OK,' he said, 'Whatever you think is best.' Peter squeezed his hand and they sat and thought some more about what they had to do next.

***

Barry turned down the CD that Beth had turned up too loud. He knew his aunt and uncle didn't mind him playing his music in his room but he knew Peter was tired and he didn't want him disturbed unnecessarily. Beth sat on his bed and looked through one of his fashion magazines. She flicked through it looking at all of the glamorous, skinny models and tutted. 'Slaves... That's what they are,' she said. Barry looked over at her as he touched up the makeup around his eyes and looked at her reflection in the mirror that sat on his dresser.

His room was not that of a typical young man's. The walls were plastered with posters of Liza Minnelli and his dresser was covered in little bottles of cream, trays with an assortment of different coloured make-ups and enough perfume to drown in. He heard Beth rummage around under his bed and he heard her wolf-whistle, as she retrieved a magazine.

He turned and watched as she flicked the pages of his Gay Times magazine. 'He's a bit of all right,' she said as she admired a semi-naked young man posing with a book covering his nether regions. 'Pity about the book though.'

Barry grabbed the magazine from her and chucked it back under his bed. 'I dread to think what you use that for,' said Beth as she pulled out a small lolly and unwrapped it from its plastic jacket. She sucked on it and her pander-like eyes seemed to narrow with each suck. She pulled it out and pointed it to Barry. 'Want one?' she said. 'They're Tooty-Fruity!' Barry shook his head and came and sat next to her on the bed, kicking his legs up and shuffling close to his friend.

'Wow, I bet this is the first time you've had a girl on your bed,' she said, grinning and sucking on her lolly. He smiled and retorted,

'Well, if you use the term girl, very loosely,' he said. Beth's pander eyes widened and she stopped sucking her lolly mid way. She looked ridiculous with the thin, white stick protruding from her black lips and her eyes blinking with rage.

'And what's that supposed to mean,' she said, sitting up and grabbing Barry by the T-Shirt, scrunching it up in a ball and causing Barry to grimace at the creases she was creating. Barry tapped her hand and told her to get off. She relented and slumped back into her original position.

'I just mean... The Goth thing... Aren't you a bit old for that now?' Beth looked at him confused. Barry ran his hands through her hair and admired it. 'I mean I love your hair and the colour is great but...' He stretched the skin around her eyes and shook his head. 'The eye-thing has got to go.' Beth watched him as he stretched over to his dresser and pulled out some cleaning wipes. He began to wipe away the black mask that covered her eyes. She started to object and Barry slapped her hands away. 'Trust me. I'm a professional,' he said as he carefully wiped away the black sludge around her eyes and the white pancake that covered her fresh face below.

Beth felt naked without her pander makeup and she began to panic. Barry told her to wait as he brought over a small tray of eye makeup and a little brush. He dabbed the brush into some sparkly purple eye shadow and carefully brushed it across the top of each of Beth's eyes. He worked, occasionally sitting back to admire his creation and watched the fear on Beth's face gradually increase.

'There,' he said, sitting back on his ankles and standing up. He pulled her over the mirror and told her to look. Beth looked at him and he could see she was scared. 'Trust me, you look fab,' said

Barry as he pushed her onto the small stool in front of his dresser.

Beth looked in the mirror. Gone were the big black circles she had lived with all through her teenage years; gone was the pale complexion and the morbid exterior. She didn't recognise the beautiful girl Barry had uncovered. She stared at her eyes. The little bit of purple that he had applied really did accentuate their beauty and match the colour of her hair. Her skin looked so fresh, so clear.

She had become used to not looking in mirrors, not looking at her reflection if she could help it but now what she saw in the mirror, she liked. She looked at her lips. They were still black and she felt if she was going to cast away her immature ideas, then she had to finish the job Barry had started. She pulled out some of the wet wipes and scraped off the black, greasy lipstick. Barry could see where she was going and he handed her a small purple-tipped lipstick. She spread it over her skinny lips and rubbed them together.

Barry pulled her shoulders back and they looked at the new Beth in the mirror together. Beth smiled. She liked it and Barry felt proud of the transformation. 'Now that's a girl I wouldn't mind having on my bed,' said Barry. Beth looked at him and saw he expression change as he realised what he had just said. They both burst out laughing and Barry went weak at the knees.

***

Bill had already laid the table when they heard the youngsters upstairs rolling around on the floor and screaming. Peter smiled as he stirred the bolognaise sauce and tasted it, dipping his tongue into the sauce on the wooden spoon he was using to stir it with. 'It's good that Barry has found a new friend – well I mean an old friend,' said Peter. Bill nodded as he drained the spaghetti into the sink and stood back, allowing the steam to miss his head. His glasses steamed up as he moved the heavy pot over to the bench. He couldn't see where he was going so he had to look over the top of his glasses until he found his destination.

'Yes. I worry about him not having many friends...you know like him...us, I mean.' Peter turned off the gas and brought the pan across to Bill, who poured it over the individual plates onto which he had already shared out the pasta.

'Yeah. I know. Maybe he'll meet a nice boy and settle down soon,' said Bill. Peter thought about the time when Barry would eventually want to fly the nest. He'd miss him, he thought.

They heard the thunder of their steps as they ran down stairs and burst into the kitchen, full of energy. Barry pushed Beth forward, holding his creation proudly by the shoulders. Beth stood, like a doll, nervous at the expected reaction. 'What do you think?' asked Barry. Peter looked up and smiled. Bill pulled his piny off and also looked at Beth.

'Wow! What a difference,' said Peter. 'You look fabulous!' Beth blushed and this time, because she was not hidden behind a layer of morbid-white makeup, everyone could see her fresh and youthful cheeks flush pink. She looked so much more human and Peter commented that before, he thought she looked like death warmed up but now, she looked beautiful. Barry gleamed with pride and Beth sank into her seat with slight embarrassment but also with a contented glow.

Bill placed the hot food in front of Beth and she tucked in greedily. He was a little surprised, as he thought girls of her age never ate anything, trying desperately to maintain their slender figures. He was pleased that Beth didn't match that cliché and he liked that she obviously enjoyed his home cooking.

They all sat and enjoyed their meal, chatting about life and about Beth's job at the chemist. Bill asked her if she wanted to be a pharmacist and she told him that she wanted to be a singer and that she had a band that she sang for whenever they could get a bar to give them a gig. Peter was impressed. He remembered when he first started out on the drag scene and how difficult it was to get started.

He told them about some of the sleazy clubs he had worked in and Bill nodded and confirmed the outrageous stories that he told them. Barry sat in a daze as his uncle Peter relayed his outrageous anecdotes and they all laughed and giggled when he told them about the number of times he'd been propositioned by drunken straight men, thinking he was a woman.

Barry leant over his plate, being careful not to get the tomato sauce on his clean T-Shirt and slurped up a long length of spaghetti. He licked his lips, enjoying the warm, home-made sauce and said,' So, how are we going to keep tabs on the doctor, when we can't keep up with him in his car?'

Peter nodded, dabbing his chin with a paper napkin. 'Yes. That's a problem. Maybe it would make more sense if I followed him and you two did Greg instead. Beth sipped on her carton of Ribena she had brought with her and nodded in agreement. 'That's that sorted,' said Peter, looking at his watch. 'I've got to get ready for tonight's... gig,' he chose the word carefully and glanced at Beth. Beth grinned and asked if she could come along.

'I've never seen you in full drag,' she said, slurping the dregs out of the carton. Peter frowned at the unpleasant sound it made and said it was okay. 'It will be nice to see you all made up and in your Dolly frock.' Peter stood up, raised his nose in the air, as if affronted, straightened his skirt and said,

'It's not frock, my dear. It's a dress. Us professionals call them dresses.' He waved his skirt and minced out of the kitchen and up the stairs to his bedroom, saying 'Uh! Really, a frock indeed!' Barry grinned at Beth as if to say, I told you so.

***

The performance lasted almost an hour and Beth loved every minute of it. At first she found it strange being surrounded by lots of camp young men, in their white T-shirts and with their shaven heads. She thought they all looked so stereotypical and she was glad she was unique. It wasn't long before she relaxed and enjoyed the music, letting her hair down and swinging to the beat. She watched as Peter came up to her and sang directly to her one of his favourite songs. The buzz of the microphone softened his voice and she smiled as he winked at her, swinging his own hips to the tune.

Barry brought her a drink and she sat back at the table with him. 'She's very good,' she said, nodding towards Peter on the stage. Barry nodded back, sucking on the straw in his glass of Martini and lemonade. Beth noticed a young man looking over the crowd towards them. She knew he couldn't be interested in her so she nudged Barry and whispered in his ear. 'I think that fella fancies you.' She pointed him out and Barry blushed.

'Not when I'm working,' he said over the din of the speakers. Beth looked confused.

'Working? You call this working?' Barry grinned, glancing over at the handsome young stud across the room. He was good looking, he thought but he had his rules.

'Why don't you go and talk to him. He's got a nice smile.' Barry looked over at the man again. She was right. He had nice white teeth and looked a similar age to himself. He wore the typical white T-shirt and tight jeans and Barry thought he was quite beautiful.

'No, Peter's due off in ten minutes. He'll need me in the dressing room.' Beth slumped back into her chair and said,

'Fair enough! It up to you if you want to end up a lonely old spinster.' Barry smiled but looked over at the young man, who had given up trying to catch his eye and sighed into his glass.

Beth had never seen inside a proper dressing room before. On the few occasions her band had managed to get a gig, they were never given a dressing room; they had to get changed in the van in the car park. She looked at the light bulb-ringed mirror and thought that was a bit of a cliché and she watched as Peter wiped his face clean of its makeup and Barry lift off the glorious white Dolly wig and place it in the case made especially for it. She could see the outline of the heavy wig still impressed into Peter's forehead and the beads of sweat ran down his face as he cleaned away the remnants of Dolly. Peter looked at her in the reflection of the mirror.

'What did you think, my dear,' he asked as he peeled off his eyelashes and undid the enormous earrings that hung from each lobe.

'Bloody brilliant!' she said, forgetting Peter's dislike of

swearing. He overlooked it and waited for more praise from his newest fan. Beth looked at him, his face now clear of makeup and continued, realising he wanted more. 'I loved your singing,' Peter bowed his head graciously, 'And the way you hold the audience – such charisma!' Peter blushed modestly and said, brushing his thinning hair across his scalp,

'You can come again, my dear!' They all laughed and Beth watched as Barry grabbed Peter's big rubber breasts and lifted them into their case. She noticed how different Peter looked flat-chested and she thought he looked odd – he looked like a man.

Bill came in and Beth had to stand against the wall in the small room to let him past. He started packing up all of Peter's things and Beth offered to help him take things back to the car. 'Oh! You are a dear,' said Bill, heavily laden with bags and dresses on hangers.

Barry stood to one side and Let Peter rise, regally. Beth cleared the way and they all headed out of the club and back to the car park.

'Can we drop you off Beth?' asked Bill as he closed the boot of the car. Barry and Peter were already sitting in the back seat and Barry was still fussing over Peter's makeup. She popped her head in the door and felt the warm air of the heater stroke her chilled face. She said goodbye to the two on the back seat and told Bill she was okay – she didn't live far and she would walk. He nodded and she waved them off as she felt the cold air of the night nip at her thin waist.

Beth looked around the almost-empty car park and wondered where she should go tonight. The roof of the building in front of her was covered in a light dusting of frost except for one area, which remained clear. She knew it was going to be a cold night. She headed for the fire escape and looked up, knowing that the only chance of a warm bed lay at the top. She climbed the metal frame of the escape ladder and headed for the roof.

The heat vent from the takeaway gave off a warmness that she needed and she curled herself up close to it and closed her eyes.

Nine

They had agreed to meet in the cafe near the Metro station and Barry was already there when Beth arrived. He watched her as she came in. She looked frozen to the bone and she had her long coat buttoned up to the collar. Barry noticed her fish net stockings that she had been wearing the day before and in fact, whenever they had been together. He wondered if they were really sensible for this type of weather and then he remembered his uncle's saying: Us women have to suffer to please our men! And he put the thought to the back of his mind.

Beth looked at the menu and at the hot, sizzling fry-ups that the waitress carried out to other tables and she breathed in the warm, belly-filling aroma and then ordered a cup of tea. 'Aren't you going to have something?' asked Barry, biting into his sausage sandwich and drinking his mug of tea. Beth shook her head and placed the small cup on the table before she swung her legs under it. It was difficult to bend in the tightly-fastened, full-length coat but the thought of letting in any cold air made Beth make do and sit, buttoned up like a mummy.

Barry thought it strange but he focused on his sandwich and Beth watched him and she felt a little faint. She sat up, trying not to think about the beautiful smells that surrounded her and she said, 'So, what time does this Greg character usually turn up?' Barry shrugged his shoulders.

'Peter said he saw him about half past nine last time, so about then I guess.' He looked at his watch and decided it was too early to leave, so he finished off the first half of his sandwich. He looked at Beth looking at the other half and he watched her eyes, staring at it. 'Do you want that other half,' said Barry nodding to the remaining feast before Beth and said he was full and couldn't finish it.

Beth looked at him. She could feel her stomach aching with emptiness and the smell of the brown sauce and grease made her yearn for the sandwich. 'Er...Better not,' she said. 'All that fat isn't good for you.' Barry looked at her and he could tell that she really wanted it. He sensed there was something else too but he couldn't quite figure it out.

'Well, no doubt, we'll be walking it off today following this Greg around.' She looked at him and smiled. She slid the plate over to her and took a bite of the sandwich. Her cold lips wrapped themselves around the cheap bread and she felt the warm meaty sausage slip between her teeth. She made short work of it and when Barry looked up again, it was gone. Beth smiled and unbuttoned the top two buttons of her coat; she was feeling better now and was keen to get on with the job in hand.

Barry stood up and suggested they get on. Beth agreed and followed him out on to the street. They could see the agency and decided to start by calling in and pretending to be house buyers. Beth was pleased to be in out of the cold and she looped Barry's arm and behaved like a customer as they looked at the boards with details of the houses for sale.

Barry noticed the staff watching them and giggled, wondering what they were thinking. The two of them must not look like their usual customers, he thought; Beth in her Goth uniform and him in his stylish, but slightly camp, attire.

They looked up at the images of the mansion houses on offer. 'Bloody hell! Whispered Barry as he pointed to a large Georgian house for sale. 'Two point eight million! They've got to be kidding!' He heard a voice behind them and they turned, still locked together in their loop and a middle-class lady with her hair tied up in a smart, brown bun, glanced at them as they presented themselves front-on. Her face changed as she noticed Barry wearing makeup and Beth's tall, bedraggled purple hair.

The lady forced a smile and said, 'Can I be of any service?' Barry tried to hold a smirk and said they were just looking, thanks. She nodded and returned to her desk. Beth dragged Barry over to look at an even bigger house and she pointed to the picture of the swimming pool. He agreed it must be wonderful to have your own pool but then he noticed a picture out of the corner of his eye. It was Joe's house. He recognised the big white front door and he studied the details. He pulled out his notebook and wrote down what he thought might be important. The lady at the desk watched him and was about to come over and tell him about the property when the phone on her desk rang.

Beth pulled Barry back and forward around the small agency

and Barry overheard the conversation the lady was having with the caller.

'Sorry, Greg's not in today. It's his day off. Can I take a message?' Barry pulled on Beth's arm as she drooled over the big houses and large, well-kept lawns.

'Did you hear that?' he asked and she turned not aware of the telephone conversation. 'We're wasting our time...He not in today!' Beth frowned.

***

Peter looked at the speedometer. He was doing almost seventy in a sixty zone. 'Bloody Idiot!' said Peter as he tried to keep up with the car ahead of him. The expensive Mercedes turned off the motorway and Peter had to cut in front of another car to make the exit himself. He was sweating. He wasn't used to this sort of driving. Bill usually did most of the driving and Peter knew he would be curled up on the back seat if could see how Peter had to drive to keep up with Dr Collins.

Peter looked in the rear view mirror and noticed a bead of sweat trickling down his forehead. He wanted to wipe it away but he didn't want to lose his quarry. Peter flicked his head to one side and tried to force the droplet off his brow. He sat at the traffic lights, twitching and shaking his head until he noticed the man in the car in the next lane watching him. Peter giggled. They must have thought he was having some sort of fit, he thought. He used the time to get a hanky from his bag and he mopped his brow, smiling at the man in the next lane.

The lights changed and the Mercedes was off. Peter hadn't noticed. He was still watching the other man and noticed him pull away. Peter looked up and saw the lights change again to red. He watched as the Mercedes turned off the high street into a back lane. He couldn't move. The light was still on red and he panicked, thinking he had lost him. The lights changed and Peter turned off down the same street, hoping that he could catch up with the doctor.

Peter couldn't see the car anywhere on the road and he sighed. He decided he might as well drive to the end and turn back towards home. He looked to the right and he spotted the car parked in a car park at the back of what looked like a commercial building. Peter pulled up and decided to get out and investigate.

The sign above the parking space said, 'Parking for Customers of Saville & Co Only.' That didn't tell him much, thought Peter so he decided to walk around to the front of the building and see what Saville & Co did.

The front of the street was very grand. Late Georgian, thought Peter. The buildings all were fronted with twelve-paned sash windows and their doors were grand and foreboding. Peter walked along the palatial avenue and looked at the brass signs to the side of each door. 'Saville & Co – Solicitors' Peter read the sign and was impressed by its fancy marble frame.

He thought for a moment and rubbed his chin. He wouldn't find out much out on the street, he thought. But what reason did he have to go in? He took a deep breath and pulled open the heavy door.

The reception was very elegant and the professional young lady behind the desk smiled at him and waited for him to speak. Peter hesitated. What was he doing here, he thought. 'Er...'He said looking around him for inspiration. He noticed a box on the desk behind the lady with old-looking documents, tied up with red ribbons. Peter looked at her and smiled.

'I'd like to have a will drawn up for me and my Hus...' he stopped, realising what he was about to say may sound odd, 'Wife,' he finished. The young woman smiled and said that wouldn't be a problem and asked if he had an appointment. Peter shook his head.

'Can I just take your name,' she said as she pulled a pad of paper in front of her and waited for Peter's answer. Peter froze. He knew it best not to give his real name – detectives on the TV never did. He quickly looked about the woman's desk and noticed the stamps hanging on a circular rack to her left,

'Stamp. Mr Stamp.' He smiled and she asked him to take a seat. Peter sat and looked around the waiting room, thinking what on earth was he doing here and what was he going to do next.

He looked up at the grand clock above the reception desk and he checked it against his own watch. He wasn't sure if he was cut out to be doing this sort of thing and he wondered if he should just make an excuse and leave. He noticed the woman watching him and looking at his bright umbrella.

He had borrowed it from Barry. It was his favourite and Peter had to promise to look after it. Peter looked at it. The bright pink and yellow folds of its skin looked out of place in the reserved greyness of the solicitor's office and he understood her interest in it. He smiled and told her he had to borrow it from a friend. She nodded and returned to her work.

He felt uncomfortable and he needed to pee. He fidgeted in his seat and his nerves made it worse. He stood up and asked the young lady if there was a customer toilet he could use. She pointed him to a door and gave him directions. He thanked her and headed for the door.

As he stood at the urinal he heard two other men come in and stand at the stalls further down the row. Peter, with his face glued to the wall in front listened as they chatted and peed in unison. They were very upper class, thought Peter - Definitely public school types.

'I've got everything we need set up and the Winslock will's being typed up as we speak.' He heard the older man say. Peter finished up and went over to the sink to wash his hands. 'All I need is a copy of the signature and we're set.' The two men joined him at the sink and they nodded to him as he dried his hands on the air dryer. Peter couldn't hear anything more over the noise of the dryer and wished he'd thought about it before using it. He turned, about to leave when he recognised one of the men. It was Dr Collins. Peter froze, frightened of being recognised. Then he remembered he had never actually met the doctor, so he wouldn't recognise him anyway. He needed to quickly think of a reason not to leave. The others noticed him hover by the door and then Peter spotted the vending machine on the wall.

It was a condom vending machine and he thought what a strange place to put one. Never mind, he thought, it gave him those extra few second to delay his exit. He fumbled around in his pocket for change and took his time as he listened to their conversation.

'What about witnesses. Are we using the same ones as last time?' said Dr Collins. Peter found a pound coin, thinking that would be enough. He looked at the slot and read the label. £3 each it said. Cricky, thought Peter. It had been many years since he had bought such things and he thought it outrageous to charge such a price.

'No, I think it wise we select different witnesses this time... you know, to be on the safe side.' Dr Collins nodded and looked over at Peter fumbling with his change. 'I think I can get a couple sorted out – provided we bung them a few quid,' said Dr Collins.

Peter put his money in the slot and watched as the small packet dropped into the shoot at the bottom. He took his time and pretended to read the back of the condom packet. What am I doing? He thought. Who reads the back of a condom packet?

The older man straitened his tie in the mirror and Dr Collins slapped him on the back. 'I'll give you a call,' he said as he left. The older man noticed Peter still hanging around, fidgeting with the condom in his hand and he pointed his eyes towards an open toilet cubicle. Peter had seen that look before and he knew what it meant. He put the condom in his jacket pocket and left for the reception.

The young woman noticed his return and she told him that Mr Saville was free to see him now. Peter had forgotten about the reason he was supposed to be here and he collected his umbrella and told her that he had changed his mind. He left her with her chin hanging down in surprise. He headed for the street but the doctor had gone.

It didn't matter, he had found out what he had wanted to hear and he felt proud of his achievement. He couldn't wait to get back and tell the others.

'So should we just go back to yours,' asked Beth as Barry looked up and down the street, looking lost. Beth liked the idea of staying in the warm and she knew she'd get a nice lunch if she went back to Peter's.

'No. It seems daft to have come all this way and not achieved anything,' said Barry, looking at his watch and looking up the street again. He stood, as if there was an idea formulating in his mind and Beth watched him.

'Well?' she snapped, feeling the cold air begin to rise up her coat again. She wished she had thought to bring more clothes when she had decided to leave home. It was a difficult time - a stressful time and she acted on the spur of the moment, not thinking about things like clothes or money.

'Here,' said Barry, holding out his hand. Beth took it gratefully, expecting to be taken back to the metro station to get back to Barry's warm and cosy house. Barry dragged her in the opposite direction and headed up the street. Beth was confused.

'Where we going?' she said, like an uncooperative child, being tugged by its mother to the dentist. Barry just grinned and replied,

'I've got an idea.'

Beth didn't recognise the street and Barry told her to behave herself as they approached the big house he had visited previously. They stopped at the gate and Barry noticed a small but expensive car parked in the driveway. That hadn't been there before, he thought. It was the sort of car you saw a lot in areas like this; small, flashy and totally impractical. He noticed the old man in the front room. The view from the road allowed them to see directly into his living room and Barry could see the back of the head of the man he was talking to. He recognised the back of this head, he thought – it was Greg's. Barry watched and Beth wondered why he was looking at this house and not heading back to the metro.

'Who lives here?' she asked, now curious why Barry was looking into someone else's front room. She thought it a bit rude and tugged his arm to get him to come away.

'Look,' he said, pulling her by the sleeve. He pointed at the window. 'Don't you recognise him?' Beth looked and saw Greg. She froze, not sure what to do next. They both stood and watched as the old man led Greg into a back room they couldn't see.

Barry tugged on Beth's sleeve and told her to follow him. 'Where are you going,' she said in a hushed voice as she looked around to see if they were being observed. Barry crept around the back, along the gravel drive, which no matter how lightly they tread, it could not disguise their approach.

He noticed a light on in the rear of the property and he crouched down under the window. By the smell coming from the small gap of the open window, he could tell it was the kitchen. They could hear the two men talking and it wasn't clear what they were saying but Barry recognised flirting when he heard it. He had heard enough of it in the gay bars he worked in over the years and it was clear that Greg was coming on to the old man. Beth knelt beside him and placed her ear as near to the gap as she could. Barry looked up and noticed her big hair was sticking above the windowsill and would easily be seen from inside. He pulled her down and indicated to her hair. She looked bemused for a second and then got what he was trying to say and ducked even lower.

They heard a sound around the front of the house and voices. Barry crept along the driveway, keeping close to the wall, where the gravel was thinner and made less noise. He carefully popped his head around the corner and caught a glimpse of Greg standing at the front door. Beth wanted to see too but Barry held her back. He slipped just enough of his head out so he could watch them with his right eye.

Greg hugged the man and kissed him gently on the cheek. 'I'll call round tomorrow and we can try on those new boxers you got me for my birthday,' he said giggling like a schoolboy. The old man, excitedly said,

'Oh Yes. I'd like that very much!' Greg kissed him again and got into his sports car and blew the old man a kiss as he drove off. Barry watched as the old man smiled and watched as his new young friend drove away in his expensive car. Barry shook his head and pulled Beth along to the gate.

'Bastard!' he said as he thought about what Greg was doing to the poor old man. Beth understood and she squeezed his hand and said,

'Let's go home.'

Ten

Peter was in a good mood and he sat on the sofa, smiling as Beth and Barry came in. He looked at them, dying to tell them about his day. Bill was in the kitchen and shouted out, 'Is that the kids?'

Beth wasn't sure about being called a kid but it was nice to be referred to as a member of the family. She liked it at Peter's house. It was always warm and friendly. They were such nice people and she felt at home there.

Bill popped his head around the door and confirmed his own question. 'Ooh, you look cold Beth. Why don't you put the fire on and get warmed up.' Beth needed no further encouragement and she knelt in front of the electric fire and switched it on. Peter noticed a tear in her fish-net stockings and he noticed how pale her legs were.

It was an old fashioned fire it and had two long electric bars that heated up quickly and gave off a reassuring glow. She pulled her big boots under her and sat Buda-style by the fire.

Peter watched her and could see she didn't look comfortable. 'Why don't you take those big boots off Beth?' He could see they were up to her knees and he was sure they couldn't be comfortable to sit on. Beth smiled and started to unbuckle the twenty or so buckles that ran the full length of each boot.

'Cricky,' said Peter. 'Those must take you a week to get on and off.' Beth smiled and slipped off the first boot and put it by the side of the fire to warm.

Barry was itching to tell them his story and Peter could see him writhing with energy. 'So how did it go?' asked Peter, deciding to let Barry go first and put him out of his misery. Barry came and sat on the sofa next to Peter and Bill came in, still carrying a tea-towel and propped himself against the edge of the sofa. Barry told them about how they thought they'd had a wasted trip and about his intention to call on the old man and try to get to know him. He told them about Greg and how he heard him flirting with him. Peter nodded, recognising the style.

'So that confirms he's their target then,' said Peter, still itching to tell them about his adventure. Barry nodded. He looked sad and Bill touched him on the shoulder, recognising Barry's pain.

'We won't let anything happen to that old man. Don't worry,' said Bill, stroking his shoulder. Barry looked up at his aunty and nodded.

Beth could see Peter was near bursting point and she asked him if he had any luck. Peter's eyes glowed as he told his tale. He told them about the car chase and the solicitor's office. He told them about the conversation he overheard in the gents and Beth held her hand over her mouth in disbelief at what he had heard.

'So, they're definitely going to do it again, then?' she said stretching her skinny legs out in front of the fire and warming her small feet against the bars. Peter nodded and said,

'Looks like it. The solicitor's obviously bent and he's setting up the will side of things; the doctor is probably poisoning the victims and the gigolo is the one who draws them in.' Bill held the tea-towel up to his mouth and then, realising it wasn't hygienic, lowered it and scrunched it up.

'Well, we don't know about the poisoning bit of it, do we? I mean there's no proof of that is there?' said Beth, feeling remarkably at home and wondering what Bill was going to make them for lunch.

Bill was looking uneasy and stood up about to go back to his dishes. 'Shouldn't we just pass this information on to the police and let them take over?' The three of them all looked at him in horror. Barry shook his head and Beth lost interest in the fire. Peter stood up and patted him on the arm softly, saying,

'Not just yet. Let's make sure we've got enough for them to do a good job and put these buggers behind bars!' Barry and Beth nodded and Bill returned to the kitchen and said,

'OK, as you think best dear.'

***

Beth had enjoyed her day. It had been nice to be involved in something exciting and it was nice to be in a family again. She sat on the sofa between Barry and Peter as they watched Coronation Street. Peter had his feet up on a small footrest and she watched him as he gazed at the TV, totally lost in the story and his favourite characters.

Barry lay low in his seat, his legs propped on the coffee table and his little pink socks shoeless. Barry held onto her Arm and he snuggled in like a boyfriend might do. She giggled to herself, watching Barry grip her arm, his fingers wrapped under it and pressed against the side of her breast. She knew if Barry had been straight, he would be enjoying the close contact but she knew Barry was oblivious to the fact that he was touching her breast and she liked the fact that she could relax, safe in the knowledge Barry didn't even notice or care she had breasts.

She thought about what had happened at home; she thought about that final night before she decided she'd had enough and stormed out, not thinking where she might go.

Her father had been drinking again. He often came home smelling of whiskey and she hated that smell; she hated the feel of his warm breath against her cheek as he stood too close and shouted at her. Beth tried to focus on the TV but she could hear the rain on the window and the harsh wind tugging at the big bush in the garden, occasionally beating it against the window as a gust of autumn wind shook its thin branches. She didn't want to leave the comfort of Peter's warm home and face the harsh reality of sleeping on the street.

She wrapped her arm around Barry's shoulder and held him tight against her chest. She needed comfort; she needed someone to hold her. Barry, still oblivious to his surroundings and grinning at the actions of the characters, didn't notice as she squeezed him closer.

Her father was a violent man. Her mother had died from breast cancer when she was twelve and she had been left in his care, despite her requests that she be allowed to stay with her gran. Her father had never got over the loss of his wife and he mourned for her, soothing his pain with whiskey.

Beth had taken over the responsibility of running the house and looking after her dad. It was only when he developed an interest in his growing daughter that Beth's life changed for the worse. She was a pretty child and by the age of fifteen her developing body had caught the eye of her father.

Without the protection of family members or guardians, it wasn't long before her father had taken her innocence. He threatened her with a beating if she told anyone and this continued up until the age of seventeen. She had become his slave – to do with as he pleased and to throw away when he was finished.

Beth had suffered from depression since her mother had died and she wished she had someone to talk to during that difficult time. Her father only ever let her out of the house to do the shopping and to fetch him more whiskey, frightened if she spent time with people, his secret would be revealed.

She had adopted the Goth way of life as a way to hide; her big hair could be wrapped around her face and her long, black coat obscured her body, keeping her safe from the eyes of men.

Peter laughed as the final scene ended and he placed his warm, soft hand on her thigh. Beth had never felt threatened by Peter. He was a man but not in the same way as other men. She thought of him as an aunty. 'Anybody fancy a cuppa?' he said as he squeezed her thigh and got up to head for the kitchen. Barry slumped onto Beth as the space created by Peter leaving made her sink into the void.

'Get off, you big poof!' said Beth as she propped Barry back up and slipped out from under him. He giggled and spread himself out on the full length of the sofa and flicked channels with the remote.

Beth joined Peter in the kitchen. She wanted to be of some help; she wanted to feel useful. After all, she had done everything at home – the cooking, the cleaning and looked after the bills, everything. Peter looked at her and noticed the tear in her stocking again. He didn't say anything, not sure if he should.

Peter looked at the clock and then lifted the net curtain and looked out at the garden. It was getting dark and he said they would probably get a frost again tonight. Beth shuddered at the thought of another night on the roof of the takeaway, huddle close to the air vent for warmth. Peter turned, his kind smile gently spreading across his face as he looked at Beth. In the strip light of the kitchen Peter could see the she looked different; she looked concerned.

'Is there anything up, my dear?' he said, as he pushed the door to the kitchen slightly ajar, quietening the sound of the game show

Barry was now watching. Peter looked at Beth's eyes. They looked nice, now that Barry had scraped away all of that black muck but he could see the tremble of her body, the gentle rock of her legs, as if they were about to give way beneath her. He watched as the emotion began to well up inside her and he new she was about to explode with something – he didn't know what but he knew there was something coming.

He held her by the elbow and what he was expecting came. Her eyes filled with tears and her cheeks wrinkled. She sniffed and rubbed the tears that had begun to fall across her beautiful cheeks and Peter just knew he had to hold her. He pulled her to his chest and she buried her face into him and cried. Peter stroked her back, not sure what was going on; he just knew she needed him right now and he squeezed her close and waited until she was ready to talk.

Bill came in, finished having a bath upstairs. He opened the door and saw Peter cradling Beth in his arms. Peter gently shook his head and indicated to Bill to leave them be. Bill could see Beth was in distress and he nodded, quietly pulling the door closed behind him and joining Barry on the sofa.

Peter pulled out a chair and sat Beth down in it. She had stopped sobbing and looked at Peter's gentle, caring eyes. 'Sorry,' she said, wiping her eyes with her sleeve. Peter handed her a small, flowery box of tissues and she took a few, blowing her small nose and mopping the dampness from around her eyes. 'I must look like a right fool,' she said, breathing in deeply and trying to compose herself.

Peter sat on the chair next to her and held her hand. 'Now, what's this all about?' he said. Beth looked into his kind face. She could see the outline of his makeup and his faint covering of blusher over each cheek. She looked at his smile and felt reassured that she was safe.

'I've left home,' she said, sniffing. Peter looked confused. 'I left home on Tuesday and I've been sleeping rough ever since.' Peter's eyes widened. He couldn't believe it.

'But it's been freezing the last few nights. How on earth have you survived the cold?' He pulled her to his chest and hugged her. 'You poor dear.'

Beth snuggled into Peter's chest. She felt safe and relief that her story was out. She went on to tell Peter about her father and the life she had at home, since her mother died. Peter sat, holding a tissue up to his mouth, trying to hold back the tears himself. She finished her tale and she slumped back into her seat, unsure what would happen next. Peter waited for a moment, rubbing his chin.

He stood up, pulled open the kitchen door and shouted, 'Barry!' Beth looked at him, unsure what he was doing. Barry came in, still grinning at the comedy sketch he had been watching with his aunty Bill. He glanced at Beth and noticed her tear-stained face. His grin dropped and his expression changed to that of concern. He was just about to ask what had happened when Peter held him by the shoulders and said,

'Go up to the spare room and make up the bed.' Barry looked at him, not sure why he was being given such instructions. 'Beth is moving in,' said Peter. Barry glanced across at Beth and he grinned and nodded. Before he could ask any further questions, Peter swung him around by the shoulders and patted him on the bottom, pushing him out of the kitchen. He turned and faced Beth, who had a look of shock on her face.

'Are you sure?' she asked, still trembling with shock and wiping the last tear from her eye. Peter saw the beginnings of a smile forming at the corners of her thin lips and he smiled and said,

'Of course, my dear. It will be nice to have another woman about the house.' Beth smiled and hugged Peter. 'Now get upstairs and clean your room!' announced Peter, like any mother should do to her children, he thought.

Beth smiled, kissed Peter on the cheek and ran out of the kitchen, kissing her new aunty on the cheek to and darted up the stairs to the spare room.

Eleven

Peter sat in his car and watched as people came and went into the surgery. He could see the doctor's Mercedes parked to the side of the building and he thought about the conversation he had with the solicitor in the gents. 'Thieving bugger,' he said under his breath as he looked at the expensive car. Peter wondered how many times he had done it before and how many innocent old men he had slaughtered to buy his expensive trinkets.

He was bored; he had been there since nine and as he looked at his watch it said ten twenty. He huffed and tapped his steering wheel, as he always did when he was bored. He wasn't even sure what good it would do to keep following the doctor. He knew what he had planned and he knew the old man was in danger but did he need to keep following him, he wondered. His mind wandered from topic to topic and he thought about Beth.

Bill had agreed to help her recover her things from her father's place when she knew he would be in the pub. Peter was pleased that she now seemed more settled, having her own clothes and a few of her possessions in her new room and he was pleased that he was able to help her.

He had sent Barry and Beth to keep an eye on the Greg character. Again, he wasn't sure how much more they could do but at least he knew that if the doctor and Greg were occupied, then the old man was still safe.

He guessed if the solicitor was getting the will ready and Greg was obviously buttering up the old man, how long was it going to be before they attempted to kill him? A shudder ran down Peter's spine. The thought of them killing the innocent old man made him shiver with disgust.

Peter was pleased he had Bill. To be alone when you are old must be horrible, he thought. He remembered the day Bill and him had their Civil Partnership ceremony. It was a wonderful day and Peter felt like a blushing bride as Bill stood by his side in the registry office and they exchanged their vows. He really loved Bill and hoped they would continue to have the wonderful relationship they had enjoyed for the last twenty-five years. Peter smiled as he remembered the things he and Bill had done during their time together.

He was so involved in his memories, that he hadn't noticed the doctor's car pulling out of its space and leaving the car park. It was the lights on its rear that caught his attention as it braked before turning left.

'Here we go again,' said Peter as he started the engine and tried to catch up with the doctor. He pulled up behind him at the traffic lights and noticed him looking in his rear-view mirror at Peter. He wondered if he would remember him from the gents and Peter looked to the side giving him a little chance as possible to get a good look at his face. The lights changed and the Mercedes sped off ahead.

Peter's little hatchback didn't have the power to catch up with him and Peter watched as the performance car turned off down the slip road and headed towards the city centre. It was several minutes before Peter spotted him again. He watched him as he stood in front of the machine buying a parking ticket. He was on his mobile and didn't notice as Peter pulled into the empty parking bay a few cars up from his.

Peter looked for change as he waited and wanted to be ready to buy his ticket and catch up with him before he lost sight of him again. The doctor returned to his car and placed the ticket in his windscreen, still talking to someone on his phone. He had his hands full, looking for something in a small leather portfolio he carried under his other arm. He placed the slim case onto his bonnet and rummaged through the papers. Peter thought this would be a good time to get his own ticket, whilst the doctor was tied up with his caller. He slipped out, fed the machine and deposited the ticket in the small window of his car.

The doctor finished his call and put away the papers he had been referring to whilst on the phone and zipped up the case. Peter faced the other way, pretending to look at a notice board hung there to advise customers about closing times and other council information.

He followed the doctor through the shopping centre and down the escalator into the basement of the mall. He was surprised to see him enter a rough-looking cafe opposite the butchers and Peter watched as he took a seat near the back of the cafe in a small alcove, tucked to one side. He had his back to the window, so Peter felt confident about following him in.

He bought a cup of tea and sat as close to the alcove as he could without the doctor being able to see him. The walls of the cafe were lined with greasy-looking mirrors and peter could see the doctor sat at his table. Fortunately the wall the doctor faced had no mirrors and Peter knew he wouldn't be able to see him.

He wondered why on earth the doctor had decided to come to such a place. The cafe was grimy and not the sort of place Peter would normally consider eating at. Its tables were covered in cheap Formica, cracked with age and stained with years of use. The floor was disgusting and the smell of burgers and chip fat was quite off-putting.

Peter looked at the cup of tea he had been given. The edge of the cup still had lipstick around it from its previous user and Peter pushed it away and frowned at the thought of drinking from it. He looked around the cafe and it was filled with the lower echelons of society. A man in the corner looked like he had too much to drink and he struggled to negotiate an egg and sausage sandwich into his whiskered mouth.

Another woman sat and stretched her long black tights along her legs and straightened the seams while she waited for her current customer to bring her a cup of tea. The man returned and grouped her under the table as she sipped on the grubby cup. She giggled and rubbed his leg in return.

Peter looked at the sad characters and he was grateful he had Bill and Barry – and now Beth, he thought. He watched as a young couple came in. She pushed a pushchair containing a screaming baby and he waded forward, oblivious to the screaming child and looked around the cafe as if expecting to meet someone. Peter looked at him. He wore the typical baseball cap and tracksuit bottoms, again tucked into his white sports socks and he shouted at the girl he had in tow as she got in his way.

He watched the creature as he strutted his way to the back of the cafe and Peter looked in the mirror to see him standing by the table the doctor was sitting at.

'Alright?' said the young Chav as he plonked himself down opposite the doctor. The girl was obviously struggling to get the pushchair past the narrow gap between the tables but the young man ignored her plight and shouted at her to hurry up and sit down.

'Did ya bring the money?' said the thug and the doctor nodded. The young mother sat the screaming child on her knee and bounced it up and down. The doctor took out a wad of notes and flashed it quickly in front of them. Peter watched as the young man's eyes swelled with desire as he watched the notes being returned to the doctor's inside jacket pocket. The girl smiled at him and she managed to quieten the baby.

Peter watched as the doctor unzipped the case and pulled out a thick, folded document. He unfolded it and got out his gold-coloured pen. He pointed to a spot on the paper and handed the man his pen. The young man admired the gold pen and looked at the paper before him. 'Here?' he said pointing at the thick parchment. 'Sign your name and then write your name and address beneath it and the date,' He looked at his expensive-looking watch and said, 'Twenty third of November 2010'. The young man leant across the paper and looked closely at his words as he carefully scribbled his name and concentrated as he tried to remember his address. He sat up proudly and grinned as if he deserved a prize for literary achievement.

The doctor checked his writing and nodded. He passed the document across to the girl and gave the pen to her. She looked at the long text and frowned. 'What's it for,' she said as she held the pen in mid air. The young man slapped her in the arm,

'Never mind what it's frigging for, just sign it!' The girl sank her head and signed her name. She filled in her address and dated the form, handing back the pen to the doctor. The young man watched her as she passed the gold pen back to him and he frowned at her, as if to say, stupid girl.

The doctor looked again at both signatures and addresses and grinned. He slipped the document back into the case and the young man said,

'And the two hundred?' The doctor nodded and pulled out the pile of folded notes and handed it to the man. His face lit up as he counted the notes and he quickly pushed it into his jeans pocket. 'Cheers,' he said and he pushed the girl out of his way and marched off to the door. The girl struggled to get the small child back into its pushchair and the doctor helped her.

'Thanks,' she said and the doctor took his leather case and left the cafe. Peter felt the doctor brush past his back and he heard him mutter, 'Sorry'. Peter froze and didn't dare turn around. The doctor didn't wait for a response and Peter watched him as he walked down the shopping mall back to the car park. Peter smiled and looked at himself in the mirror.

***

Beth was bored. They had followed Greg for most of the morning and all he had done was traipse them back and forward around Jesmond and Gosforth showing various types of couples different houses and flats. She looked at her watch and told Barry she was due in at work at one. He agreed it was proving to be a waste of time following Greg and they sat on the wall opposite the metro station and wondered if they should give up.

'Well I've got to go to work, so it's up to you if you want to keep following him,' said Beth as she finished off a packet of crisps she'd bought from the newsagents in the station. Barry shook his head,

'Na. I think it's pointless. What's he likely to do, whilst he working?' Beth scrunched up the empty bag and tossed it into the bin by the wall and jumped up and sat next to Barry. She put her arm around him and sat and swung their feet idly as they waited for Beth's metro train to arrive.

'Here it is,' she said as she jumped down from the wall. 'I'll see you at home after work.' Barry waved her off as the metro pulled away from the station and he sat and wondered what he should do. He looked at his watch and it was only twelve thirty five.

He was worried about the old man. He knew the gang of con men were getting ready to do their worst and Barry didn't want to stand by and let that happen. He paced back and forth along the pavement and he ignored the strange looks he got from onlookers. He thought about how he could help the old man; he thought about what he could do to stop the con men getting to him. He racked his brains but he came up with nothing. He decided to walk back up Osborne Road and head towards the old man's house. Maybe he would think of something before he got there, he thought.

He needed a drink and he decided to pop into the Co-Op and get a can of something. Just as he was opening the door he saw the old man coming out towards him. He held the door as the old man struggled with his three shopping bags. 'Thank you,' said the old man and he nodded at Barry. He recognised him and he grinned. Barry nodded and continued to hold the door. 'Oh. Hello,' said the old man again, 'Thank you...thank you.'

'No problem sir. Here, I'll let you past.' Barry let the man past and out onto the street. The man's bags looked heavy and Barry could see the thin plastic handle of one of them begin to stretch before it snapped and the bag dropped to the floor. Barry left the door and came to his aid. He picked up the apples that had rolled out of the bag and carefully placed them back. He picked up the bag and carried it by the bottom.

'Here, let me carry this for you. You're just up the street aren't you?' The old man's wrinkled face stretched as he smiled and his warm, caring eyes gleamed with gratitude.

'Oh Really? You are so kind.' Barry took one of the other bags and the old man thanked him again.

Barry wasn't used to walking so slow. The old man had difficulty walking and he obviously found the shopping trip a task. They chatted about the weather and about how cold it was getting. Barry nodded and grinned as the old man told him stories about when he was a young man and how he used to run in marathons and throw javelins. Barry was impressed and looked at the man with a greater respect.

They arrived at the door and the man fished for his keys and unlocked it. 'You'll come in for a cup of tea, I hope?' asked the old man, not waiting for an answer, as he swung open the heavy door. Barry stepped into the grand hall.

It had a cold looking, white marble floor and tall Greek-style columns around each doorway. He followed the man into the kitchen and put the bags onto a long, highly polished kitchen table, which stood in the centre of an enormous kitchen.

It was fairly traditional in design but Barry could tell it was quality and must have cost a lot. He watched as the old man pottered around, flicking on the kettle and taking things out from the carrier bags. 'Ooh!' he said, 'I think I've got some cake in here somewhere.' He dug around in the bag and pulled out a small, boxed cake. He opened it and found a knife from the rack on the kitchen bench. 'Here,' he said as he cut into it and placed a piece on a small, antique-looking tea plate and handed it to Barry.

He looked Barry up and down and looked at his skinny waist and torn, designer jeans. He went back to his jacket, which he had slung over the back of one of the kitchen chairs and pulled out his wallet. 'Here,' he said pulling out a twenty pound note. 'Get yourself a new pair of jeans, on me,' pointing at the holes in Barry's jeans. Barry waved his hand and said,

'Oh! No...No. Thanks all the same but no.' The old man looked put out and Barry recognised his upset.

'But you've been so good to me,' said the old man. 'With the shopping and everything...' He pointed to the empty bags on the counter and looked at Barry. Barry could see he wouldn't take no for an answer and he reluctantly accepted the note.

'Thank you...It really isn't necessary... but thank you anyway.' The man grinned, satisfied that he had helped out a worthy cause.

The old man put the cups on a small tray and took them through to the living room. Barry couldn't believe the size of the room. Its tall windows dominated and he could see the place he had stood and observed him and Greg from the street opposite and he noticed the grand curtains that framed the windows. They were made of heavy, quality fabric and Barry thought they would make a nice dress. He sat on the enormous sofa and sank into its luxury. He balanced the tiny teacup and its saucer on his knee and was terrified of spilling it.

'So,' said the old man as he plumped up his cushions of his high-winged armchair. 'Tell me all about yourself. Do you go to school around here?' Barry almost choked on his tea and had to catch the spray as it left his nostrils. He smiled and said,

'Er no. I'm nineteen. I left school when I was sixteen.' The old man watched and grinned. He sipped on his tea and looked at Barry, looking at his belt buckle, which read 'sexy' and noticing the touch of eye shadow around his eyes.

'So do you work then?' asked the man, shuffling in his seat and looking at the pink socks that hung over the tops of Barry's trainers. Barry, not sure what to say and wondering if it wise that he tell him that he was a private eye, investigating the con men that were about to murder him.

'No. I'm looking for work though. If you know of any jobs going, I'd be interested,' he said hastily. The old man looked at him and Barry could tell his interest in him was more than just curiosity. He smiled and looked out of the window at the garden.

'Well, as it happens, I need a gardener. I'm too old to look after the garden now and it's just too much for me to deal with.' He looked at Barry's shocked expression and continued, 'There's not much to do at this time of year but during the summer months it needs regular attention.' Barry sat up and wondered if this could be a way to keep an eye on him and prevent the con men from killing him. He nodded and tried to look excited.

'Ooh, that would be great,' he said and the old man smiled. Barry could sense he was lonely and suspected he just needed some company. Barry thought quickly and said, 'I could come round for a few hours each day and maybe clear up leaves and stuff.' The old man nodded and said,

'Would a couple of hundred pounds be okay? As its just part time' said the old man. Barry swallowed hard. He had never made that much for a part-time job before and he thought it rather excessive. Working as Peter's assistant, he was only given an allowance of seventy-five pounds and that was for a whole week.

He grinned at the old man and nodded. He felt guilty taking the old man's money and overcharging for a simple job but he knew it was his only chance to keep an eye on him.

'Excellent!' said the old man and he slapped his leg. 'You can start tomorrow!' Barry sipped on his tea and grinned.

Twelve

'You're joking!' said Bill as Peter relayed the events in the café. Bill turned off the iron he was holding and slumped into the chair opposite Peter in disbelief. 'You mean...Collins is using those two Chavs as witnesses on the wills?' Peter nodded and played with the gold chain around his neck.

'Looks like it,' he said, proud of his day's work following Collins. Bill, still shocked, continued,

'But, surely, no-one could take them seriously as witnesses? Surely, people would question how they knew the person who's will they are witnessing.'

'Apparently not. The solicitor said Joe's will was legally correct and witnessed and that was all there is to it.'

'But if we told the solicitor about the Chavs, about what Collins is up to, surely he would do something about it, wouldn't he?' Peter frowned, unsure of the answer to Bill's question.

'I don't know,' shrugged Peter.

They heard the front door slam an Barry swung in to the room and plopped himself on the sofa next to his uncle Peter. He sensed there had been some important discussion while he was away and he was keen to catch up. Bill sighed and returned to his ironing and left Peter to fill Barry in on the events in the café.

'Jeasu...' Barry was about to say and then held himself back. 'Two hundred pounds for a man's life. That's disgusting.' Peter nodded. 'Argh! These sort of creatures make me sick – They would sell their own grandmother for a handful of notes!'

Peter was surprised by Barry's outburst. He was not normally so animated and, in a way, Peter was proud that his nephew was so concerned for other people and had such strong feelings.

Barry swung his legs up on the footstool, crossed his arms and buried his chin into his chest as he thought about what he had just learnt. Peter put his arm around him and hugged him. Barry remembered his news and told Peter about his job offer.

'Ah! said Peter. 'That'll be useful. At least you can keep an eye on things and make sure nothing happens to the old gent while we try and nail these bast...' Peter stopped, realising he was about to break one of his own rules and he picked up the TV remote control as he new his favourite soap was about to start. He kicked off his shoes and swung his legs up and on to Barry's lap. Barry relaxed and straightened the creased tights wrapped around Peter's toes.

***

Bill had made a Lasagne for tea and Barry's eyes lit up as Bill proudly laid the piping hot glass dish in front of him. It smelt wonderful and Beth breathed in the aroma, thankful she was now part of the family and looking forward to tasting more of Bill's home cooking.

'Ooh, that smells lovely dear,' said Peter as Bill spooned a big slice on to the plate in front of him. 'Pass me some of those lovely new potatoes as well Beth will you my dear,' he said pointing at the bowl of steaming small potatoes covered in butter and parsley. Beth picked up the dish and passed it over and grinned at Peter.

Peter then remembered about Barry's news. 'Have you heard that Barry's got a new job?' he said, spooning himself a healthy portion of potatoes. Beth looked at Barry's smug smile and looked confused.

Barry blew onto his hot slice of lasagne and waited for it to cool. 'Yeah. I start tomorrow.' Beth looked even more confused and Peter realised that he hadn't told her the full story.

'The old gent has asked him to be his gardener,' said Peter, slicing his lasagne into six equal pieces and separating them so they cooled quicker. Barry, now with a hot mouthful and keen to quench the fire, desperately filling a glass with coke and swallowing it, continued.

'I thought it would be a good way to keep an eye on him and maybe I might be able to find out more about what that Greg is up to.' Peter nodded at his clever nephew and Bill passed around the peas.

Beth smiled and thought about it for a moment. 'What you need is a way of hearing what Greg and the old gent are talking about when you aren't there.'

'Like a bug, you mean?' said Barry.

Beth nodded and touched the tip of her tongue to the piece of lasagne on her fork. Sensing it was cool enough she ate it and began to bisect a potato. Barry's eyes widened at the thought of being a spy and planting a bug in the old gent's house.

Peter saw his dreamy state and tutted under his breath and wondered if his nephew was all that bright after all. Barry came around and pondered the idea for a second.

'Where would we get a bug from?'

Beth grinned and said, as she scraped the Bolognese sauce from around the edge of her plate, 'I know where we can get one.'

Peter and Bill both looked at her in disbelief and wondered how Beth would know about such things.

'They sell them at the pharmacy,' she said and smiled, watching her audience as they stared back incredulously. Barry grinned and said,

'Oh yes. I've seen them on the shelf next to the grappling hooks, the lock pick sets and the shoes with the built-in compass.' He grinned and looked at Beth.

'No, daft arse,' she said. 'We sell baby monitors – which are a sort of bug aren't they?' She looked at Peter for confirmation. Peter's face lit up and Barry frowned at being put in his place.

'If Barry can put a microphone somewhere where the old gent and Greg are likely to talk then we can sit and listen from close by.'

They all sat back in their seats and thought about the proposition for a moment. 'How far do these things reach?' asked Bill as he cleared away the plates. Beth wiped her mouth and replied,

'That depends on the model. The expensive ones can transmit up to fifty feet I believe.' Bill cringed at the word expensive and asked where was the money going to come from for this gadget.

'Never mind about that,' said Barry. 'The old gent will be paying for it.' The others looked at him confused and he told them about his new salary, promised to him by his employer.

'Two hundred quid for a light-footed pansy to pick up some

leaves for a few hours,' said Beth as she downed the last of her coke and helped Bill clear the table. ' He must be mad... or interested? How much did you wiggle that little bum of yours to get the price that high,' she asked with a big grin across her face.

Barry jumped up and chased Beth, screaming out of the room and up the stairs. Peter and Bill listened as Barry shouted, 'I can't help it if men find me irresistible!'

***

Barry arrived early and he glanced down the side of the house and looked at the garden. There were piles of leaves heaped up against the wall and under the big oak tree, which dominated the garden. The leaves had a curled appearance and were crisp with the night's frost, giving them a silver jacket. He watched as his breath steamed in front of him and he wished he'd worn his plain jeans as the slits in the ones he was wearing let in the cold and he felt it creep up his inner thigh.

The warm glow of the hall light was welcoming and he wished the old gent would hurry up and let him in. He saw a blurred image through the textured glass of the front door and it grew larger as the man approached. As the door swung open Barry felt the warm blanket of air surround him and saw the welcoming face of the professor.

'Come in...come in,' he said, waving his hand and grabbing Barry by the elbow. 'You must be freezing, you poor little thing. Come in and get a nice warm drink in the kitchen.'

Barry wasn't sure about being referred to as a little thing but he overlooked it and loosened his scarf as the heat from the kitchen took hold and thawed him. He looked around the room. It was really cosy, he thought. The radio was on and some gentle, cheery classical music was playing. There was a smell of bacon and warm toast and he could hear the crackle of the open fire in the adjacent living room.

The old man peeled away Barry's coat and told him to sit on

a tall wooden bar stool while he made the tea. 'What's it like out there?' he asked, as he poured the boiling water into the little teapot he had prepared earlier. Its hot steam rose like a cloud in front of the old man and he smiled as he waited for Barry's reply.

'Oh, it's freezing!' said Barry as he gratefully accepted his cup and refused the small plate of biscuits offered to him. 'I wish I'd worn a jumper now.'

The old man looked at Barry's T-Shirt and stared at it for some time, trying to figure out what it was on the front of it. Barry noticed his curiosity and he looked down at his flat chest and stretched out the fabric so the image could be seen more clearly. The man still looked none the wiser and Barry, looking at the black and white image said, 'It's Lisa Minnelli.'

The old man's fluffy eyebrows rose as he made the connection. 'Oh, Lisa. Yes, I used to like her. She has a great singing voice.' Barry grinned, pleased to find a fellow fan.

'I love her,' said Barry, sipping on his hot tea. 'I want be like her and sing on the stage and wear her brilliant outfits.' He paused for a moment and realised he was going into camp mode – something he had to keep an eye on when in certain types of company. He looked at the old man. He didn't seemed to mind and in fact Barry felt sure he liked it. The man grinned and looked at Barry's outfit.

He was wearing his black and white, Minnelli T-Shirt, his faded, ripped designer jeans, with his 'sexy' belt buckle proudly perched on his flat belly and he wore dainty black shoes, with a fake-diamond trim.

The man smiled as he surveyed Barry's slender shape and he said, 'Not quite right for doing a bit of gardening in but very nice all the same.'

Barry hadn't really thought about it. The old man was right. He had just dressed as he dis normally, forgetting he was meant to be coming to do a manual job.

'Tell you what,' said the old man. 'Just for today. Why don't you do a bit of tidying up for me around the house instead of the garden? ' He looked out of the window into the dark, unwelcoming cold of the garden and knew it was not the place for his new friend. 'You can do the garden next time and remember to bring something warm to wear.'

Barry, relieved by the old man's kind offer, grinned and nodded. Not wanting to take advantage of the old man, he stood up and straightened his outfit and said, 'So what would you like me to do?'

The professor looked a little startled by Barry's desire to get on and Barry sensed that he would probably be happy if he just sat and told him his life story. He was obviously lonely and needed the company.

The old man looked around the room and searched for tasks for Barry to do for him. He spotted some cake tins in the corner, piled high, balancing precariously on one another. He pointed at the pile and said to Barry, 'Those tins really need to go up there.' He pointed to a shelf above the clock on the kitchen wall. 'I used to do a lot of baking and I love to make cakes. But I'm too old now and I've nobody to make them for anymore.'

Barry felt sad for the old mad but he got to work and arranged the tins in piles, in size order on the kitchen worktop. The old man pulled out a kitchen chair and placed it in front of the high shelf. Barry took the larger of the tins and stepped up onto the chair. The old man stood close by and watched as Barry stretched up to the top shelf and placed the tins there as requested. Each time he stretched up, his T-Shirt rose and revealed his smooth flat stomach. Barry noticed the old man watching his belly as it came into view each time. The old man stared and grinned. Barry could tell he was titillated by it but Barry didn't mind. He didn't feel in any danger from the old man and if he could bring a little happiness to his life, he didn't mind him leering at him. After all plenty of other gay men leered at him – but was the price he paid for being gorgeous he told himself.

Barry stepped down and returned the chair to its former location. He swung around and looked around the room. 'What next,' he said, smiling at the grinning old man. The professor was in a world of his own, oblivious to Barry's words. When he came round and saw Barry waiting for his next task he pulled open one of the cupboards under the sink and passed Barry a duster and some furniture polish.

'Can you just go around and give the place the once over with these?' Barry took the cloth and can and smiled. 'You can start in the living room if you like. I'll get on and clear away these breakfast things.' He pointed Barry towards the living room and watched his bottom as he bent over and polished the brass doorknob on the door.

The room was as Barry remembered it. Its big windows dominated and the heavy curtains that had caught his eye the last time, hung in their splendour. He looked around and saw a big white marble fireplace with a big brass-coloured framed mirror above it. It was similar to the one he had seen in Joe's house. Either side of the fireplace were two tall African-looking, dog-like, creatures. They stood proud and elite and guarded the room. Along the top of the mantelpiece was a selection of silver-framed photos. Barry, intrigued and wanting to know more about the professor, thought that would be the best place to start his dusting.

He looked at the photos and the first thing he noticed was that there were no pictures of women. All the frames contained images of only two men. Barry picked up the first large frame and ran his duster across its glass surface. The image was of two young men. They looked about early twenties and they both wore old-fashioned bathing costumes. It was obviously a beach scene and Barry looked closely at the face of one of the men. It was the professor. He was a handsome man, thought Barry as he looked at the image of the two men with their arms around each other. Barry wondered if they were lovers. Even though gay relationships were not talked about back then, you could tell from the sparkle in their eyes that they were in love. Barry wondered if someday he would find someone that he could love. He put the picture back and dusted along the mantle shelf.

Another frame held an army-looking picture. It was of the two same men but posed in their stiff uniforms and staring emotionless into the camera. Even though he thought the old man looked smart in his uniform, he preferred the previous image.

The third picture was the first to be in colour. It looked strange. It's faded colours difficult to make out and its edges blurred. It had a broad white border on three of its sides and a wider white bit along the bottom. Barry had never seen one up close before but he had seen such things on TV. He knew it was a Polaroid and remembered seeing an old camera somewhere in the loft at his uncle Peter's.

The picture was very different from the two previous ones. It showed the professor and the other man kissing, lying on a picnic blanket, surrounded by buttercups. Barry smiled. It was the first real picture he could relate to. The others were restrained, hiding their true love. But this, this was the real thing, without any inhibitions.

'His name was Tom,' said a voice from over Barry's shoulder. Barry shook, startled by the sudden appearance of the professor at his side. 'He was my partner.' Barry, realising that he may be intruding, put the picture back on the shelf and said,

'Sorry. I was just dusting and was curious. I didn't mean to...'

'It's okay,' said the professor, reassuring him and patting him on the shoulder. 'We were together for nearly fifty years. It was different back then. You had to keep it under wraps or you would be sent to prison.' Barry gasped and held his small hand up to his lips.

The old man pulled down another frame and showed it to Barry. 'This was taken just before Tom died.' Barry watched as the old man stroked the image and he could sense the grief in his soul.

'He was a handsome man,' said Barry. The old professor nodded and reluctantly placed the frame back on the shelf and straightened it until it was just right.

Barry thought about the reason he was there and he trembled at the thought of any harm coming to this dear old man. He wondered if he should tell him about what Greg was up to and tell him that he intended to kill him. He bit his lip. He knew that if he told him it may stop the gang's plans for now but what about the other old men on their list. No. They had to be stopped for good and that meant either catching them in the act or gathering enough evidence for the police to put them away for a long time.

The old man looked Barry up and down again and said, 'What about you? Have you got a nice young man in your life?' Barry flushed with embarrassment and shook his head. The old man seemed surprised. He glanced down at Barry's belt buckle and smiled. 'At least you don't have to hide who you are these days.'

Barry had never really hid who he was and the thought of having to do so was alien to him. He had always been gay, always been camp and didn't care what anybody else thought about him. He looked at the big mirror and saw the image of him and the old man in its reflection; the old man, nearing the end of his life, enjoying the comfort of his cardigan, warm slippers and memories and there, standing next to him was Barry -- A camp, glamorous young gay man, inexperienced in love and his whole life waiting to unfold.

The phone rang and the professor left Barry to his dusting. Barry could hear the conversation in the kitchen clearly and he listened as best he could.

'Oh! Hello my dear,' he heard the old man say. Barry assumed it was obviously someone the old man knew. 'Oh, that'll be nice. I'll make sure the heating's on for you. We don't want you getting cold do we?' Barry didn't know what they were talking about but somehow he sensed it was Greg on the line.

'Yes. The red satin ones and the Kelvin Cline's would be nice. I'll lay them out for you. Yes... See you at seven.'

Barry then remembered the conversation he had overheard the last time he was here and the suggestion of a fashion parade of some new underwear the old man had acquired for him. Barry cringed at the thought but left it.

He continued to look around the room and take advantage of the opportunity to find his way about. The house was beautiful and Barry wondered if he would ever live somewhere as luxurious as this. The old man had obviously done well for himself and Barry wondered if professors really made that much money. Maybe his partner was wealthy. Maybe he was a film star in his time and made their fortune that way. He dusted and wiped the highly polished surfaces as he wandered about.

It was obvious that the house was well cared for and Barry felt sure that the old man probably had a regular cleaner, so his being there wasn't really that necessary. He felt guilty for a moment, taking the man's money for a job that didn't really need doing. Then he thought about it --he wasn't there to dust. He was there to save the old man's life.

Thirteen

'Okay love...Ahah...Oh, brilliant!' said Peter as he nodded and grinned talking to Pierre on the phone in the narrow hall. Barry sat on the step of the landing and peered over the banister, like an excited schoolboy. 'Ten o'clock...Ahah...Ahah' he said as he to became more animated. 'And did you manage to get the little extra I talked to you about?' He looked up at Barry and smiled. Barry, confused and intrigued came down to question his uncle's naughty smile. 'Okay my dear, see you at ten. My love to Tim!'.

'Little extra?' quizzed Barry with a wide grin spanning his face. Peter spun around on the spot and wafted his skirts.

'Never you mind!' he said. 'You'll see when we get there. Peter wafted into the sitting room and picked up his Women's Weekly.

'But is it ready?' asked Barry, jumping up and down on the spot.

'Yes. We have to be there for your final fitting at ten', said Peter, flicking the glossy pages and trying to contain his own excitement.

Barry leaped into the air and squealed like a young pig. He heard movement at the top of the stairs and rushed up to share his excitement with Beth. He halted at the top of the landing and stood back with horror. Beth, just woken from her bed, with her hair all squashed to one side like a scarecrow and her eyes all screwed up with sleep, stood at the doorway to the bathroom and said, 'What's all the screeching for?' She looked at her big watch, which she never seemed to take off and made out the time on it. 'It's only eight thirty and you're squealing like a Banshee.

Barry, disregarding her disturbing appearance, spun her around and skipped in a circle at the top of the landing. 'My dress...It's ready!' he said. 'It's finally ready!' Beth pulled his hands away and headed toward the bathroom.

'Fascinating', she said. 'Some of us who live in the real world have to go to work now, so is it all right if I have a pee?' Barry let her go and he floated into his room and turned on his CD player. Within moments, the house was filled with the sound of Liza, accompanied by Barry on the hairbrush.

Peter grinned, knowing that today was to be an exciting day for both of them and he looked forward to seeing his friend Pierre and the new dress he had paid him to make for Barry.

Beth came in, still in her pyjamas and sat on the sofa next to Peter. 'Listen to that' she said, plopping her feet up on the little foot stool and waving her bunny slippers back and forth. Peter looked over the top of his magazine and smiled.

'It his big day.' He said. Folding the magazine and stuffing it in a skinny wooden rack by the side of Peter's chair. 'He's been waiting for this day for months now.'

'Months?' questioned Beth. Peter, happy to share the inner secrets of the drag queen world, straightened the cuffs of his sweater and continued.

'Well, it's the scquins you know. Barry's dress is being hand-made by my dear friend and ex-performer Pierre. It is a lovely black number and it's absolutely covered in tiny black sequins. Each one has to be hand stitched and, as you can imagine, that takes forever!'

Beth, not really that interested in dresses or sequins, just bounced her feet on the poof and said, 'Couldn't he just get a dress from Marks and Sparks or somewhere?'

Peter looked at her with shock and forced himself to calm down before he replied. 'My dear. This is a business and in business you have to invest in your product before it starts to reward you with an income. Barry's dress is costing us eight hundred pounds and with the shoes and other bits and pieces it will more than likely tot up to be over a thousand.'

Beth's jaw dropped. 'A thousand quid, just for a frock?' Peter frowned and Beth corrected herself. 'I mean a dress'. Peter smiled.

'That's nothing. I've known some of my friends pay over two and a half for something really special. Pierre isn't cheap but he's the best in the business. Beth stood up and headed toward the door mumbling under her dress.

'A thousand quid - just for a frock.'

***

Peter and Barry sat together on the garish pink sofa and waited patiently as Pierre did something in the back of the small flat that looked over the river on the quayside. Peter felt Barry's knee vibrating with anticipation and Peter put his hand on it to calm him.

'I hope it fits', he said. 'I hope he's done the back just the way I asked him to. You remember...'

Before Barry was allowed to finish, Pierre swooshed into the room carrying a long slim dress over his arm like a bouquet of flowers and stood in front of Barry to present him with his long-awaited dress. Barry nervously stood up and touched the fabric, stroking it like a fluffy kitten. His eyes met Pierre's and they both grinned with excitement. 'Do you want to try it on?' asked Pierre as he let it hang its full length and support it by its shoulders.

Barry clamped his hand to his chest as if about to have a heart attack and, without further prompting, he slipped of his jacket and kicked of his trainers. Peter and Pierre watched as the skinny boy stripped down to his skimpy Y-fronts and stepped forward to be dressed by the famous Pierre.

'Careful!' looping the straps over his bony shoulders. 'It's taken me a lifetime to sew all these sequins and my fingers are almost down to the bone.' Barry swung around as Pierre pulled up the zip on the back of the dress and he looked in the full-length mirror that Pierre had pulled up next to the sofa.

Barry could not contain his grin, which spread across his young face. Peter looked at Barry's eyes. He had never seen him so happy and he was pleased that he was about to become the newest member of the family business. Barry swished the dress back and forth and bent his knees and leaped up and down with excitement.

Pierre pulled open a small box and pulled out a pair of sequin-covered black shoes. He handed them to Barry. 'Don't forget the shoes.'

'Oh, yes!' said Barry, again stroking the shoes before putting them on and twisting his body from side to side as he admired them in the mirror. He noticed the reflection in the mirror of his uncle Peter and he watched his proud face as he began to weep with happiness.

Peter wiped his nose as he shuffled in his seat and said, 'It's missing something,' said Peter, Pierre swung around with his hands on his hips and brushed the big bushy moustache that clung to his top lip and nodded. Barry looked bemused. What could they mean, he thought. This is the perfect dress and the shoes are just divine.

Pierre pulled open a small cupboard door and lifted out a small white cardboard box. Barry looked at Peter, who just couldn't contain his cheeky grin and looked at Pierre, who was also excited by the mystery box.

'This is a little something extra that Bill and I thought would complete the outfit perfectly for you.' Barry looked at his uncle Peter and, curious to know what he meant, lifted the lid of the box and peered inside. Barry's face illuminated with a glow and Peter watched with pride as Barry lifted the black wig from its box.

'Wow! A Minnelli wig!' said Barry as he spun it around to view it from the front. He looked over at Peter and almost leapt on top of him, wrapping is skinny arms around him and hugging him close. 'Thanks, Uncle Peter. Thanks!'

Peter began to cry and he told Barry to put it on. Pierre stood behind Barry and adjusted the wig in the mirror. He spun round to show Peter the finished look. 'What do you think?'

'Absolutely a spitting image of Liza', said Peter as he held a tissue to his mouth. Barry spun round to show Pierre and he nodded in agreement.

Fourteen

'Can you turn the heater up...It's freezing!' said Beth as she zipped up her fleece and slung its black hood over her head. Peter pushed the slider on the dashboard that controlled the temperature in the car.

'It's as high as it will go', he said, shuffling in his seat.

'I bet he's forgotten to switch it on!' said Beth wrapping her arms around her chest and burying her small hands under each armpit to keep them warm.

'I'm sure he hasn't', said Peter as he flipped up the vanity mirror and undid his seatbelt. 'I'm sure once he gets a moment he'll set it up somewhere and turn it on.'

A small flashy sports car passed them and began to enter the professor's drive. Peter nudged Beth and she popped her head out of the warm hoody. 'Look!', said Peter. 'Look. Isn't that Collin's little car?' Beth pulled off her hood and sat up in her seat properly. She watched as the young man in his expensive suit got out of the car and retrieved a small black case from the small back seat.

***

Barry had dressed for the job this time. He wore his big winter coat with its big fur-lined hood. He had bought some warm, sensible boots for working in the garden and had put on some old jeans for the occasion. He knew he looked a sight but at least he would be warm whilst doing the work for the old man.

'Ah! That's much better', said the professor as he looked at Barry and gave him a pair of work gloves. He looked out of the back door and pointed to an area by the side of the garage. 'Now, if you start by raking up all of those leaves over there and put them in these bags.' He handed Barry a roll of garden waste sacks. 'Then you can have a break and I'll put the kettle on.'

The doorbell rang and the old gentleman turned and looked up at the clock. 'Oh! That'll be Dr Collins.' He noticed the expression of concern on Barry's face and continued. 'He comes every day at this time to give me my injection.' Barry froze on the spot. Injection? Was he coming to kill the old man now, without any warning? He panicked – he needed more information.

'Injection?' he said just as the old man was about to close the door behind him.

'Oh! Nothing to worry about. I'm Diabetic and I need a daily injection of Insulin. I've always hated needles, so Dr Collin's comes every day to do it for me.'

Barry didn't know what to think. He felt the bulk of the baby monitor under his coat and he remembered he had yet to think of a place to put it. He watched as the old man headed towards the door and he knew he had to act quickly. He scanned the kitchen for a likely place to hide the microphone. He heard the front door being opened and the old man greeting the doctor. There was no time to think about it any further so Barry plonked the little white box behind an old teapot that sat on the dresser in the large and warm kitchen.

***

'Is it on?' asked Peter as Beth fiddled with the knobs on the receiver of the baby monitor. Beth extended the aerial as far as she could and balanced the box on the dashboard to give it the best chance of picking up the signal from the microphone.

'Hang on. Listen.' She turned up the volume and they both grinned as they heard the voices of the professor and Dr Collins.

'It looks cold out there,' said the old man and they heard Collins talking about the roads being icy.

'I haven't got long, so let's get down to business,' said Collins. 'Just slip your pants down for me and I'll slip it in. Promise it won't hurt.'

Peter held his hand to his mouth, unsure what was going on. Beth grinned and said, 'Dirty old bugger.' Peter slapped her on the arm.

'There. All done. You can pull up your pants now.'

Beth laughed out loud. 'Crikey, that was quick!' Peter told her to shoosh but held back a smirk of agreement.

'See you tomorrow at the same time,' said Dr Collins.

'Are you sure I can't offer you a cup of tea? I've got a nice young man doing some work in the garden for me. I'm sure he'd love to meet you.'

Peter held his hand up to his mouth again. 'Oh no! That would blow the gaff.' Beth stared at him and didn't know what he meant. 'What if he recognises Barry. Wouldn't that be awkward?' Beth looked at his worried face and asked if he had ever seen Barry before. Peter pondered for a moment and his eyes brightened. 'You're right. They haven't have they? Tut. Silly old fool'.

Barry watched through the window as he raked the leaves into neat piles. He watched as Dr Collins waved and headed to the front door. He wondered what all that was about in the kitchen but remembered he was there to do a job. The rough leather of the work gloves he wore was harsh against his soft skin and he wished he had thought to bring some moisturiser with him. He wasn't used to his sort of work and he didn't think he was cut out for it.

***

'So, do we have to sit here all day?' asked Beth, squirming in her seat. 'I'm hungry.' Peter looked at the skinny girl and remembered how she wolfed down her food when she first came around to his house with Barry. He looked at her thin legs and her long neck and wondered what she would become later in life. Would she make it as a rock singer, as she wished or, more likely, would she end up married to an accountant and have three kids.

He rummaged in his big bag and opened his purse, taking out a few pound coins. 'Here. Take this and pop along to that sandwich shop and get us a couple of hot chocolates... and if there's enough change, get a couple packets of crisps. Beth didn't need further encouragement. She swung open the car door and leapt out like a young Lamb. She bent over and stuck her head in the car door.

'Won't be long', she said as Peter wrapped his coat around his waist to keep the cold draft out created by the open door. He sat and listened to the rummaging noises in the kitchen as he heard the sound of the old man stirring what sounded like a pot of tea. Ooh I fancy a cup myself mate, he thought. He turned up the volume and heard the old man call Barry in from the garden.

***

'Now you sit yourself down there', said the old man, pointing to a tall bar stool which stood next to the marble-topped island in the centre of the kitchen. 'The tea's ready. Do you want a biscuit?' Barry thought about it but then remembered his big day and decided against it.

'No...Watching my figure,' said Barry and grinned at the old man. The professor looked over the top of his glasses and looked at Barry's petite body. Barry could tell he liked what he saw. He had seen that look many times before.

'Nonsense. You've got a nice shape,' said the old man, propping himself on the stool opposite. 'This is novel', he said. 'I don't normally sit on these things... They're just for show really.' Barry noticed him struggle to get himself up onto the stool so he came around and supported his elbow to give him a helping hand.

'Thank you my boy. You are kind.'

Barry returned to his seat and cupped his hands around the warm cup and tried to thaw his poor hands.

'So what do you get up to when you are not working?' asked the old man, sipping on his tea and staring at Barry with genuine interest. Barry thought about it and wondered if he should keep under cover or reveal his real exciting life.

'I'm training in the family business,' said Barry shuffling on the hard wicker seat of the stool. The old man raised his eyebrows with curiosity.

'Oh! That sounds interesting. What sort of business is your

family involved in?' Barry paused before continuing.

'Well, I suppose technically it's not my real family. I live with my uncle Peter and my aunty Bill.' The old man smiled.

'But I think of them as my family as I've lived with them for a long time and I love them to bits.' He sipped from the warm cup and continued. My uncle Peter is a profession female impersonator and he is well known in the north as one of the best. He specialises in Dolly Parton but he has done other characters over the years.

The professor grinned and nodded, wanting Barry to continue. 'And what part in the family business do you perform?

'Well... up until now, I was Peter's assistant. You know, helping him with his costumes, his makeup and general running around so he can focus on being brilliant on stage. But starting on Friday I'm going on stage myself for the first time. I'm really nervous but also very excited.'

The old man grinned even more and his eyes widened. 'Ah! That sounds like a lot of fun. I used to enjoy seeing the drag acts on stage at the men's clubs when I was younger. It must be very exciting performing in front of a crowd. So, will you be another Dolly, or something different?'

'I'm going to be Liza Minnelli,' said Barry proudly.

'Oh!' said the old man. 'I remember her. Wasn't she the one in Cabaret?' Barry nodded, pleased to be able to share his interest in his favourite star. Barry was about to go on and tell him about the show and what he had planned when the phone in the hall rang.

The old man shuffled off the tall stool and said, 'Sorry. Won't be a mo.' He headed into the hall to answer the annoying buzz of the phone. Barry sat and thought about the show and the list of things he had to do before Friday. He watched the fuzzy image of the professor through the textured glass of the kitchen door and listened to the conversation.

'Oooh! Hello Greg, my sweet.' Barry cringed but his attention was triggered. 'Yes, I haven't forgotten. I laid them all out on the bed and put the heating on, so you will be warm. Yes...Okay. See you at eight.'

The old man hung up and returned to the kitchen. 'That was my friend Greg,' said the professor. 'Such a nice boy and a bit of a looker, if I say so myself.' Barry forced a smile and resisted the urge to tell the old man that, in fact, Greg was planning to kill him.

Barry looked at his watch and realised he was due to finish for the day in half an hour. He knew, if they were going to know what happened at eight that night, he was going to have to move the bug into the old man's bedroom.

The professor looked at the big gold-framed clock on the kitchen wall and said, 'Time's getting on. You'd better get those remaining leaves bagged up before you finish for the day.' Barry nodded and put his cup in the sink.

'Could I use your loo before I get back to it?' said Barry as he manoeuvred himself over by the cabinet where he had concealed the baby monitor.

'Of course, my dear!' said the old man. It's just at the top of the stairs, on the right.' Barry smiled and thanked him. He wondered how he could distract the old man while he recovered the box from behind the teapot.

'Oh! Is that the phone again?' asked Barry and the old man turned and headed towards the hall, hoping to hear Greg's voice again. Barry took the opportunity to fish for the box behind the teapot and grab it. He then realised he wasn't wearing his coat, so there was no easy place to conceal it. He panicked as he heard the old man returning. 'No. You must be mistaken,' said the old man pushing on the kitchen door. Barry patted his thin and wiry body and decided the only place to conceal it was down the front of his jeans. He quickly pushed the long thin box down and adjusted it as best he could.

Barry headed for the door and said, 'I'll just pop upstairs. Won't be a jiffy.' The professor looked down at the elongated bulge in Barry's jeans and smiled.

'Would you like me to show you where it is?'

'No...no. That's okay. I'm sure I'll find it. said Barry, noticing the glance at his crotch from the old man.

Barry stepped on the bottom step of the staircase and noticed it squeak as he stood on it. He saw the bathroom as soon as he reached the top of the stairs but he knew he had to find the professor's bedroom first. He opened doors along the landing but none of them looked likely to be his room. At the end of the corridor was the last door on that floor. Barry pushed it open and heard the swoosh of the draught excluder brushing against the expensive-looking carpet. Barry popped his head around and the heat hit him in the face. This must be it, he though.

He quickly scanned the room and spotted the big bed in the centre. On its cover were half a dozen different types of men's underwear. Some boxer shorts, some skimpy briefs and a thong. Barry picked up the little thong and grimaced at the thought of Greg parading around in it.

He remembered what he was meant to be doing there and looked for a place to hide the bug. He heard the creak of the bottom step of the stairs and suspected the old man may be coming up to see if he'd got lost.

Barry noticed an old-fashioned dressing table with a big mirror on pivoting hinges sitting in front of the window. He quickly pulled out the uncomfortable box from his jeans and placed it behind the mirror, making sure the microphone was pointing in the right direction. He quickly pulled closed the bedroom door and skipped along the corridor. He just had time to flush the toilet as the old man reached the top of the stairs and he made a point of closing the bathroom door, once the professor noticed him.

He met the old man on the landing and he noticed him check out his crotch again. He looked disappointed to see the bulge had gone. 'Did you find it okay? Asked the professor. Barry nodded and said,

'Yes. I'd best get on with the garden.'

Fifteen

Beth scanned the table with its array of steaming dishes. A large roast chicken sat proudly on its plate surrounded by a variety of roast vegetables. Smaller plates and dishes clustered around it containing golden-coloured Yorkshire Puddings and baby carrots covered with a sheen of butter. Beth licked her drooling mouth and waited patiently for everyone to get seated.

Bill always made an effort for Sunday lunch. He liked it when the family got together and sat around the table and had a proper meal and shared their news. And of course, Bill loved to cook. When he was a young man he was a galley hand on a large fishing trawler and often spent weeks out at sea. He often shared his memories of that happy time working on the boats and laughed with Peter about how all these straight men would find comfort in his arms.

'Great spread,' said Peter, leaning over to help himself to the carrots. Bill just smiled and passed Beth the gravy boat. She poured the smooth steaming gravy and looked around at the other's plates so see if it was okay to start.

Barry didn't wait. He sliced into his big Yorkshire Pudding and it crunched as the knife cut through it. 'So, tonight's the big night for the professor, then?' said Barry as he spun the piece of Yorkshire pudding on his plate, soaking up some of the gravy.

'Dirty old man, you mean,' said Beth as she swallowed a mouthful of mashed potato. Peter looked her both surprised at how much she was able to get in her mouth and at what she said. He laughed.

'It's not that he's a dirty old man...It just means that that's his thing. You know, some men like twinks, some bears, some queens. We're all different!' Beth stared at him.

'Bears?' Peter giggled and explained.

'Yes, bears.' He paused for a moment for dramatic effect and continued. 'A bear is the name given to big hairy men. Gay men that are into hairy men go to bear clubs.'

Beth grinned. 'And do they have teddy bear picnics at these clubs? Peter laughed and rocked in his chair.

'I don't think discussing what happens at these things is suitable material for the dinner table,' said Peter as he looked at Bill and smiled. Beth crunched on a roast parsnip and watched Barry.

'So what's your thing, princess?'

'I wish you wouldn't call me that!' said Barry, trying to change the conversation back to the events of the evening.

'Or, haven't you popped your cherry yet? said Beth, with an evil grin. 'Still waiting for Mr Right, are we?'

Barry flushed with a dark shade of pink and stared her back with vengeance. 'For your information, Panda Bear, I had a boyfriend at school for two years!' Beth put down her knife.

'Get away! Who with. It wasn't that limp-wristed Pete in year 11?' She turned to peter and said, 'No offence.' He smiled but said nothing.

'Never you mind who it was!' said Barry. He turned at looked at Peter. 'So, what time should we be there tonight?' Beth, dropped her pursuit and looked at Peter for his answer. Bill poured himself some more gravy and said,

'You're not planning on sitting in the car all night in this weather, I hope? Rather you than me.' Peter touched him on the arm.

'It shouldn't take that long. I mean, how long can it take to parade around in your Y-fronts for the old man?' Bill continued,

'That's all well and good but...What's the point?' He looked around the room at the faces bemused by the statement. 'What do you expect to find out? Are you expecting to overhear Greg, posing in his Kelvin Klein's, and then saying, Oh! By the way, old man, Me and my mate Dr Collin's will be calling around on Tuesday at lunch time to administer a lethal dose of poison?'

Peter looked at Bill in amazement. He always had the knack of stating the obvious. Peter sat back in his chair and Barry pushed away his plate and stared at it quietly thinking.

'Bill's raised an interesting point,' said Barry, pulling the plate back in front of him. 'The purpose of us doing all of this is to gather evidence for the police to pick Collins and Greg up, isn't it?' He looked at the others and they all nodded in agreement. 'Then one thing we need to be doing is recording everything! I mean, it's okay that we hear them say stuff but it would be better if we actually had a recording of everything that is said, in case it's needed for evidence in court.'

Bill stood up and began clearing away the plates. 'More expense, I suppose?' Barry let him take his plate and replied.

'No. I've got an old tape recorder upstairs. We can just plug that in to the baby monitor and it will record everything.' Peter looked at his nephew and smiled proudly, acknowledging his brilliance.

Peter suddenly jerked and held his hand to his mouth. 'Oh my god! We'll miss Stars in Their Eyes. It's the final tonight!' Barry's expression changed. They had both been watching every week, enjoying the different acts performing and the response from the judges. They were both looking forward to the final and, Peter was right, it was tonight they would find out the winner.

'You'll have to tape it for me dear,' said Peter grabbing onto Bill's arm as he passed with a pile of dirty plates.

'Okay, okay. I will, I will.'

'He's right though,' said Beth stacking the mugs on to a little tray and getting up from her seat. 'What can we really expect to hear tonight from this little kinky fashion parade?'

'I don't know but we know they are planning to make their move soon, so we'd best be there, just in case,' said Barry passing Beth his empty mug.

***

'Dave Hiscup?' said Beth as she continued to quiz Barry on the back-seat of the small hatchback. Barry just shook his head and grinned.

'I'm not telling you!' Beth slumped back and tapped her long thick stockings.

'Eddy Winslow? She looked at Barry again, knowing she must be right this time. Barry shook his head. 'That's the only gay boys I knew of at school. It must be one of them. She slapped Barry's arm and Peter watched her in the rear-view mirror and grinned. Barry sat grinning, guarding his secret.

Peter pulled the car into the old man's street and was surprised.

It was very different to when they were last there. The road was now filled with posh cars, taking every available space. Peter looked at the spot where he had parked last time and he noticed it was occupied by a big, expensive-looking car.

'Damn!' he said under his breath. The others noticed and looked out of the windscreen.

'Where're we going to park.' Asked Beth, scanning up and down the street for a space. Peter shook his head and then spotted a space about a hundred feet ahead. Barry spotted the same space but then said,

'Too far!' Peter looked at him, confused. 'It's too far for the intercom to reach.' He said. Peter tapped the steering wheel, not sure to do next. 'Round the back,' said Barry. 'There's a back alley. We can park there.' He patted Peter on the shoulder and pointed directions as he turned off the main street and down a narrow, cobbled-stoned lane that ran parallel to the main street.

'We can't park here!' said Peter. 'It's double yellows!'

'Never mind that. If anyone comes, we'll move. For now, it'll do. Pull up at the back of number forty-four and turn off your lights.' Beth butted in.

'But leave the heater on.' Barry looked at his watch and it was ten to eight.

'Better get this set up.' He said, positioning the intercom and tape recorder on the dashboard and turning it on. He stretched out the aerial and turned up the volume. The box came to life and crackled.

'It didn't do that last time,' said Beth. Barry twisted the box to see if it improved the signal.

'The red ones first, I think,' said the voice from the box. Barry grinned and looked at Beth. He sat back and waited for the show to begin. Peter opened a pack of Minstrels and passed it around.

Very quiet voices suddenly became louder and they recognised the voice of Greg. 'Ooh! It's very warm in here. I'd better take off some of these clothes.'

'Oh! Here we go.' Sid Beth.

'Shush!' said Barry digging her in the ribs.

They listened as Greg slipped out of his suit and down to his boxer shorts. They could hear the old man's breathing increase and Peter smiled imagining the scene he was listening to play out before his imagination.

'Oh yes!' said the old man. 'That is very nice.' Barry looked at Beth's big eyes in the dimly-lit back-seat of the car and grinned. Beth was about to say,

'Dirty old...' when Greg butted in.

'I'll have to take these off to try on the others. You wouldn't peak, will you?' he said in a boyish voice.

'No, no. I'll avert my eyes.' He said.

'I wouldn't!' said Barry as he moved closer to the speaker of the baby monitor. 'That Greg's not a bad looking guy.' Beth dragged him back into his seat and put her arm around him.

'Down boy!' she said gripping Barry's shoulders firmly. 'Remember. Your saving yourself for Mr Right!'

Peter glanced at them both in the rear-view mirror and told them to shush. They sat an listened as the old man had palpitations each time Greg tried on the different saucy underwear. Beth was getting bored and it was cold in the car.

'How long do we have to listen to this horny old fart getting his rocks off watching that skinny twiglet parade his little booty in front of him?' Barry nudged her as he sensed the party may be over.

'Anyway, You know it's Mrs Featherwhich's birthday on Tuesday? You remember? They nice lady in number twenty four?' The professor hummed under his breath and then replied.

'Oh yes. Mrs Featherwhich! I go to the senior centre with her on the bus sometimes.'

'Well, she's eighty on Tuesday, so I've got her a card and I'm getting all of the locals to sign it for her.'

'Oh! You are a nice boy. What a kind thing to do. Not many young people like you take the time to be nice to us older folk these days.'

Barry growled, knowing the game Greg was playing with the old man. He was about to give his opinion of Greg when Peter cut him short. 'Listen...'

They heard Greg rummage in his case. 'Would you like to sign it?' he asked.

'Oh yes!' said the old man. 'I haven't got my reading glasses.

I'll have to go down stairs and get them.'

'That's okay,' said Greg. 'Here, I'll take your hand and show you where to sign your name. Peter stirred, sensing something was not right. Barry shuffled forward to listen closer and Beth joined him.

'Here, just sign you normal signature... just there.'

'I'd like to write a little message, if I may.' They heard Greg panic under his breath.

'No, best not. It's only a small card and I have a lot of other signatures to get yet.'

'Oh! Fair enough,' said the old man and they listened as he scratched his signature on the card with the expensive fountain pen Greg had given him. 'My! It is a thick card, isn't it?' said the old man as he had a chance to hold it in his hand.

'Yes, I bought an expensive one with nice thick embossed card both sides. I thought she deserved the best.'

'What's he up to?' asked Barry.

'I don't know...but I don't think it sounds good.' Peter noticed some headlights in the rear-view mirror and they were approaching. The vehicle behind tooted its horn and Peter knew he would have to move. 'The show's over for tonight,' said Peter as he turned on the engine and pulled the small car out of the back alley.

***

Peter turned off the television and swung his feet up onto Beth's legs. Beth knew that meant he wanted her to massage his feet. 'I knew she'd win. I can spot talent a mile off,' said Peter as he kicked of his slippers. She looked over at Barry who was just finishing off his can of coke, slouched in the armchair. 'You tell Beth,' he said. 'Tell her how I have an eye for talent!'

Barry nodded and said. 'It's true, Uncle Pete's a natural at spotting those that have it in them to make it in the business and those that wouldn't survive the hard world of show business.'

Beth assumed that Barry meant the drag queen business and

thought it best not to give her real opinion about what she though about that. She looked down at Peter's feet, wriggling on her lap. She didn't really want to give Peter a foot massage but She thought she had better. - After all, she was part of the family now and she was grateful for that. She took Peter's big toe and revolved it slowly.

'Ooh! That's nice,' said Peter. 'You can come again!' Beth just smiled and didn't really know what she was doing.

Bill, who was in the kitchen, came through and said he was going up to bed. Peter yawned and agreed that it had been a long day and they should all call it a night. Barry pulled himself up off the armchair and turned off the light on the sideboard. 'You comin'?,' he said, looking at Beth, brushing the bits of fluff off her skirt left by Peters woolly socks.

'Suppose so,' she said. 'It just seems like a bit of a wasted day.' Barry looked at her confused. 'Well, I mean... We haven't really achieved much when you think about it.' Barry sat on the arm of the chair and started to take out the hairpins from the back of Beth's hair and pull out the long strands of hair that they had been holding up.

'Umh!' said Barry. 'It's just that card thing. I can't figure out what that was all about.' Beth sat and stared into space.

'Maybe he was being truthful and it was just a birthday card,' said Beth, as she took Barry's hand and turned off the living room light. 'Anyway. Will you help me with my hair?' Barry pushed her up the stairs and directed her to his room.

He checked the radiator to see if it had any residual heat and pulled off his trainers. Beth sat at his dressing table and looked at the reflection before her. Barry stripped off his t-shirt and jeans and pulled on some pyjamas. Beth watched in the mirror and commented that she didn't know he wore pyjamas.

'I do when it's cold like this.' He slipped his little slippers on and came over to the mirror and began to undo the remaining hair clips and fingered out her hair until it was loose enough to brush. He lent over her shoulder, pressing against her skinny frame and pulled a hairbrush out of the stand that held an array of similar make-up brushes and combs.

'Why was the card so thick?' Mumbled Barry as he pulled the

brush through the long strands of Beth's hair. Beth looked at him in the reflection of the mirror. 'That's what is bugging me.' He said, bringing the strands together and wrapping them with an elasticated hair band. Barry patted her on the shoulders and told her that he was done. He kicked off his slippers and got into bed tucking the duvet under his chin, trying to keep warm.

Beth headed towards the door and smiled at Barry. 'I'll be off to my bed then.' She paused and continued. 'Unless... You'd like a real woman to keep you warm tonight?' Barry laughed out lout and shook his head.

'No. I'm still thinking about Greg in his underpants. Thanks all the same.'

Sixteen

There was a layer of frost on the lawn when Barry arrived and the gutters had small icicles hanging from their rims. It was cold and Barry missed his warm bed. He wasn't used to being up so early and he wondered what he was doing there. The front door opened and the heat from the old man's hallway wafted over Barry and he enjoyed the thawing feeling.

'Ooh you do look cold, my boy! Come in and get into the kitchen.' The old man pulled Barry by the elbow and pushed the big door closed. Barry shuffled into the kitchen and took his usual stool. 'Tea?' asked the old professor, shaking the kettle and filling it from the kitchen tap. Barry just nodded, not wanting to unbutton his top button just yet. The old man came around to his side and looked at Barry's coat, with it's sheen of icy morning due. 'Here, let's have this coat off and I'll put it on the radiator to warm up for you.' 'Thanks,' said Barry as he pulled his arms out of the coat and felt the warm air of the kitchen envelop him.
'The forecast said we were in for a cold snap. Possibly even some snow, they say.' He emptied the hot water into the teapot and a welcoming cloud of steam rose from the pot as the professor stirred it. He poured some tea into Barry's usual mug and handed it to him. Barry accepted it and wrapped his frozen fingers around its hot cylindrical body. The old man stood at the window and looked out at the garden. 'It looks unlikely you'll be able to do much in the garden today. The ground's just too frozen.' He turned and smiled at Barry and Barry felt relief that he wouldn't have to go back into the cold again. At least not just yet. 'Is there anything I can do for you around the house today?' asked Barry, hopeful for a chance to stay in the warm but still be there to make sure the old man was okay. The professor looked at his watch and replied. 'Well. Mage, my cleaner, is due in at eleven, so best not do any cleaning. It might make her feel unneeded.' Barry though it kind that he thought of his cleaner's feeling like that. Barry nodded, 'Sure. I understand,' said Barry, sipping on the warming tea. The old man realised something and turned to Barry. 'Magazines!' he said, quite animated, raising his finger

as if he'd had a eureka moment. He pulled Barry off his stool and held him with his warm frail hand. Barry felt safe. The old man pulled on a cord that was hanging from the ceiling in a small side-cupboard Barry had never noticed before. He pointed to a pile of old magazines stacked neatly on a row of two shelves.

'I use to be into model railway and I collected the magazines but now I'm too old for it and I've been meaning to get shot of these for some time. He picked up a copy of Train Monthly and flicked through its pages. He turned it to show Barry the Cover. 'The Flying Scotsman. A beautiful piece of engineering.' Barry watched as his eyes widened as he flicked through the pages.

'Anyway. I think its time they were recycled. It's the recycling bin collection today, so if you can get all of these into the bin before they turn up, that would be a start. Then you can sort out the garage for me.' Barry asked for a box to transport the magazines to the bin and the old man obliged with an old wicker basket. The recycling wheelie bin was in the back yard, only feet away from were they had been encamped the night before and Barry spotted it's frozen blue lid. He tugged at it but it was frozen shut. The old man watched from the doorway and noticed the problem. He disappeared for a moment and returned with the kettle in his hands. 'Here. Use this. The water should still be hot enough to melt the ice.' Just then the telephone rang and the old man handed Barry the kettle and retreated into the warmth of his hallway. Barry carefully poured the hot water around the lid and listened as the ice cracked, releasing its hold on the bin lid. He quickly flipped over the heavy bin lid and was about to pour the contents of his basket into the bin when he noticed something strange sitting on top of a full bin bag.   It was a garish-looking birthday card. Barry's imagination was immediately struck. Could this be the card Greg had asked the old man to sign. And if so, why was it in the bin? Barry reached into the smelly bin, being careful not to get his t-shirt dirty and picked up the card. He suddenly realised that he may have put his fingerprints on it without thinking and he hissed at his own stupidity. He quickly reached into his back jeans pocket and pulled out a handkerchief his Aunty Bill had made for him.

He picked up the card and looked at it. It was quite cheap and nasty - the sort of thing you would get from a petrol station. He flipped open the cover expecting to find the professor's signature. Barry's eyes widened at what he saw.

There was no signature on the card and no other sign of handwriting. The thin card had a small rectangle shape cut-out near the bottom and there were two loops of ink just above it. Barry heard the old man returning so quickly tucked the card in his inner coat pocket.

'Almost done,' said Barry, tipping the contents of the basket into the bin. Another couple of trips should do it.'

***

Peter and Beth sat on the sofa with their feet in shallow plastic bowls. Peter tipped in the contents of a small bottle and Beth smiled and noticed the minty smell. Peter looked at the label on the bottle over the top of his glasses and read out the text. 'Relaxing Spearmint Foot wash - Takes away the worries of the day' He smirked. 'At two pounds fifty a bottle , it better had!' Beth laughed and sat back, rubbing her feet together in the warm and soothing liquid.

'Barry didn't want to go this morning,' said Peter as he wriggled his toes. 'I had to almost drag him out of bed.' Beth bit her top lip and prevented herself from saying what came to mind. She just nodded. 'When I told him the money he would get would pay for the last few bits and pieces he needed for his show, he soon came around.'

'That's on Friday. Isn't it?' asked Beth as she rubbed the back of her ankles and splashed the warm water over her feet. Peter sat back and nodded.

'Yes. I'm so proud. I do hope he'll be okay on the night. I know he's very nervous.'

'He'll do great. I've seen him practicing in his room and he's a right little diva!' Peter agreed.

'I've asked Eric, the owner of the club, if I can bring in Barry early this afternoon to have a bit of practice on the stage and get him used to it before his debut on Friday.' Peter lifted his foot and dabbed it with a towel, before placing it on the carpet and doing the same with the other. 'Well, I don't know about you but I think that stuff is just over-priced bubble bath!'

Beth remained, paddling in the warm water. 'Do you think we are any further forward with this case then?' asked Beth. Peter looked around for the case she was talking about then realised she meant the Joe thing. He slumped back into the seat and huffed under his breath.

'I don't know' he said, 'It seems we have something and then we have nothing!' Beth nodded. 'I mean. We spent last night listening to that ridiculous Y-front party thing and what have we learned from it? Absolutely nothing!' Beth butted in.

'We learned that the professor's a bit kinky and a sad old queen!' Peter frowned at her.

'That's not really fair. The old man may have an odd fetish but at the end of the day, he is just lonely. Barry told us of how he had a partner whom he loved and now he's gone.' Beth felt a little startled to be told off like that.

'It's very different when you are gay. When your partner dies, people don't really understand and just think, well, it's just two men. But I can really feel for the old man. I don't know what I'd do if I ever lost Bill.' Beth noticed a small tear forming in Peter's eye and pulled him toward her and put her arm around him.

'That's not going to happen. You'll be together for a long time.' Peter wiped his eye with the corner of his folded handkerchief.

'One of us will go eventually and one of us will be left alone - just like the old man.' Beth hugged Peter and rocked slowly.

'I'm sorry. I didn't mean to upset you.' Peter lifted her arm from his shoulder and gave her a kiss on the cheek as he stood up and pushed his handkerchief in his piny pocket.

'Don't be daft. You mean well. Now is that the kettle I can hear boiling?' Beth understood the hint and skipped into the kitchen to make the tea.

***

Barry felt hot. The hottest he had felt all morning. Humping boxes around a garage was not what he was designed for. He was an up-and-coming star! He looked down at his designer-ripped jeans and he could see several marks that would require a pre-soak, he thought.

The professor looked at the new, tidy area that was meant to be the garage but contained no car nor any sign of there ever being one. He was pleased and patted Barry on the back. Barry wondered if the pat maybe lingered a little longer than necessary but he thought it didn't matter. If the old man got pleasure from touching him, then he didn't mind.

'Have you got time for another cuppa before you go?' asked the professor. Barry looked at his watch and he knew he would have to go if he was to get ready for his practice session later that afternoon.

'No. Not really. I'm due on stage at twelve.' Barry liked the sound of that. He felt proud to be able to say it and for it be actually true. The old man's eyes widened.

'Ah! Is today the big day then?'

Barry smiled, proud that the big day was coming up. 'No. This is just a practice run, so to speak. The big day is Friday night.' The professor nodded, also proud that his new-found friend is doing something that makes him so happy.

'Can I come and see you on Friday? I haven't been to a drag club in many years.' Barry was aghast. His very first fan! 'I'll have to get a taxi but I'm sure I'll find the way. What time are you due on?'

Barry became flustered. He was pleased that the old man wanted to see him perform but he already had too many things to think about without chaperoning him to the club to watch his debut. He paused for a moment.

'I go on about nine o'clock, I think.' Barry tried to think of ways to put him off but he watched him as he pulled down the train calendar from the wall and wrote on it with a black biro.

'Nine o'clock. Barry, staring at G. Club.' He said as he wrote the reminder on the calendar. Barry Heard the words 'star' and was blinded by them before he could dissuade the professor.

'I have a friend. A nice girl. Beth. She's going. I'll ask her if she will bring you along with her - just so you know where to go etc. I'll make sure you get VIP seats and everything.' The old man smiled at the kindness.

'Beth, eh? Not a girlfriend, I think?' Barry repelled by the thought quickly added,

'No! Just a friend who happens to be a girl. She's very friendly and I trust her to look after you and not let all those horny young men pester you in the club.' The old man's eyes widened even further at the thought.

'Oh. I don't mind,' he said and they both laughed.

Seventeen

The club looked strange without any clubbers or staff. Apart from an old gent brushing down the stage's surface with a wide and worn-out-looking broom, the only other people to be seen were a rough-looking man in overalls rolling a barrel along the floor in the direction of the main bar and a young man in a cheap suit talking to the barman. The barman polished glasses with his cloth as they spoke but also seemed to be flirting with the young man as Barry recognised the look.

Barry though he recognised the cute bum of the man in the suit but he dismissed the thought. He was here to do a job. Barry was excited and breathed in the stale air of the club, excited to be finally there, not as Peter's sidekick but as the main attraction.

Peter spotted the manager and pulled Barry with him to be introduced. They both put down what they were carrying and Barry straightened his clothes. The old man with a big hairy moustache balanced on his top lip looked at Barry. He stared at him, gradually working his way down and lingering on any bits that he liked.

'This is Barry,' said Peter as he tried to balance the heavy case between his feet. Barry held out his hand, as if to be kissed like the queen but then realised and turned it ninety degrees and shook the man's hand. The man still looked at Barry, this time walking behind him to see what delights he could find there. Barry felt uncomfortable but he put up with it. Peter noticed his concern and just smiled and winked.

'Yes. Very nice,' said the man. 'And you'll be?' Barry butted in.

'Liza Minnelli'. The man smiled and held out Barry's arms to see his skinny frame.

'And you have the outfit?' he asked, still enjoying holding Barry's hand. Peter nodded.

'We are all geared up. Dress, Shoes, wig and of course, talent!' The man grinned and left them to it, saying he would pop back and watch once Barry's set up. Suddenly, Barry felt nervous. Did he have to impress this creep before he could be guaranteed his debut on Friday? Peter sensed the question.

'Don't worry about Eric. He's harmless. He'll like you even if you make a complete arse of it!' Barry didn't look too reassured, so Peter continued. 'He's a chicken-chaser. As long as you are young and pretty, which you undoubtedly are', Peter added, 'He will love whatever you do. Just avoid being lured into the gents by him - He has a reputation!'

Barry picked up his things and headed toward the dressing room he had visited before, as Peter's assistant for many years. This time the room looked different. It was his room and he was going to be the performer. Peter had agreed to help him and reverse rolls for the day.

'Let's just dump these things for now and I'll show you the stage. Barry looked up and took Peter's welcoming hand.

It was bigger than he had imagined it would be. It looked a lot smaller from the audience side. Peter swung his arms around like Julie Andrews in the scene from Sound of Music and he was obviously at home there. 'The stage, my dear, is your territory. You and you alone are in charge of it and you must let the audience know that right from the beginning. Don't be afraid to move around. We've both seen the ammeters stand up here like planks of wood. You are a professional and you must use the space you have to show off your talent to its best effect.'

Barry was honoured that his Uncle Peter was sharing his golden nuggets of professional performer knowledge and he was determined to take all the advice he could get. He was surprised by how bright the lights were and how hot it was on stage because of them. He could see all of the empty seats in front of the stage and, if he squinted, he could see the bar behind them.

The young man in the cheap suit was still there and he turned to face Barry, drinking from his glass. Barry recognised the face instantly. Sergeant Finkle!, he thought. That young police office he had liked that assisted the older detective McGarry. He wondered what he was doing here again. Had he possibly further information to pass on to him and his Uncle Peter?

'Patsy!' he heard his uncle shout. 'Well I never. Frank Hamilton. After all these years!' Barry looked over at the man Peter was talking to at the edge of the side of the stage. 'Barry. Come and meet one of Manchester's biggest artists, Patsy Cline

- AKA Frank Hamilton.' Barry joined them and Peter introduced him as the hottest new talent in Newcastle, if not the world, which Barry felt proud of. Barry could see that Peter was pleased to see his old friend but he wanted to know why Finkle was here.

'I'm just going to get a drink at the bar,' said Barry and Peter just nodded, engrossed in catching up with his old friend.

Finkle smiled as Barry approached the bar. He looked a lot more relaxed than the last time he had seen him. He hadn't noticed if McGarry was with him or not.

'Hello,' said Finkle, as Barry stood at the bar and ordered a coke from the barman. Barry nodded and asked if his inspector was with him. 'No. He let's me do these smaller cases on my own these days.'

'So, your not here to see me then?' asked Barry, disappointed at the prospect of no further progression in the murder investigation. Finkle looked up and down at Barry's slim body and smiled. He adjusted back to his professional roll and continued.

'Well. No. I'm investigating the use of counterfeit five pound notes being passed off as genuine in bars like this in the area.' Barry thought how dull. Barry noticed Finkle look at him again, that way he thought he saw him look at him the first time they met. 'So, why would you think I would be interested in speaking to you? Have you done something that may be of interest to the police?' He smiled, knowing that he was playing with Barry.

Barry knew what he was up to but answered anyway. 'No. I'd hoped you'd have some more information about the Joe Trolley case?' Finkle looked at him blankly. Then he remembered.

'Er...No. That case is still closed, as far as I know.' He looked at Barry straight-on and Barry noticed he had really nice grey eyes. He thought he was probably about a similar age to himself, maybe a little older and he had a nice figure - for a policeman. Finkle noticed the look and asked Barry if he was helping his uncle with his act again.

'No. I'm performing myself of Friday, so this is just a warm up and dress rehearsal sort of thing.' Finkle's eyes lit up.

'Really? I bet you'd look really great on stage.' Barry was confused. Is this the same person that almost climbed the walls in the dressing room to avoid brushing against him? Not sure if he was taking the mick or being genuine, Barry was unsure of what to say next.

'What I mean is... I mean, I think you...' Finkle paused to compose his thoughts. 'What I mean is, I really like you. I asked the inspector if I could take this case, just on the off-chance, that you'd be here and I could get a chance to say hello.'

Finkle blushed and Barry thought it was really cute. 'I've come a few times to the drag nights but I must have missed you. I'd hoped we could have a drink and maybe, talk?'

Barry's professional-mode was about to kick in and say no - this is business but he couldn't bring himself to say the words he had said so many times before. He looked again at Finkle and then at his cheap suit and back to his beautiful grey eyes. There was something about those eyes that just mesmerised him. Finkle blushed again and Barry smiled at him reassuringly.

'Does the inspector know you hang around gay bars on your nights off?' Finkle grinned and replied,

'Crickey! No! He doesn't feel comfortable coming to places like this, so he was more that happy when I said I'd deal with the case.' Barry frowned.

'Places like this?'

Finkle recognised he'd made another blunder and quickly tried to correct it. He put his hand on Barry's forearm and squeezed it gently. 'No, no, that's not what I mean... Damn it! I'm just not very good at this am I?' Barry liked the feel of his hand on his arm. It had been a long time since his school-yard romance and he felt the need for it again. Finkle smiled and revealed his polished white teeth.

Barry noticed his uncle Peter watching from the stage and he knew he had stuff to do. 'Finkle?' Barry said slowly. 'What sort of name is that? Does your mother call you Finkle?' Again, Finkle blushed.

'Sorry. Justin... My name is Justin.' He paused and then asked. 'Do you like skating?' Barry thought about the idea of going skating with Finkle, he meant Justin and it wasn't a bad idea. At least it would give them a chance to talk without any funny business.

'Yes. I do. But I am very busy preparing for my big night on

Friday,' said Barry, aware that he was keeping his uncle waiting. Justin squeezed his forearm again and Barry swooned. 'Okay, then. I can do tomorrow afternoon, if you are free?'

'I'm on a weeks holiday, starting at the end of this shift.' He grinned and Barry thought his beautiful grey eyes sparkled. 'I'll meet you outside the ice rink at one.' Barry nodded and pulled his arm away. He couldn't help one last glance back as he watched the young man in the cheap suit leave through the side door to the club.

'Wasn't that...?'

'Justin?' Barry nodded.

'Who,' said Peter. I thought he was that young police fellow... What's his name again?'

'Finkle?' Peter nodded, looking confused. 'It is. Justin Finkle and we are going out on a date tomorrow at one.' Peter's face dropped with initial shock but the corners of his mouth curled upwards and spread a great big smile across his face.

'Good on ya,' said Peter admiring his maturing nephew. He then did his uncle job of just checking. 'Are you sure?' Barry beamed back an even larger smile and Peter knew that he was. Peter took his hand and led him back to the dressing room. 'Ooh! I just can't wait to tell Bill. He'll be over the moon.'

'It's only a date, uncle,' said Barry, trying to convince himself that he shouldn't get too excited either.

Barry stood in the centre of the stage and Peter took a front row seat in the centre of the facing chairs. Peter was so proud. All of his planning and the cooperation of so many different people had led to this and he bounced in his seat with excitement, waiting for the music to start. He realised he hadn't already done it, so he pressed the play button on the remote control and watched as Barry began to swing to the music of 'All that Jazz.'

Barry worked the microphone like a professional and, remembering what his uncle has said about using the stage, he swished the microphone lead back and forth and danced equally at each side of the stage.

Peter weeped with joy and dabbed his eyes with his, ever-present, handkerchief. Eric came and sat next to him in one of the metal chairs, bedazzled by the performance. 'He's got a nice little body, hasn't he. That dress really shows it off!' Peter ignored the remark.

'So is he good enough for Friday then?' asked Peter looking between Barry and Eric.

'Yeh! Definitely.' Peter smiled and sat back and let Barry finish the piece.

Eighteen

'Can I pay that please' said Peter as he slid the unfolded electricity bill under the thick glass screen of the bank cashier's counter. He opened his purse and counted out the correct money before sliding it under the glass. The cashier typed something into her computer and stamped the bill with a heavy metal-framed rubber stamp before handing the paper back to Peter with a printed receipt. 'Thank you, my dear' he said as he turned to leave.

He recognised a voice over his shoulder, a few windows down from the counter he had just been at. He looked at the odd couple. An elderly man and a pretty young man in a smart white suite wearing expensive, tan-coloured shoes. It was the professor and Greg.

Not wanting to been seen, Peter quickly turned and looked for somewhere he could hide himself but still be able to see what they were up to. He decided to stand behind some artificial greenery the bank used to section off a small area where the could talk to customers privately about bank loans and mortgages. There was nobody sitting there, so he pretended to look at some of the literature and watched the odd couple at the counter.

He was too far away to hear the conversation but he watched as the old man signed a slip of paper and handed it to the cashier. Peter was curious why Greg was with him and startled when he heard a voice behind him say, 'That particular credit card has a very good interest rate at the moment.' Peter looked behind him to see a skinny girl in her early twenties and wearing a smart, but too-tight, business two-piece suit staring at him.

'Sorry...What?' he said, not sure if she was talking to him. The smiling girl nodded towards the leaflet he was pretending to read and said,

'Twenty seven percent for the first three months and then twenty nine percent after that.' Peter looked at the folded paper in his hands, still curious to know what Greg was up to.

'Oh! No... I was just flicking through. I'm happy with the card I've already got. Thanks anyway.' The girl, still smiling, left him to his perusal as he pretended to look at other leaflets.

He watched as the old man was handed what looked like a

bundle of bank notes, which Greg quickly relieved him of and thanked the cashier before escorting the old man to the exit.

'Bastard', mumbled Peter under his voice as he realised what Greg was up to. Peter was fuming and was determined to follow them and see what else Greg was planning to get out of the old professor. He began to walk towards the door and to try and catch up with them when he heard the skinny girl's voice again.

'We could probably beat your current card providers deal, if you want to take a seat, I'll look at the computer.' Peter twitched, not wanting to be rude to the young girl but also aware that the two were getting away. He watched out of the bank window as he saw Greg helping the old man into his car and he knew he'd lost them anyway. He politely declined the skinny girl's offer and decided to go to the butcher to order the turkey for Christmas lunch.

***

'Forty two pounds for a turkey!' said Peter as he plonked his heavy shopping bags down on the kitchen table. Bill looked up from his paper and nodded.

'Yes, I know. But Bob's turkeys are the best. You've got to admit that?' Peter thought for a moment, tilting his head on one side, like a puppy contemplating which side of his food bowl to eat first, and finally nodding in agreement.

'Yes. You're right. I remember that year we decided to try something cheaper from the supermarket - what a disaster that was.' Bill nodded and stood up to help Peter unpack the bags and put things away. Peter remembered the drama at the bank and told Bill as he folded up the carrier bags and put them back into the shopping bag ready for their next use.

'Never!', said Bill as he pulled out the box of tea bags and flipped the lid. 'How much do you think it was?'

'I don't know but it looked like a few thousand, at least,' said Peter, kicking off his boots and slipping his feet into the slippers Bill had left by the radiator in preparation for his return.

'That's what Agnus had said they did with Joe's bank before...'
Bill paused for a moment and ignored the old, steaming kettle,
struggling to turn itself off even though it was boiling away with
fury. Peter noticed and flicked the switch.

'Before they killed him?', said Peter. Bill looked down and just
continued with making the tea. 'Well! That's not going to happen
this time - We'll make sure of that!' Bill looked Peter in the eye
and held onto his forearms.

'Shouldn't we just pass this on to the police? Let them deal
with it?' Peter pulled Bill close and wrapped his arms around
Bill's waist.

'We will...as soon as we have enough evidence to give them
and make sure these bast...' He stopping himself and took a deep
breath, 'Well you know, are put away for a long time.'

'Anyway, the reason for the extra-expensive turkey this year is
that I thought I'd better order a bigger one, now we have Beth.' Bill
looked at Peter and they both grinned, remembering Beth's hearty
appetite. Peter carried the small tea tray through into the living
room and placed it on the coffee table in front of the comfy sofa.
He noticed the Christmas tree Bill had been busy decorating and
fingered some of the old decorations hanging from its branches.

'You've done a good job with the tree. I'd forgotten we had
some of these old decs.'

'Yes. That one there is from my grandmother. It must be eighty
plus years old,' said Bill as he joined Peter at the tree and adjusted
some of the tinsel.

'I hope I still have that much sparkle when I'm eighty,' said
Peter as he pulled Bill close and kissed him on the cheek. Bill
told him to stop being daft and pulled him down onto the sofa and
handed him a cup of tea.

Peter snuggled down and said he was looking forward to
Christmas and to Barry's debut. Bill agreed. He too was excited
about Barry's big day. Bill snuggled in and said,

'There is still a lot of preparation to do and I still have to finish
the decorating and write out all the remaining cards and buy the
presents. The last posting day for Christmas is Saturday, so I'd
better get the cards done by Friday. That reminds me. I'll have to
go to the post office and buy some more stamps.'

Peter remembered the stamps he'd picked up from Joe's desk. 'There's a load of stamps in my jacket pocket - help yourself.' Bill asked Peter what they should get Beth for Christmas and Peter pondered the question, rubbing his chin as he did when thinking.

'You know...I don't really know! What's she into? I don't even know what sort of music she likes.' Bill nudged him in the side and sat up straight.

'Good job we've got a man on the inside, then isn't it?' said Bill as pulled the empty mug from Peter's fingers and put it onto the small tray. 'I asked Barry and, apparently, Beth's always wanted to be a photographer.' Peter looked pleased that Beth was into something sensible like photography.

'We'll get her a camera!' said Peter, picking up the remote control and switching on the tv.

'Hang on. I wasn't thinking of that much expense!' said Bill, as he stood at the entrance to the small kitchen with the tray.

'Oh! Don't be so tight. Beth's one of the family...and she's really brought Barry out of his shell.'

Bill muttered under his breath. 'Shell?'

Nineteen

Barry bought his metro train ticket from the grubby machine at the station entrance and Beth clung to his arm. He didn't know why she had wanted to come with him. 'To see you off', she said. Which although thoughtful, made Barry even more nervous. He was having second thoughts and he wasn't sure if he should be getting back into a relationship at this difficult and busy time in his life.

Beth could sense he was nervous but she was excited for Barry and wanted him to have a boyfriend and not end up a spinster, as she kept reminding him. 'Just try and relax. And remember... You're in charge. Don't let him boss you about,' said Beth as she gripped his arm more firmly.

'Ow! Mind the leather!' said Barry, as he prised her grip off his sleeve. Barry wasn't sure if wearing his leather jacket was a good idea or not. Maybe it was a bit old-fashioned now - but he liked it and that was what matters, he thought.

The metro train approached and Beth became more excited. Barry separated his companion for her clutch and said he would see her later. Beth rummaged around in her pocket, trying to find something. The doors to the train opened and Barry began to head towards them. 'See ya,' he said.

'Wait. Stop!' said Beth as she picked up Barry's hand and placed the mysterious object in it and pushed him on to the train just as its doors began to close. Beth grinned and Barry waved as the train pulled out of the station. He glanced down at his hand to see what she had given him and smirked when he saw it was a small foil packet containing a condom.

It was only a short ride to the city centre and Barry stepped of the train and looked at his watch. He knew he was going to be early and he thought it best if he didn't seem too keen. He decided to look around the shops and try to take his mind off the date ahead of him.

It had been two years since he had been on a proper date. His glamorous life as Peter's assistant and training to become Newcastle's next drag star had taken up most of his thoughts recently. But he admitted to himself, when he thought about Finkle his heart fluttered; when he looked into his eyes, something stirred within him. Something that he had been suppressing for so long. Now it was time to be attended to.

His school boyfriend, Terry White, was his last love. They had met at the age of fourteen and were together for two years. When they first met they soon realised they were kindred spirits and both fancied each other rotten. Barry missed Terry and he was devastated when his parents decided to move to Sydney, Australia. Barry remembered the tears - tears that had to be hidden from Terry's parents, as he didn't have the confidence to come out to his parents and Barry remembered saying goodbye to Terry, waving him off at the airport, wanting so much to give him a goodbye hug and kiss but unable to without blowing the cover of his best friend. Barry wiped away a tear that had began to form in the corner of his eye and checked his reflection in a shop window to make sure there was no evidence that his police sergeant may detect.

It was five to one and Barry, nervous and wondering if he should just go home, crossed the road opposite the ice rink and spotted a young man wearing a thick, warm-looking parker-type coat, a white T-shirt, some smart jeans and designer trainers. It was Finkle and Barry was pleasantly surprised at how nice he looked out of that awful cheap suit. Finkle noticed Barry approaching and pushed himself away from the wall he was leaning against.

Barry was pleased he wasn't the first to have arrived - giving him the edge he thought. Not wanting to seem desperate, even though Barry did want to be there, he was desperate, in a sense. He wasn't sure exactly what for at the moment but he just knew that he wanted to be there.

Finkle grinned and his white teeth were revealed as his skinny lips separated. Barry didn't know how to greet him. In his normal circle of gay friends, he'd just give them a hug and a kiss on the cheek but as he didn't really know Finkle properly he wasn't sure if he should shake his hand or just say hi.

Finkle wasn't so shy. He put out his hand and as Barry took it he quickly pulled him close and pecked him on the cheek. 'Hi. How ya doing?' asked Finkle as Barry, pleasantly surprised by the open display of affection, nodded and replied,

'OK. I'm okay. Thanks.' Barry sensed he may be coming off as a bit of an idiot so remembered Beth's advice and decided to take charge of the situation before Finkle did.

'I haven't been here for years' said Barry, as he looked up at the old, grand building the council had turned into a public ice rink and leisure centre a few years ago. He was brave and offered his hand to Finkle and said, 'Let's go in. It's a little cold out here.' Finkle smiled, realising the blunder.

'I don't think it's likely to be much warmer in the ice rink. Why don't we have a coffee first?' Barry, looked down and then remembered to keep his head up. Okay, so he made another blunder -- of course it would be colder inside. It's an ice rink! Why was he turning into an idiot? Why was he behaving like an innocent schoolgirl. Barry looked at Finkle's beautiful grey eyes again and this answered his own questions.

The coffee bar at the centre was quite busy but Barry found them a quite corner where they could talk without too much noise from the screaming kids, skating on the ice opposite the big observation window at the side of the cafe.

The fake-leather, buffet-style, wide seats would easily accommodate two people but Barry thought it best they sat opposite one another -- as it was their first date. 'So, you said you were on a week's holiday,' asked Barry, making the first move. Finkle nodded, drinking from his paper cup of hot chocolate. Barry noticed the creamy foam of chocolate left on Finkle's top lip and had to divert his eyes as he imagined kissing those skinny but lovely chocolatey lips.

'Yeah! A whole week away from dead bodies and drug dealer raids. It will be nice to put my feet up for a while and spend some time with friends...' He looked into Barry's eyes.' Old and new.' He looked at Barry, who looked quite pale, waiting for a response.

Barry pulled himself together and said, 'Wow! That must be exciting work. Do you really have to deal with murders?' He stared at Finkle's eyes and watched as his pupils widened.

'Yes...Occasionally. Not that often but about every few weeks.' He sensed Barry's curiosity but he didn't want to talk about work, so he changed the subject. 'Anyway! Isn't it your big day on Friday? I bet you can't wait. I'll be there. Already got my ticket.' He pulled out a slip of paper from his jeans pocket and showed it to Barry.

Barry had never seen a ticket for one of the drag shows. Being on the performer side of the business he never needed a ticket, so it was a thrill to see his name printed on the little piece of paper, listed as one of the performers. He made a mental note to get a copy for his scrapbook of fame.

Barry handed back the ticket and asked if Finkle liked drag shows. Finkle paused for a moment, realising that his answer could make or break any future relationship he hoped might happen, before he answered. 'I've seen your uncle perform and he's brilliant!' Barry sipped on his coffee, realising it had no sugar in it, and grinned. 'He's a real pro and the way he commands his audience shows he's one, if not the, best in the business.' Barry continued to grin, knowing what Finkle was saying is all true.

'I'm really looking forward to seeing you on stage on Friday.' He put his hand on top of Barry's and rubbed the back of his hand with his thumb. Barry felt waves of heat rush through his body and his jeans suddenly felt tighter.

Barry closed his eyes for a second and tried to focus on the question. Was he asked a question? He couldn't remember. As Justin's hand caressed the skin on the back of his hand his left leg began to spasm and he had to put his left hand under the table to take control of it again. Deep breaths, he told himself... deep breaths.

'Er...Yeah! Uncle Pete's the best.' Barry slipped his hand from under that of Justin's. Yes, he had decided he will now call him Justin, rather than Finkle. He had earned that. 'So, tell me a bit about yourself,' said Barry as he rummaged in his pocket for some sweeteners. He pulled out a little sachet and was about to sprinkle it into his cup when he realised it was the condom Beth had given him and not the sweeteners he wanted.

Justin glanced at the small packet and Barry quickly put it back in his coat pocket and pulled out a sachet of sweeteners. 'Er...You were telling me about yourself. Are you from Newcastle originally?' asked Barry desperate to move onto something, anything.

Justin resumed his position, taking hold of Barry's right hand again and stroking it with that hypnotic rhythm that Barry yearned for again. 'No. I'm a Londoner. I came up here when I qualified as a sergeant and I've lived up here for just over a year now.' Barry listened as he went on to tell him about how he was brought up on a council estate and how his mother died when he was eleven and how he'd spent most of his teenage years in different foster homes until he was sixteen and made the break and went to college.

Barry was keen to know about everything he could about Justin and he didn't want this conversation to end. Justin had finished his drink and shuffled in his seat. Barry felt his foot rub against his and linger there. Barry decided it was time to skate and stood up, offering his hand again to Justin.

Justin swung his long legs from under the table and pulled on the sleeves of his thick coat, buttoning it up under his chin. Barry thought he looked quite cute with only his face showing, surrounded by the big, fury rim of his coat.

They headed for the rink and paid for their hire skates at the small kiosk by the entrance. They sat on the provided stools and tied the long laces of each boot. 'I haven't skated for a long time,' said Barry. 'So forgive me if I make a fool of myself.'

Justin helped him up onto his feet and they waddled, arm in arm, towards the door. Once on the ice Justin left go of Barry's arm and raced to the centre of the rink, where he spun around and then swayed from side to side as he showed off his talent and expertise as a skater. Barry was surprised but pleased that he was more than just a policeman and actually had an artistic side to him. He was beginning to like Justin.

Barry pushed himself off and moved along the ice confidently. It had been a while since he last skated but it was coming back to him. He decided to show Justin that he could do turns and a spin, if he tried. He built up some speed and twisted his body ready to turn but he must have been doing something wrong, as the skates beneath him weren't taking him in the direction he wanted to go and he felt himself begin to topple. His instinct was to scream but he thought Justin might not appreciate that.

The pain in his bottom was bad and he wanted to go home and sit in a warm bath but he knew he couldn't. He heard the swish of skates approaching and he was sprayed with a wave of ice as Justin came to his rescue. 'You alright?' asked Justin, showing genuine concern. He offered Barry his arm and helped him to his feet. 'You really hit the floor with some umph!' he said as he made sure Barry could stand and steady himself.

Barry pointed towards the door. 'Do you mind?..'

'Course not,' said Justin, pulling Barry along like a sled of bruised tomatoes. 'You poor thing. It's all my fault.' Barry shook his head and squeezed his arm.

'No. Don't be daft. It's just me trying to impress. Bloody fool, I know,' said Barry as he limped across to the stools and pulled off his skates.

'Does it hurt?' asked Justin, gingerly nodding towards Barry's behind. Barry just nodded, embarrassed by his sore bottom. 'If I knew you better, I'd offer to rub it for you,' said Justin with a big smile across his face.

'Maybe one day --but not on a first date!' said Barry and they both laughed as they hobbled out of the ice rink, arm in arm, and into the busy street.

Justin put his arm through Barry's and they crossed the road and headed up the high street. 'Do you fancy a burger?' asked Justin. 'I think we need to get you somewhere warm and let you recover.' Barry felt a nice warm feeling about Justin. He had shown a side of him that the initial persona of the police sergeant had concealed. Justin was a gentle and caring young man. He genuinely wanted to help Barry and look after him.

Barry had never experienced this situation before. After all, it was always him that looked after other people. Not the other way around. 'Yeah! That would be nice,' he replied.

Justin helped Barry into his seat and helped him off with his jacket. He admired it and held it up to have a closer look at it. 'I like this,' he said running his hand over the worn but smooth leather fabric. 'A real classic. You can't go wrong with a leather jacket, can you?' he asked as he gently hung it on a hook by the side of the cubicle they were sat in.

'Yeah! My uncle Peter and Aunty Bill bought it for my eighteenth birthday. I was over the moon!" Justin held back a snigger at the "Aunty Bill" line but also felt it nice to have such a close relationship with a parent, which he never had.

Justin ordered a big burger and fries and Barry thought it best to have a chicken burger with salad. When Justin questioned his selection he reminded him that he was a performer and he needed to watch his figure. Justin glanced over Barry's skinny body and nodded slowly, noting his incredibly flat stomach and boyish body.

'I like you the way you are but don't deprive yourself of a an occasional French fry just to keep other people happy.' Barry was flattered that Justin said he liked him and ignored the comment about fries.

'So, are you investigating any murders at the moment?' asked Barry as the waitress placed his plate in front of him and felt uncomfortable with her customer's conversation. Justin waited until she had gone before answering.

'No. Nothing like that at the moment. This time of year is generally quite for murders.' Barry thought that was a fascinating topic -- he didn't think murdering was a seasonal activity and he was about to question Justin further when he was interrupted.

'I'm not really supposed to talk about such things... off duty. You know?' Barry understood but at the same time was disappointed. Justin noticed his enthusiasm slump and thought he'd better say something.

'So, what ever happened about your friend who died and you thought he'd been killed for his money? What was his name?.. Trolley?'

Barry sat up. 'Yes. Joe Trolley.'

Justin, realising he was on a topic that Barry wanted to talk about, bit into his burger and listened carefully, as if interviewing a suspect.

'Well...' said Barry. Pausing to make sure he got all of the facts in the right order. 'As you know, we found out that Dr. Collins and Greg,' Justin interrupted,

'The Gigolo?' Barry nodded.

'Were planning on killing another old man. The old professor. But when we told your Inspector McGarry, he wasn't interested and you closed the case, saying there wasn't any evidence to prove it.' Justin nodded and continued to eat his burger.

'Well... We've been sort of watching over the old man to make sure he's not hurt and we've also been gathering evidence for you.' Justin smirked but tried to hold it in. Barry noticed the smirk but continued anyway, determined to tell his story.

'We've been following Dr. Collin's and Greg to keep an eye on them and to find out what they are up to.' Justin's eyebrows rose and he put down his burger.

'Woah!' he said. 'You've been what?' He wiped his chin with a napkin and sat back in his seat. Barry, keen to continue with the saga, didn't know what to make of it and began to continue. Justin raised his hand to stop Barry.

"We've been after Dr. Collins for a long time. He's a clever criminal. He knows what he's doing and we've never been able to pin anything on him. We suspect he may have killed before but we've never been able to prove it.' Justin put his hand back on top of Barry's and said,

'He's dangerous. Keep away from him!' Barry was shocked. First by the news that police knew Collins was a murderer and second that they haven't been able to prove it once. Barry put his hand on top of Justin's to reassure him that he was okay and he wasn't taking any risks.

'It's okay. We're keeping at a safe distance. We're always in pairs and we take turns so he won't recognise us.' Justin still wasn't sure and squeezed Barry's hand, obviously worried for him. Barry liked the fact that Justin must like him enough to care about his safety.

Barry went on to tell his story about how they had found out about the wills being forged and witnessed by fake witnesses, how Greg was buttering up the old professor and about the Y-front parade. Justin laughed at this point but continued to listen.

Barry told him about the card with the cut-out in it and then Justin stopped him mid-sentence. 'I've seen that before,' he said. He let go of Barry's hand and put his hand to his chin, just the way his uncle Peter does when he's thinking. 'There was a similar card in the evidence bag for a similar murder case we dealt with a few months ago. Turns out, according to my boss, McGarry, its a common method used by con men to get their victims to sign things. Important things like contracts and...' Barry butted in,

'Wills?'

Justin nodded. 'Yeah! Wills! Apparently, if you cut out a hole in a card or other non-important bit of paper, then stick that over something that you want to be signed, that any normal person wouldn't sign without questioning what they are signing, then get the victim to sign where the hole is, they don't know they're actually signing the document below.

Barry was engrossed. 'So, you think the professor might have just signed a new will, without being aware of it?' Justin nodded and put his hand back on top of Barry's. 'Wow! It's a good job I kept it, isn't it?'

Justin looked serious and came across more as a policeman than as his date. Barry wasn't sure if he liked the change in role. 'Really, Barry. I'd rather you left this to the police. I don't like the idea of you getting hurt.'

'We came to the police but you won't listen to us. You think we are just a bunch of amateurs and won't take us seriously!' said Barry pulling away his hand to force his point. Justin dropped his head.

'You're right. Your right,' he said holding up both hands as if backing off from a gunman. 'I will have a word with McGarry when I get back to work next week and see if he thinks it's worth looking into again. I mean if we can get any prints off the card you have or any other DNA evidence, then that might be enough to persuade him.' Barry cringed for a moment.

'Ah!' he said, remembering how he had forgotten about prints and DNA evidence when he fished the card out of the bin. 'There might be a slight problem with that...I might have, accidentally, handled the card without thinking and it probably has my prints all over it!' Barry replayed the words in his mind he had stated only moments before: "You think we are just a bunch of amateurs!"

Justin smiled and kept his thoughts to himself. 'All the same, it could be the evidence we need to re-open the case.'

Barry pushed away his plate. He had no appetite and was feeling low. Justin squeezed his hand again and rubbed his knee against Barry's under the table. Barry looked up and giggled. 'Stop it. People might see,' he said in a boyish voice. A voice he realised he hadn't used since his relationship with Terry.

Twenty

Beth was waiting by the window when Barry returned and all three of them had gathered in the front room to greet him as he opened the front door. Beth was clearly excited and jumped up and down on the spot like an excited schoolgirl.

Barry dropped his bag on the sofa and looked a the three watching him and smiling. Beth couldn't contain herself and asked, 'So... how did it go?'

'My bum's sore,' said Barry and he watched as all three of their jaws dropped in sync and as Peter swooned, as if about to faint. Bill propped him up.

'What?' said Barry as he rubbed his bruised behind and looked at their blank expressions. 'I fell on the ice and hurt my backside.'

Peter and Bill rushed around the sofa and gently cradled Barry in their arms. 'Oh! My poor dear,' said Peter as he helped Barry down on to the sofa and instructed Bill to make some tea. Beth couldn't contain herself. She burst out laughing. Barry looked up at her covering her small mouth with her hand, trying to hold back the giggles.

'Sorry princess. You alright?' She came and sat down next to him. 'I'll rub some cream on later, if you want.' Barry looked Beth in the eye, not sure if she was taunting him. Peter looked in the shortbread biscuit tin in the sideboard they used for first aid to see if there might be something suitable. He lifted the glasses that hung on a lanyard around his neck and pushed them onto his nose and read the small print on the back of a green bottle Barry had never seen before.

'This should do the trick,' he said, handing the bottle to Beth and sitting in the armchair opposite. 'If you rub that in it should relieve some of the pain.' Barry looked at Beth, who was grinning wildly.

'You're not seeing my bum,' he said, beginning to giggle. Beth tried to keep a straight face and paused, trying to keep her laughter under control.

'Don't be silly. You're hurt. You need someone to rub in the cream, if you want it to heal quickly.' Barry was about to protest when Peter butted in.

'You don't want to be black and blue on Friday, do you? And remember, that dress you're wearing has a low-cut back!' Barry's face suddenly became serious. He hadn't thought about that. He pulled himself up and then pulled Beth by the arm and told her,

'Come on. Upstairs to my bedroom!' Beth giggled but held back.

'Poor lad,' said Peter as he flicked through the newspaper, clipping out a coupon for 20p off moisturiser. 'I hope the rest of the date went without any other problems.' He looked over at Bill who was reading his book on lamp posts. Bill put his finger to mark where he was up to and looked over the top of his small, round spectacles.

'Yes. I hope so. It would be nice if Barry found a nicc boy to setting down with.' Peter nodded but then after thinking for a moment, he thought of something.

'I'd really miss him if he decided to get married to this Finkle character. I mean I'd be really happy if he finds love...but I'd also really miss him if he moved out.' Bill looked over the top of his spectacles again and responded with a slow nod and said,

'It's only a first date. Who said anything about them getting married?' Peter giggled and returned to his newspaper. They heard Beth and Barry coming down the stairs and both looked towards the door.

'Here he is!' said Beth as she led Barry, now wearing soft jogging pants, to the sofa and gently eased him down into his original seat. Peter and Bill looked at Beth for her diagnosis.

'Not as bad as it seems. He's got a little bruising on his buttocks but nothing serious.' She grinned at the embarrassed Barry. 'Otherwise, not a bad looking little bum. Barry flushed even pinker and placed his hands over his face.

Bill handed him his tea and he sat back, trying to compose himself. Beth squashed herself in the small gap between Barry and the end of the sofa. Peter put down his paper and took a sip of tea. 'Did you have a nice time...other than you falling on your ars...' he paused for a second, 'falling.'

Barry smiled. 'Yes, I did.' The others waited for him to continue and he realised they wanted more. Barry went on to tell them about the talks they had and about how Justin kept wanting to hold his hand and how romantic it all was. Peter sat and grinned, pleased that his adopted son was happy and may be on the verge of finding a boyfriend.

Barry described Justin's beautiful grey eyes and how they had mesmerised him from the first time he had saw him. Beth was excited for Barry. She questioned him about everything: 'What was he wearing? Was he on time? Did he pay? Are you going to see him again.?'

'He said he'll be at my debut on Friday.' Barry mentioned the ticket Justin had showed him and how he wanted to get a copy for his scrapbook. Peter said he would ask at the venue and would get him one.

'He says, because of his job, he has to keep his being gay under cover --sort of thing!' Bill nodded. 'He says the people at work all know he's gay but McGarry is very strict and he has to be "straight-acting" during office hours.'

Peter put his handkerchief to his mouth and said, 'How awful!'

Barry put his empty cup on the coffee table and put his two fingers to his lips, as if considering something before he spoke. 'Justin told me about doctor Collins and about how they have suspected him for murdering before but how they haven't been able to prove it.'

Peter held his handkerchief tighter and said, under his breath, 'Jesus!' Everyone looked at Peter, not used to such exclamations. Peter just waved Barry to continue.

'He said Collin's had been questioned in connection with a similar murder a few months ago but Justin said he's a very clever criminal and they have never been able to get enough evidence to convict him -- so he always walks free!' Barry looked around for their response.

'He warned me to be very careful. He said Collin's is very dangerous and Justin was genuinely concerned for my safety.' Barry smiled, proud that his Justin cared about him. Peter looked nervous.

'Right! That's it!' said Peter as he stood up and looked out of the net curtains at the front room window. 'We have to stop all this right now!' Bill stood up and joined Peter, putting his arm around his waist.

'Peter's right,' he said. 'It's just too dangerous!' Barry looked shocked and Beth screwed up her face. She looked at Barry and then at the others.

'Does that mean we just let these bastards kill the old professor then? Do we just go back to our boring little lives watching tv and dragging it out on stage?' She looked at each one of them in turn and, as each one of their faces dropped, realising they couldn't just leave the old man to die. She stood up and said,

'I say we carry on!.. Yes, it's dangerous...but a man's life is at stake here. If we don't protect him and he is killed, how could we live with it for the rest of our lives?' Slowly each of them nodded in agreement.

Peter rubbed his chin and paced back and forth in front of the window. The others waited patiently, whilst their leader conjured up a plan. 'Buddies!' he said. The others looked up confused.

'Buddies!' said Peter again. He looked at their blank expressions and continued

'OK. The new rule is: If anyone of us is following Collins or Greg or anyone else, we must always be in pairs.' The others looked at each other and nodded in agreement.

'Always keep our distance and never be alone with any of them!' he continued. Barry butted in again and told them about what Justin had told him about the card he had found in the bin.

'It sounds like they might be getting ready to do the dirty deed,' said Beth as she adjusted the strap at the top of her big boot. Barry nodded.

'Yeah! And if Greg's taking money out of the old man's account that could also be a clue that they're getting ready.' He nudged Beth in the side and she shuffled over a bit to let him sit up straight.

'You'd better come with me when I'm at the professor's tomorrow. We'll have to think of a reason for me taking you with me though,' said Barry, aware of his sore bottom.

'Well, he knows you're gay, so I can't be you girlfriend,' said Beth with her usual witty grin. 'Maybe we could say, I'm your nurse and I have to apply cream to your botty every few hours!'

Barry elbowed her in the side and said, 'Very funny.' He thought about it for a moment and suggested that Beth could be a writer and doing a book on gay history. The old man could tell her all about what it was like when he was young and about it being illegal.'

Beth looked at him and said, 'Illegal...Really?'

***

Beth hadn't wanted to get up so early. She had become accustomed to the cosy life, living in Peter's house and she usually didn't get up before ten. Barry had to drag her out of bed and remind her that she was going with him to the professor's house. They stopped in at WH Smith's on the way to get spiral-topped notebook as Beth had forgotten she was playing the part of a writer today.

The professor noticed Beth's big purple hair as he opened the door and a smile stretched across his face as he welcomed them both into the warmth of his home. Barry put his arm around Beth and introduced her.

'I hope you don't mind but I've brought a friend along. This is Beth and she's a writer, who I thought you might like to meet.' The old man looked at her extravagant long black coat and her silly, over-the-top boots and then again at her enormous purple hair, sticking out in every direction. He smiled again.

'Hello. Nice to meet you,' said Beth, holding out her black gloved hand.

'Come in...Come in,' said the professor closing the big door behind them and pushing them into the warmth of the kitchen. 'A writer. Oh! That is exciting.' He filled the kettle and pulled out some tea bags from a small gold tin. Barry took off his coat and made himself at home.

'Beth's writing a book about gay history and I thought you might like to talk to her and give her some material for the book...I hope you don't mind?' The old man swung around with the tea tray.

'Mind? No... I 'd love to. A book. Wow! That must be so exciting for you my dear.' He touched Beth's arm. 'Here. Let me hang that big coat up for you. He helped her off with it and hung it on the hook on the back of the door. 'Should we go into to the living room?' he said, conscious of his manners. Beth said she was happy in the kitchen.

'I'd better make a start on the garden as soon as I've drunk this,' said Barry and he nudged Beth to say something.

'You've got a lovely home here...Mr?

'Gerald Winslock...But just call me Gerald.' He replied, making himself comfortable on the kitchen stool. 'And, thank you.' He looked around the room. 'My partner bought this house nearly twelve years ago and we've been...were very happy here. He died five years ago and I've lived here on my own since.'

Barry nodded towards the notebook she was holding and she remembered she was supposed to be doing research. She flipped the cover over and wrote down the old man's name with the biro she had bought with the notebook.

'I'm sorry. That must have been a difficult time for you,' she said. The old man dropped his head for a moment and then raised it again.

'Yes it was. Tom and I were together for neatly fifty years. I really miss him.' Beth looked at Barry, who was nearly in tears.

Barry jumped down from his stool and put his coat back on. 'What would you like me to do today Gerald?' The old man looked out at the garden, not that interested anymore.

'Oh! If you could pick up all those apples that have dropped. They'll only rot if left.' Barry, without further instruction, pulled open the kitchen door and headed for the garden, leaving Beth in the nice warm kitchen, grinning through the window at him out in the cold.

Beth glanced at her watch. It was nearly ten thirty and she wondered how long she could keep up the pretence that she was a writer. She waited as the old man fished around in a cupboard to the side and watched him as he brought three thick, leather-bound, albums towards her. He placed them on the kitchen island that Beth was sitting at and he pulled up his own stool and sat next to her.

'This was taken of me when I was twelve,' said the old man as he pointed to an old black and white photograph of a little boy in a full-body swimming costume. Beth thought it looked like the photos you see in museums. Very stiff and posed.

'Even at that age, I knew I was gay.' He looked at Beth's pen and noticed it wasn't moving. She wrote down some notes and the old man continued his history lesson. 'Of course, back then, there was no such thing as "Gay" or "Lesbian". It just wasn't even thought of. Such things certainly weren't talked about and as a boy of twelve I didn't even know that such things were possible. All I knew was I liked other boys.'

Beth jumped as the front door bell rang. Gerald looked up at the clock on the kitchen wall and touched Beth on the arm again. 'Sorry...That'll be Dr Collins. He comes everyday at this time to give me my Insulin injection. Won't be a tick.' He shuffled off his stool and went to answer the door.

Beth panicked. She ran to the back door and banged on the glass, trying to attract Barry's attention. He looked up from his apple collecting and noticed the strange look on Beth's face and her waving hand, indicating for him to come in.

'What's up?' he said as he wiped his feet on the door mat.

'Collins is here. He's come to give the old man his injection!' Barry held her shaking body.

'It's okay. He comes everyday about this time. I'm normally in the garden but the old man tells me when he's been.

'What if it's...you know... THE injection?' Whispered Beth. Barry looked at her intense stare and thought about it.

'No! He wouldn't do it if he knew there were other people here, would he?' They turned as Gerald and Dr. Collins entered the kitchen.

'This is my gardener, Barry and this young lady is a journalist, writing about gay history and she's currently interviewing me for her book.' He smiled proudly. Collins looked at them both and especially at Beth's hair.

'Er...yes. Nice to meet you both.' He turned to Gerald and said he didn't have a lot of time and could they do this in another room. The old gent led him into the living room by the elbow and asked about his day and his family.

'Are you sure?' asked Beth, still nervous about the old man.

'Yes! Don't worry. I'd better get back to the garden.' He pulled open the door and returned to his apples.

A few minutes later he heard Gerald saying goodbye to Collins at the front door and waving him off. Collin's mobile phone rang just as he was getting into his expensive Mercedes car and Barry pricked up his ears and tried to listen, hugging behind the corner of the wall.

'Greg? Hi. No... I couldn't. There were people there. No... some daft girl and a camp queen he's employed as a gardener. I know... You've got to laugh! Yes...Tonight at seven. Where? The Angel's Arms. OK. See you then.'

Twenty One

'Do you think Peter would give me driving lessons?' asked Beth as she pulled on the long strands of purple hair sticking out above her forehead. Barry watched as she teased each bunch of hair and twisted it like a curling tong before stretching it to its maximum length and releasing it.

'I don't know. Have you asked him?' he replied shuffling in his seat and pressing on the back of the seat in front of him with his knees in the grubby metro train carriage. Beth continued to pull at her hair and Barry continued to watch as the scenes from the window flitted past at a comfortable speed.

'It would be very useful if one of us could drive. It would save us having to use the metro and we could come and go as we please,' said Beth as she slipped her arm through Barry's and rested her head on his shoulder. Barry noticed as an old lady nodded at him as she stepped off the train, indicating she thought they made a cute couple. Barry smiled and didn't care.

'Will you ask him for me?' Barry shuffled in his seat some more and replied,

'Ask him yourself, you lazy cow.'

Beth spun around and stared Barry directly in the eye. She thumped him on his upper arm and he giggled as she mounted him and held his arms like a screaming girl. Barry noticed the train was slowing down and he yelped, 'OK...OK. I give in. Get off me you scary creature. This is our stop!'

The metro pulled to a stop and the doors hissed as they opened. Barry pulled Beth onto the platform and she re-linked her arms with his as they skipped out of the station. It was a short walk to the pub and, as planned, they would arrive early to suss out the place before the two con-men were due to turn up.

The old oak door with its frosted glass panel swung open and the welcoming heat wafted over them and thawed their tingling bodies. Beth headed for the bar, almost by instinct but Barry took the time to look around at the bustling scene. It wasn't the sort of place he was used to going in. There were no camp young men hanging around watching his every move. There were no drag queens on stage, just a tired old jukebox in the corner playing some country and western song he didn't recognise. The place smelt of smoke and beer and the carpet felt grimy under foot.

Beth returned carrying two glasses and two packets of crisps hung between her lips. 'Where are we sitting?' she said, keen to offload her bounty. Barry scoured the room. It was divided into an open area with tall stools and small tables, only big enough to hold a few glasses and at the other end, there were several small booths, separated by frosted glass and which were lined either side with big leather-buttoned benches. Barry pointed towards a free booth and Beth headed in that direction.

'Bit of a dump, isn't it?' said Beth as she placed the two glasses down and pulled the crisp packets from her lips. Barry just nodded. He noticed a problem instantly.

'There's nowhere we can hide when they get here.' Beth wasn't sure what he was talking about until she too looked around the room. He was right. The open area was just that, too open. Greg and the doctor would see them if the hung around there. The booths, although somewhat private, still didn't provide a suitable location to avoid being seen.

Barry looked at the big clock on the wall behind the bar. It was already a quarter to seven and they would be here in a minute. Barry watched as an old man in a cloth cap got up from his table and downed the dregs in his glass. He put on his raincoat and pulled out a large newspaper from its side pocket and left in on his table as he headed for the door.

'Just a mo,' said Barry as he quickly trotted over to the table and retrieved the newspaper. It was one of the large broadsheets and Barry opened it out and pulled it up to his face, as if he was reading it. 'What do you think?' he said from behind the paper.

Beth smiled and looked at Barry's socks which were sticking out above his dainty trainers. 'I'm not sure if the average reader of the Times usually wears white frilly socks but who am I to know.' Barry flipped the corner of the newspaper down and looked at his socks. He uncrossed his legs and pulled the denim of his jeans so the top of his socks were covered.

'There. Is that better?'

Beth nodded. 'But what about me? Dr Collins saw me at the old professor's, so he would recognise me if he saw me here.'

Barry looked up at Beth's big hair. Even a broadsheet couldn't cover that, he thought. Reluctantly, he passed his wooly hat over to her and told her to put it on.

Beth pulled it over her massive hair and tried to tuck the wild strands in to it delicately. Barry noticed Greg coming in through the entrance and quickly helped Beth to shove the remaining strands of purple hair into the hat. Beth looked ridiculous - like a Rastafarian nun but it didn't matter. He indicated that Beth should sit with her back to the room and he raised his paper to cover himself.

Greg was joined at the bar by Dr. Collins, just as he received the drinks he'd ordered from a very overweight barman with several days growth on his wrinkled chin. Beth asked Barry what was going on. Barry kicked her leg under the table to say be quiet as he carefully peeked out of the corner of his paper to watch as the couple looked for a booth but when they could not find an empty one they took their place at one of the tall tables in the centre of the room.

Dr Collins lit a slender cigar and put the gold-coloured lighter back in his jacket pocket. Greg smiled at him and Barry could see they were chatting and laughing about something. They were too far away to make anything out and Barry felt disheartened.

'I can't hear what they are saying,' said Barry as he lifted his drink behind the paper and took a sip. Beth began to turn around and she was kicked by Barry again.

'Ow!' she said. 'Stop doing that!'

There was a pause and then Barry said, 'This is a waste of time.' Beth nodded. 'Should we just go?' Barry was about to fold up his paper and make a quick exit when the people in the next booth got up and left. Greg spotted the vacant booth and indicated to Dr. Collins that he should follow him as they slid into the leather-bound cubby hole.

The only thing between them now was the thin glass screen. Barry indicated to Beth to swing around and sit next to him with their backs to the glass barrier. Barry squeezed Beth's hand with excitement at their good fortune.

***

Peter was ironing Barry's dress for the big night and Bill was baking some fruit cake in the kitchen. 'It feels odd doing this myself now. I can't remember the last time I ironed something,' said Peter as he straitened out the seams on the dress and applied the steam iron. Bill stuck his head through the door and said, 'What was that dear - I had my head in the oven?'

'I was just saying, I haven't lifted an iron in years.' Bill nodded, half expecting something more substantial.

'Well, you are star, my dear! That's what you have your people for - to look after you, so you can focus on being fabulous!' Peter blushed and he knew Bill was right.

'I wonder how they are getting on. I should have went myself.' Peter put down the iron and rubbed his chin. 'I hope they are okay. I'm worried about them.' Bill came through and placed his hand on Peters shoulder.

'Barry can look after himself,' said Bill reassuringly. Peter raised his eyebrow indicating he wasn't sure about that, when Bill continued, 'He's with Beth. She'll look after him.' Peter dropped his eyebrow and returned to his ironing.

Peter glanced up at the wall above the sideboard. It was covered in Christmas cards. He smiled. 'We seem to get more cards every year,' he said, folding up the ironing board and putting it away in the under stairs cupboard.

'I know. It's nice in a way. It shows how popular you are. But it's a pain in another way.' Peter looked at him confused. 'It means I have to send out cards in return.' Peter nodded. 'I've already done about fifty but there's still that pile on the sideboard waiting to be posted.

There was a small ching sound from the kitchen and Bill returned to see to his cake. Peter sat down on the sofa with his clip board and pen. 'I still have to work out the final bits of Barry's routine on Friday.'

***

Barry lay his head back against the hard wooden frame of the glass screen and listened to the conversation of the con men. Greg was talking about his job and Collin's about his new car. Barry looked at Beth and raised both eyebrows and pretended to yawn. Beth smiled and squeezed his hand in acknowledgment.

'So did you get the last of the cash,' asked Dr Collin's, taking a sip from his gin and tonic.

'Yes. I take him every week at the same time and he takes out 5k.' Beth squeezed Barry's hand so hard he let out a little yelp and tugged it away. 'Managed to collect forty five k so far. Do you want your half sent to the usual account?'

Barry nudged Beth and whispered in her ear. 'We forgot to bring the tape recorder.' Beth winked at him and opened her coat to show him the tape recorder spinning as it took down everything that was being said.

'Yeah. That'll come in handy,' said Dr. Collins as he got up to get another round of drinks. 'Same again?'

Barry noticed Bath's leg bouncing gently against his leg and thought she must either be excited or nervous. He whispered in her ear. 'You okay?' She nodded and whispered in return,

'I need to go.'

'But we've only just got hear and it sounds like we might get what we need on tape, if we stay. Why do you want to go now?' Beth stared at his and bit her bottom lip.

'No, I mean I need the ladies.' Barry grinned and realised his misunderstanding. He pushed her away and then remembered the tape recorder in her jacket. He indicated for her to leave it with him and he positioned it against the edge of the glass barrier, so it would pick up the conversation more easily.

Dr. Collins returned with fresh drinks and lit another cigar. Barry hated the smell and waved the newspaper gently, as not to attract attention but sufficient to keep the smoke away from him.

'Have you got the stuff?' asked Greg. Dr. Collins, unsure what he meant replied,

'Stuff? Oh, I see what you mean. The injection? Yes, I have it

155

in my Bag.'

Barry shuffled in his seat. This is it, he thought, they are talking about the poison. He looked along the corridor to see if Beth was coming anytime soon and he pressed his ear against the glass, not wanting to miss anything.

'When do you plan to give it to him?' Asked Greg, sipping nervously on his drink.

'I was planning to do it this week but that bloody kid is always there whenever I go to give him his insulin.' Greg sipped on his drink and thought for a moment.

'He's never there whenever I've gone over to the old man's, so he must only work during the daytime. Maybe you could give it to him later in the day.'

Barry spotted Beth returning. She made a point of keeping her face turned away as she approached, just in case they should look her way. They didn't notice the odd-looking girl in the inflated wooly hat and she resumed her seat. Barry raised his finger to his lips and indicated for her to be quiet. She shuffled her bottom up close against Barry and lay her head back and listened in on the conversation.

'Yes, I suppose so. I'll ring him in the morning and tell him I'll come on Thursday at four.' Greg smiled and raised his glass.

'Here's to another successful job!'

Barry fumed at this last remark. Is killing a poor, defenceless old man a job? He thought and Beth noticed the fury in his eyes. She put her arm around him and held him, knowing that in his current state he may jump up and say something to the evil pair sitting next to them.

'Shh... Calm down. We have enough for the police now. We can finally get them...Don't you see?' Barry gripped her by the arms, furious and wanting to lash out at the con-men but then, as his mind cleared, he realised she was right. He slumped back into his seat and smiled. They now knew when and where they were going to kill the old man. All they had to do now was tell the police and the old man would be saved.

Twenty Two

Beth listened at the door of the living room as Barry spoke to Finkle on the phone in the hall. 'Come and have some breakfast,' said Peter as he wrapped his flannel dressing gown around his legs under the table and poured himself some tea from the steaming pot. Beth looked at the hot breakfast just laid out by Bill and the temptation was just too great for her. She left Barry to his call and slid herself under the table and buttered herself some toast, nudging a piece under each of the two fried eggs on her plate.

They heard Barry putting down the phone and watched him as he joined them at the table. He too was ravenous and he tucked in without noticing his audience waiting for the news they all wanted. 'Well?' said Beth as she scraped some baked beans from her plate and squashed them against a piece of sausage. Barry looked up and then, realising what they wanted, began to recall the contents of the phone call.

'Well. I told Justin,' Beth looked at him and asked who Justin was. 'Finkle?' Beth acknowledged the name and indicated for Barry to continue. 'Finkle... I mean Justin said that was great that we have this new evidence and he will tell McGarry as soon as he gets into work for his afternoon shift. He said he was sure that this would be enough for them to re-open the case and McGarry would probably want to listen to the tape as soon as possible. He's asked me to meet him at the police station at one o'clock.

Peter smiled and sat back in his chair. 'I'd better come with you,' he said, rubbing his chin and taking a sip from his cup. Beth butted in and said she wanted to come as well and maybe Peter could give her a driving lesson on the way. Peter stopped mid-slurp and looked at Beth. She was grinning.

'Driving lesson?' said Peter. 'Oh my dear, I wouldn't be any good at that sort of thing... Best ask Bill. His nerves are stronger than mine.'

Barry smirked and said, 'I'm not getting in a car with her at the wheel! My career has only just began. I want to be in one piece for Friday night!' Beth whacked him on the arm and replied.

'Yes. And I'm sure we all know which piece Justin wants to see...' Peter interrupted her.

'Now, now. Lets be good little children and up you pop to your rooms and give your uncle and aunty a bit of piece and quiet. Barry and Beth both turned to look at Peter, in his regal parental pose, pointing to the door. They laughed, pushed their chairs under the table and each kissed Peter on the cheek, saying,

'Yes, Uncle Peter.'

***

McGarry was expecting them this time and they were escorted into his office by Finkle. Justin smiled at Barry as he held open the door for him and he was about to give Barry a wink when he noticed McGarry watching him and was told to close the door.

'Do you have the tape?' asked McGarry. Barry nodded and nudged Peter who was playing nervously with his collar. Peter fished the tape out of his bag and handed it to the inspector. He examined the tape and read the label printed on its side. 'Bananarama. Umh!' he said and placed the tape into a machine on his desk. He pressed the big old-fashioned clunky button and sat back in his chair and put his hands behind his head to listen. He then remembered the last time Peter was in his office and he dropped his arms to his side and smiled at Peter.

Barry handed McGarry a piece of paper and told him that he had also transcribed the tape to save a bit of time. Justin smiled, proud of his new boyfriend. The inspector read it through and listened to the tape. Peter hadn't heard the tape yet, so he was enthralled as the conversation progressed.

Barry watched the expression of the inspector change as the con-men confirmed the day and time they planned to carry out the murder and he sat up from his inclined chair and stopped the tape. 'Brilliant! That is exactly what we need. Not solid evidence...' Barry interrupted him.

'Not solid? What do you mean?' Peter gripped him by the arm and told the inspector to continue.

'Not solid in the sense that we don't know exactly what

they were referring to. They could be talking about something completely different.' Barry was about to butt in again but the inspector continued. 'But, it is definitely enough for us to follow up on.' He turned and swung his chair back again. They all listened and waited as McGarry thought about his next move.

'OK. Thank you for coming in and thank you for the tape. It has been most helpful. Finkle will show you out.' He indicated to Finkle to get the door. Peter and Barry looked at each other and Peter's jaw dropped. Barry stood up and turned to McGarry.

'Hang on! Is that it?' McGarry looked at him, not sure what he meant. 'What about the old professor? They said they are going to kill him on tomorrow at four o'clock.' The inspector stood up and indicated them towards the door.

'Yes, yes. We will take it from here. We'll make sure the old man comes to no harm.' Barry was furious and Justin could see in his eyes he felt they was getting a raw deal. Justin butted in.

'Well, sir. They have brought us enough evidence for a successful prosecution. Maybe we should let them help us put this one to bed.' He glanced at Barry with suggestive eyes and Barry blushed. McGarry noticed the look and sighed. He sat down and told Justin to close the door.

'Okay,' he said. 'We really need to catch these men red-handed. If we can arrange to be at the old man's house at four tomorrow and grab Collins in the act, then that is our best bet of putting him away for good.' Barry looked at Justin, in his cheap suit and white shirt and nylon blue tie. He looked at his shoes. They were very worn and looked rather tatty. He wondered how much a police sergeant got paid. It can't be that much, he thought, if he couldn't afford a decent pair of shoes.

McGarry looked at his watch and swung around in his chair. 'I'll get on to the undercover lads and see if we can arrange something for tomorrow. Finkle, if you take Mr Grills and Mr Sidewick into the interview room, we'll need a complete statement from them both.

Peter felt nervous at the thought of being interrogated by the police on an official basis. He began to twitch and a bead of sweat formed on his brow. Barry recognised the signs and held Peter's hand and gave it a little squeeze. Barry asked if they both needed to be interviewed, as he was sure he could give them all the information they needed. Peter felt a wave of relief pass across his shoulders and then McGarry said,

'No. Sorry. If we are to build a solid case against these two, then we need all the evidence we can get. The more witnesses we have the better it will go in court.'

Justin touched Barry on the arm and opened the door. Barry looked into Justin's beautiful grey eyes and smiled, knowing it was going to be alright.

***

The interview took almost an hour and Peter looked frazzled as he left the small, sterile room and headed along the narrow corridor to the exit. Barry supported him by the elbow and Justin followed them to the end of the corridor and entered the code to unlock the door.

'I get off at nine if you want to do something,' said Justin as Barry passed him in the doorway. 'Maybe we could catch a late film or go for a drink, or something? Barry smiled at him and nodded.

'I'll text you once I get uncle Peter home and settled. It's been a traumatic time for him.' Justin smiled then looked either side of him and then lent over and kissed Barry on the lips. Barry, at first startled by the action, also looked ahead to see his uncle heading for the car park and then pulled Justin by the neck and kissed him passionately. Justin got the message and said,

'Later then?' Barry nodded and let the heavy fire door swing behind him as he skipped towards his uncle and linked his arm through his.

'You took your time,' said Peter as he fished for his keys. 'More questions?' Barry just blushed and replied,

'Something like that.'

The drive home was longer than usual. Roadworks kept them sitting in a traffic jam for almost twenty minutes. Barry was fidgety. His head was full of thoughts and he hardly noticed Peter's presence. 'We really should go over your routine for Friday again when we get back. I want to see your stage actions again.' Barry wasn't really listening and just looked out of the window, oblivious to Peter's conversation.

Peter looked across at Barry and noticed his grinning face. 'What are you so happy about? I found the whole thing very draining personally.' Barry didn't respond and continued to stare into space. ' Barry!' shouted Peter, nudging him in the arm.

Barry turned, quite startled. ' What? What was that uncle Peter?'

'Are you all right?' asked Peter, now concerned that the interview may have had a more dramatic effect on Barry than it had done on himself.

'Oh. Yes... I'm fine.' He shuffled in his seat and noticed that they were close to the chemist where Beth worked. 'We might see Beth if this traffic jam doesn't get a move on.' Minutes later the stream of cars nudged forward to where they were directly opposite the chemist window.

'There she is,' said Peter, waving dramatically, trying to catch her attention. She was serving an old lady with a wicker shopping trolley and seemed to be showing her a tube of some sort.

'Looks like she's selling more haemorrhoid cream,' said Barry as the car nudged a little bit further forward. He noticed Beth look up and spot the car outside. Barry pulled a face and stuck out his tongue. Peter noticed the gesture and slapped him on the thigh.

'Stop it,' said Peter as suddenly the jam began to clear and he had to move forward. Peter remembered something and asked Barry, 'What do you think we should get Beth for Christmas?'

'A boyfriend,' said Barry.

'No, seriously. You said she was interested in photography. Bill and I thought she might like a camera. What do you think?'

'Yeah! I know she's dragged me around the photography exhibition in the town hall a few times, so I know she likes pictures. She seems to know a bit about it too. She once dragged me into a camera shop and pointed out what the professionals use.'

'I don't suppose she makes much from her part-time job', said Peter, turning down a side street and checking his rear-view mirror.

'No. Probably not.'

'Where was this shop?' asked Peter.

'Oh! It's up there,' Barry pointed to a place further up the high street. ' It's expensive though.' Peter's bit his bottom lip. 'The cameras Beth was showing me were thousands.'

Peter said, 'Umh! But I suppose they would be able to give us advice about what would be suitable and at a more affordable price.' Barry nodded.

'I expect so.'

Peter turned the car and headed in the direction of the shop. Barry gave directions and Peter was able to find a near-by parking space. ' That was lucky,' said Peter. Barry's mobile phone buzzed in his pocket. He had forgotten he's put it on silent in the interview room. He looked at its small screen and read the text message.

'Looking forward to tonight. Justin. X' Barry grinned and considered replying but decided that he didn't want to get into sending girly back and forth messages -- That just wasn't him. He put the phone back in his jeans pocket and helped Peter out of the car.

The shop was small and not much bigger than their front room, thought Peter. Its walls were lined with all sorts of cameras, bags, tripods and other gadgets Peter didn't recognise. Behind a glass-topped counter stood a thin, weedy man with thick-rimmed spectacles and wearing a diamond-checked armless jumper. Peter remembered those from the seventies and he was pleased they had come back into fashion.

Barry pointed to the camera that Beth had shown him in a tall glass case. The man behind the counter, thinking he was about to make a big sale, joined them and said, 'Yes. The Nixon X985BN. One of the best cameras on the market. A true professionals camera.'

Peter put his reading glasses on and looked at the tiny price tag next to the camera. £2300 it said. Peter said, 'Jesu...' and Barry sniggered.

The salesman butted in. 'Yes. Not the cheapest camera on the market. But if you are a true professional, then this is definitely the one for you.'

The man looked at Peter, in his lime green blouse and pink,

snug-fitting jacket and, then realising Peter maybe wasn't the customer here, he turned towards Barry. Barry smiled at him and as he watched the man glance up and down and decided he wasn't going to make a big sale today after all.

Peter put away his reading glasses and said,' We have a close friend who we want to buy a camera for. She isn't a professional -- just a beginner, I think?' He looked towards Barry for confirmation. He nodded and added,

'But we are on a small budget. What can you recommend?' The man, no longer interested, returned to his counter and pointed towards a shelf by the door.

'Any of those should do.' Peter pulled Barry by the elbow and looked at the cameras on the shelf. They didn't look anywhere as impressive as the expensive one but the prices were more in their league.

Peter pointed to one and asked Barry's opinion. Barry wasn't that interested, so just agreed. Peter paid for the camera and left the shop knowing that was another task ticked off his list.

Twenty Three

The back door of the white, anonymous van swung open and Justin offered his hand to Barry and pulled him in. It was very cramped and the smell wasn't pleasant. Several different faces appeared out of the gloom and as the door shut behind them a small internal light was switched on.

The small van had wooden benches either side of it and fixed to one side was a make-shift table. Sat on the table were various electronic boxes with big knobs and switches stuck to their fronts. Barry instantly recognised it from TV police shows he occasionally watched with his uncle Peter. It was a police surveillance van. He felt proud to be involved.

One of the faces was that of inspector McGarry. He smiled at Barry and noticing his excitement, tried to make Barry focus on him and forget the beeps and squeaks coming from radios and gadgets around them. 'Now Barry. I've asked you here because we are going to need your help.'

A loud message came through on one of the men's radios and McGarry indicated for him to turn it down, pointing to it and then pointing at the floor repeatedly. 'We all know that the suspects are planning the attack this afternoon.' Barry nodded.   'Well, it would be very helpful if I could get a couple of my tech boys into the house so they can set up some equipment beforehand.' Barry's eyebrows raised with excitement. 'And we need you to take the old man out for about an hour, so they can do their work.' He looked at Barry for his response.

Barry nodded rapidly. His leg began to quiver and Justin, who was sitting next to him in the dim light noticed. Justin casually brushed the back of his index finger against Barry's thigh to calm him.

'We want to get a hidden camera in the room and a mic, so we have plenty of evidence.' Barry suddenly thought of something.

'You are not just going to watch from here and then run in when you see him get his syringe out?' He began to panic that the old professor might be at risk if they didn't get to him in time. McGarry held up his hand, with its yellow, nicotine-stained, fingers and reassured him.

'No...no. The video is only for extra evidence. I plan to have all of us in the house watching Collin's every move. As soon as we see him doing anything that looks dangerous, we'll pounce. BUT!' he said, raising his voice.' This is important! To get a successful attempted murder prosecution, we must see him with the syringe in his hand.'

Barry looked at Justin, who just smiled and tried to remain professional. He returned his gaze to the inspector and nodded. 'What time do you normally start your gardening job?'

Barry pulled back the tight sleeve of his winter coat and looked at his watch. It was eight-thirty. 'About nine, normally,' he said, releasing the sleeve and letting it re-cover his watch.

'Excellent!' said McGarry. 'Could you get him out of the house by nine-thirty?' Barry thought about it for a moment and couldn't think what excuse he could use to persuade the old man to go out so quickly.

'That might be difficult. We don't normally go out when I'm there, so what reason could I use to get him to come out with me?'

McGarry indicated for Justin to open the door and said, "Oh! I'm sure you'll come up with something. Just leave the back door unlocked and we'll let ourselves in." With this Justin shuffled towards Barry and nudged him to get out. Justin got out with him and closed the door behind him.

It was cold and there was still a heavy frost on the pavement. Justin pulled on the zip on the front of Barry's coat and pulled it higher, making sure Barry was kept warm. 'You do your best. You are very creative person and I'm sure you'll think of something.' He looked around, as he always did and then kissed Barry on the lips and patted him on the bottom.

Justin was about to get back in the van when Barry thought of something. 'Wait!' he said grabbing Justin's sleeve. 'What about this afternoon? What time should I be here? What...' Justin put his finger to Barry's lips to stop the flow of questions and smiled.

'Don't worry. I'll text you later with the details... My beauty' He stared deeply into Barry's eyes and kissed him again. Barry swooned and had to concentrate to remain upright.

***

Barry decided to arrive early, to give him that little extra time to come up with a reason to take the old man out. He was welcomed with the usual smile and warmth when the old professor opened the door.

'Come in, come in, my boy. It looks freezing out there!' said the old professor as he headed for the kitchen. He had the teapot ready and was about to flick the switch of the kettle when Barry had his brainstorm.

'Wait! Before you make the tea!' The old man turned, looking quite surprised to be stopped from his usual routine. 'Today is my birthday!' said Barry, grinning like an idiot. 'And I'd like to take you out for a birthday breakfast. There's that lovely little cafe down the road and I thought we might have a bacon sandwich to celebrate.' He watched the old man's face as it illuminated and his bushy white eyebrows stretched across his wrinkled face.

'Oh! My boy! How wonderful. Let me give you a kiss.' He opened his arms and let the professor hug him and peck him on the cheek. 'I had no idea! Wow! Your birthday?'

Barry felt guilty about lying to the old man but he knew it was in a good cause. He looked at the clock on the kitchen wall and knew he didn't have much time.

'But I can make us a bacon sandwich, if you like.' He pulled back the net curtain and looked out at the garden. 'It doesn't look very nice out there. Here, you put your feet up in the living room and I'll get the bacon on.' He started to unzip Barry's coat and Barry panicked.

He held the old man's hand and said, 'No...no. I'd rather go out. I feel like celebrating!' He quickly scanned his brain for any inducement he could offer. 'Have you seen the new waiter there? Oh! He's beautiful!' The old man's eyes widened like a cat that just spotted a mouse and Barry knew he had him hooked.

'Yes, I saw him last time I was in. He's called Pedro. He's only about eighteen but he has that classical Greek Adonis look... you know what I mean? Very slim and a really gorgeous.' Barry smiled as he reeled in his catch. 'Yeah. Shame he's into older men. I was chatting to him only the other day and he was telling me how he didn't make much as a waiter and he'd love to be a house boy for some older man. Apparently he has a thing for older men -- so no chance for me then!' Barry watched as the old man drooled and seemed lost in a world of his own.

Barry looked at the clock again and it was nearly nine fifteen. 'He only works the early shift, so if we left now I could introduce you.' Barry nervously looked at the clock again and returned his gaze to the professor but he wasn't there. He swung around and saw him putting his coat on in the hall and wrapping a big scarf around his frail neck.

'Ready when you are,' said the old man. 'Come on, birthday boy. We don't want to be late.' Barry grinned knowing his ploy had worked.

He suddenly remembered the inspector's instructions and he told the old man that he would just check the back door was locked and he'd be right with him.

Barry checked the old man wasn't watching as he turned the key of the lock on the back door and made sure it was unlocked. He bent down and slid the old bolt to the left and he felt the door give a little, letting in some cold air.

Barry linked the old man's arm as they turned left at the gate and headed down the street. Barry spotted the white van and noticed McGarry in the front passenger seat. He casually nodded to him as they passed the van and the inspector smiled in return.

The pace was slow and Barry wasn't used to it. He hadn't really noticed how frail the old man was before but now it made him even more angry that someone could think of hurting him.

As they turned the corner onto the high street Barry looked behind them and saw the tech guys unloading their cases and heading down the back lane to the old man's house. 'It's just along here,' said Barry and he gripped the old man's arm tighter, feeling his excitement.

Barry swung open the heavy aluminium door to the cafe and noticed it was quite empty. He scanned the room and, as expected, there was no pretty young waiter. 'You get us a table and I'll order the bacon sandwiches.' He released his arm and noticed the old man glancing around the small cafe, hoping to spot the beautiful creature he was told about.

Barry felt bad. He didn't like lying to the old man. He ordered two bacon sandwiches and a pot of tea for two. He chatted with the girl behind the counter and occasionally glanced across at the professor.

'She said it won't be long,' said Barry as he pulled off his heavy coat and swung it over the back of the cane chair. The old man looked up at him expectantly. 'She says Pedro doesn't work here anymore.' The old man deflated like an old party balloon. Barry felt really bad.

'Never mind...There's plenty more pretty young things in the sea, as they say,' said Barry, trying to make amends for his betrayal. Just then the young girl placed a pot of tea in front of them and two sets of cutlery, wrapped in paper napkins. She returned moments later with two small plates and placed them in front of them

Trying to change the subject, Barry said, 'Oh! These look good.' He opened up his bun and squirted some ketchup from the dispenser over the bacon. The old professor seemed to come around and poured the tea out.

'Anyway,' said the old man. 'Today's your birthday!' Barry nodded guiltily and hid his embarrassment behind his sandwich. 'Have you got anything special planned?'

Barry was still chewing a fatty bit of bacon rind, so couldn't answer immediately. He shook his head slowly. 'No. We thought, as tomorrow is my debut, we may as well combine he two and have a party after the show.' He swallowed the mouthful and licked around his teeth before he continued. 'I hope you will come and join us tomorrow night, after the show.'

The old professor's eyes widened again as he remembered the debut. 'Oh Yes! I'm looking forward to seeing you in your dress. Liza, you said?' Barry nodded and took another bite. 'Your friend... the writer, Beth?' Again Barry nodded. 'You said she would call on me and take me to the venue?'

Barry swallowed the last of his breakfast and wiped his lips with the napkin. 'Yeah! Beth will pick you up around eight and take you on the metro. I go on after Peter at nine, so she'll get you there in plenty time and I've arranged for VIP seats and everything.'

The old man's face glowed. 'Beth... Such a colourful character and so butch in those big boots. And does she have a nice girlfriend?' Barry was taking a sip of tea and almost choked at the question.

'Er... I don't know. Maybe you could ask her when you see her tomorrow.' Barry knew he was being naughty but the thought of seeing her reaction when the old man asked, was worth it.

He looked at his watch and he knew he had to keep the old man talking for at least another forty-five minutes before they could head back. He looked at the old man in front of him. If he only knew what was about to happen. That someone, someone he knew and trusted, was going to kill him at four o'clock. Barry shuddered.

'I once thought about treading the boards,' said the old man, holding up his hands and doing a little dance in his seat. 'But my farther wanted me to go into science, so I never got the chance.' Barry noticed his obvious disappointment.

'I'm sure you would have looked great on stage.' The old man smiled.

'Do you think so?'

'Definitely,' said Barry, pouring out some more tea. 'So,' he said, trying to think of things to say. 'What are your plans for today?

The old man sat back in his chair and pondered the question. 'Well, let me think... Dr Collin's normally comes around in the morning to do my insulin injection but I got a call from him yesterday to tell me he would be late today... something about a staff meeting he couldn't get out of. He's coming at four instead.'

Barry cringed, knowing more than the old man about what exactly he was coming for. 'I normally have a nap after lunch and then later on this evening I usually give my friend Jeffrey a call and we natter on about trains for a while. Then I'm normally in bed by seven these days... Not a very exciting life... anymore.'

Barry grinned. 'So! You'll be out past bedtime tomorrow night... You naughty boy!' The old man nodded, laughed and sipped on his tea.

There was an obvious silence and Barry was relieved when the professor got back onto the topic of his debut. 'So what made you decide to become a drag queen?'

Barry smiled and told the professor about his early years as a young gay man and how his uncle Peter and aunty Bill adopted him and how he was brought into the world of glamour and dresses and performing. He told him about how he felt the first time he saw his uncle on stage and how brilliant it all was and how he just knew from that point onwards that he wanted to be on that stage.

The old man grinned, taking in all of Barry's enthusiasm and watching him as he waved his arms around dramatically at the table. The girl behind the counter also watched and smiled. Barry had an audience and he was happy.

The old man was startled by Barry's phone buzzing on the table. 'Sorry about that,' said Barry as he pressed the button and read the text:

'All done. I'll ring you later. Justin. X'

Twenty Four

Peter was checking the hemline of Barry's dress. Pulling it here and there until it looked right. 'Now, turn around and let me look at you.' He twisted Barry's body to the left and right and watched as the tight-fitting fabric moved with his moves.

'I can see a problem,' he said, kneeling in front of Barry's waistline and sitting back as he swished back and forth. Barry gave a look of horror.

'What? Is it the sequins?' Peter shook his head. Barry looked down his skinny front and moved, observing the fabric as it moved to try and see what Peter could see. 'I can't see what you mean.'

Peter pointed directly at Barry's crotch. 'I can see you bits.' Barry blushed. 'It's time to make the big decision every drag queen has to make at some point in their career.' Barry smiled, puzzled by what was to come.

'You have to decide whether you are going to be a tucker or wear a cup.' Barry blushed again and raised both eyebrows, not knowing the answer. 'When I first started out you had no option but to tuck your bits down, between your legs but - trust me, you don't want to go there. Now most professionals use a cup. Much more comfortable and looks more natural.'

Barry didn't know what to say. He was very close to his uncle but he had never had to talk about 'his bits' with him before. 'I... I... don't know.' Barry blushed and giggled. 'I haven't got much down there but I don't like the idea of squashing what I have got between my legs.'

Peter giggled to. He got up and popped across the landing to his room and returned with a small paper envelope. 'It was Bill that brought it up a few days ago. I'd completely forgot about it. Here, we got one for you - just in case.' He handed Barry the envelope and Barry looked at it. 'One size fits all, it says on the packet, so it should be okay.'

Barry couldn't control his embarrassment. Peter sensed it and put his arm around him. 'It's okay. There comes a time in every boy's life when their parents have to give them "the talk" and that was it.'

Barry fumbled with the smooth plastic object and tried to figure out which way was up. Peter told him to go into the bathroom and slip it down his underpants and come back and let him look. Barry did as he was told and a few minutes later returned, red-faced.

'Ah! Much better' said Peter as he tensioned the fabric down across Barry's wiry body. 'Everything nicely hidden.'

***

Beth looked up as Peter passed her on the sofa. 'Is he finally ready?'

'Yes! He is. Isn't it exciting?' Peter did a little skip and went in to the kitchen to put the kettle on. Bill was in there rolling out some pastry. 'Oh! This looks nice. What are you making?'

Bill wiped his flour-covered hands on his apron and pushed Peter out of the way so he could get access to the cupboard behind him. 'Steak and kidney pie,' replied Bill. He stuck his head around the door to check where Beth was and closed the door slowly behind him.

'Did you give it to him?' asked Bill with a cheeky smile. Peter nodded and grinned. ' Did he like it?'

Peter laughed out loud. 'Like it?'

'You know what I mean... Was he pleased?' Just then in came Barry, hugged his aunty and thanked him. Beth was curious why everybody was in the kitchen and why they were laughing. She came in and they all went silent.

'What's the joke?'

Barry smirked and Peter held his handkerchief to his mouth, holding back a giggle.

'Oh! Nothing dear... just man's talk.'

Beth looked at the three of them. One was wearing a dress, one was in an apron and one wearing more makeup the she was and wondered where these men were.

Barry's phone rang in his room upstairs and he darted out of the kitchen, hitching up his dress. 'Go girl!' said Beth as he rushed past.

'It'll be Justin,' he yelled as he thundered up the staircase.

Peter brought the tea tray trough to the sitting room and Bill and Beth joined him there. 'Yes, of course. He said he would ring Barry to arrange things for this afternoon,' said Peter. He held his handkerchief to his mouth and continued. 'Oh! I do hope the old man's going to be alright. What if Collins turns up early?'

'Barry said the police have the house under constant surveillance. If they see Collins before the expected time, they have orders to intercept him,' said Beth as she pulled off her boots and put her feet on the small fury poof by the coffee table.

Bill picked up his newspaper and slid his glasses down onto his nose. 'I hope they catch the bast... bugger, red-handed and put him away for life.' Peter nodded in agreement.

'He's gotten away with it before. How can we make sure he doesn't this time?' said Beth as she began selecting which strand of hair to twirl next.

'Leave it to the police now!' said Bill as he looked over the top of his paper. 'There's nothing more we can do to help. Don't get involved!' Peter was quite surprised by his assertive husband. It was not like him at all.

Reluctantly, Peter agreed with Bill. 'Yes, we need to forget about it... Leave it to the police. We have to focus on Barry's big night tomorrow. I'm sure the police don't want us getting involved any further.'

Barry rushed down stairs with his phone still in his hand, talking to Justin. 'The police need your help to catch the con-men!'

Peter's face turned pale. He glanced over at Bill who he could see was shaking his head behind his paper. 'They need someone to distract the old professor at the door, whilst they slip in to the house and hide themselves in readiness for Collins' arrival.'

Barry indicated he needed an answer quickly. 'Why can't they have one of the police do it?' asked Peter. Bill nodded in agreement and Beth frowned. Barry relayed the answer to Justin and listened to the reply.

'Cutbacks,' he said. 'Not enough staff available today. They don't want to involve a civilian but McGarry would rather you did it, as the old man hasn't met you before.' Barry watched Peter as he mused over the proposition.

Peter nodded and checked out of the corner of his eye to see Bill raise his paper again. Barry went back up to his room, still talking to Justin. His tone had changed and he was now back to his boyish, flirty voice he kept just for Justin.

'Sorry hubby,' he said as he looked over to Bill. 'I couldn't let the old man down at this late stage. He went over and kissed the top of Bill's head and nuzzled into his neck.

'Okay, okay. As long as I can come with you. Just to make sure you are alright.' Peter nodded and cleared away the tea things.

Barry returned, full of excitement and beaming. He plonked himself next to Beth and shuffled her over a bit so he could swing his legs up onto the armrest of the sofa.

'You two seem to be getting on well,' she said. 'You'll be getting married and having kids at this rate.' Barry giggled.

'Maybe.'

Beth stopped twirling her hair and pulled Barry's head down onto her lap. He stretched his legs out further long the armrest. 'So, do you really like him then?' she asked, running her fingers through his hair and parting it.

'Yes.'

'And do you think he may be the one?'

'Who knows!'

Beth continued to play with Barry's hair and picked up a strand and began, out of habit, to twirl it. Barry slapped her hand away. 'So... Have you?'

'Have I what?'

'You know...Done the business yet?'

Barry grinned but did not reply. 'You have, haven't you?' Again Barry just grinned but said nothing. 'You dirty girl!' They heard a rustle of paper and both looked over to see Bill sitting there reading his paper.

'Don't mind me,' he said and raised his paper again.

***

Bill parked the car as close to the old professor's house as he could. Peter, Beth and Barry sat next to him in the car and waited for further instructions. Barry fiddled with his phone and texted Justin to tell him they had arrived. Barry noticed the white van, still parked where had been all day.

A few seconds later they watched as the rear door of the van opened and out stepped Justin. He looked around cautiously and headed down the pavement towards them. Beth began to sing, 'Prince Charming... Prince Charming.' Barry elbowed her in her side and told her to shut up.

Peter rolled down his window and the cold air flooded in. Justin lowered himself to the level of the others and smiled.

'Thanks for agreeing to do this Mr Grills,' he said. He looked at the other members of the group and nodded. 'Barry...' He looked at Beth and she gave her name in a girly voice.

Peter touched Bill on the thigh and said, 'This is Bill, my husband.' Beth mumbled under her breath, 'And your future father-in-law.' Justin smiled and nodded.

'Now, all we need you to do is go to Mr Winslock's front door and keep him talking for long enough for us to sneak in around the back. We've already made sure there is an unlocked window on the ground floor.'

He looked over at Barry. 'It would be useful if we had someone who knows the layout with us, as we won't have much time to hide ourselves, once we are in. We don't want to distress the old man, so it is best he doesn't know that we are there.' They all nodded in unison.

Justin looked at his watch. It was quarter to four. 'You had best get going Peter. We'll tell the van driver to flash his lights, once we radio him to tell him we are in.' He held open the door for Peter and offered his hand to Barry in the back seat to assist him out of the small hatchback. Beth said, 'Take care.'

Peter headed to the house. He wasn't really sure what he was going to say to the old man. Barry had said he was very friendly and liked to chat, so it shouldn't be that difficult. He got a signal from one of the group to proceed and he walked along the narrow path that led to the front door. Even thought it was getting dark already, Peter could see the quality of the property.

He rang the big brass doorbell and waited patiently. The hall light came on and the door was opened by the old man. He smiled when he saw Peter and Peter returned the gesture.

'Hello. I'm sorry to bother you,' said Peter. The old man grinned and hugged the door, aware that the cold air was coming in. 'No problem,' he said.

'I represent the local residents' association for this area and I'm just asking residents for their opinion about the council's proposal to install speed bumps in this road.' Peter smiled, quite surprised by his own ingenuity.

The old man didn't look interested. 'Oh! No, I don't really mind. I mean, if it stops people speeding, then it's a good thing.' Peter looked over the old man's shoulder and spotted the policemen quickly concealing themselves in cupboards and adjacent rooms.

Peter looked for any sign of flashing lights from the van at the entrance to the garden but nothing. The old man said,' Okay. Thank you. Must go -- all the cold air's coming in.'

'Oh, sorry about that.' He began to panic. 'Just one more thing. I thought I recognised your face. Aren't you Mr Winslock?' The old man re-opened the door and smiled.

'Yes, that's right. Do I know you?' Peter had to think quickly in order to continue the farce.

'Didn't you used to go out with that lady at number forty two. You know the blond with the big... Oh! What was her name.' The old man shook his head and Peter saw the headlights of the van flash. 'No? Oh! Sorry to have bothered you then. Have a pleasant evening.' Peter made his getaway, his part in this undercover operation complete.

***

McGarry and another officer were in the living room, hiding behind the curtains. Another two men were in the under stairs cupboard and Barry and Justin were in the old pantry cupboard in the kitchen, the one Barry had recently cleared out for the old man.

Justin looked at his watch. It was totally dark in the cupboard but its fluorescent numbers glowed the time of 3:56. He felt Barry behind him and rubbed his bottom against his crotch. Barry slapped him on the arm, aware that he wasn't meant to make any sound for risk of giving them game away.

Justin very gently pushed the door ajar to form a tiny gap, which he could see out of. He could see the old professor in the kitchen boiling the kettle and getting ready for his expected visitor. Justin held his radio, ready to alert the others as soon as he saw Collins with his needle. He checked his watch again. 3:57.

He could feel Barry's breath on the back of his neck and he stepped back a little to enjoy it further. He stepped on Barry's toe and he let out a muffled, 'Ow!' Justin quickly checked the gap and he saw the professor turn towards them, curious where the noise had come from. He put down his tea towel and headed towards the cupboard. Just as he put his hand on the knob to open it, the front door bell rang.

'Ah! Dr. Collins.' He changed direction and headed for the front door. Justin and Barry slumped against each other and sighed. They listened as best they could to the muffled sounds in the hallway.

'Come into the kitchen. It's warmest in here. That's the problem with these big old houses -- they're so difficult to keep warm in the winter. Tea?'

Collins looked around the room, suspicious of everything. 'You alone Gerald?' he asked. The old man confirmed that he was and asked about the doctor's day. He seemed nervous. He was not the usual, confident professional he normally portrayed.

'Haven't got a lot of time as usual, so can we get on?'

'Sure,' said the old professor. 'Where do you want me?' The doctor rummaged in his Bag and pulled out a small bottle and a new syringe. Justin primed himself and Barry could feel his whole body tense up against his.

Justin watched as Collins Filled the syringe from the small bottle and then he shouted into his radio, 'Go...Go...Go.' He pushed open the cupboard door and grabbed the arm of the doctor. The other men took his other arm and pulled it behind his back and pushed it upwards. Justin gave the man the remaining arm and he was handcuffed. The professor was in shock, still standing with the back of his trousers pulled down, revealing his buttock.

'What...what is going on?' he said, stumbling out of the way of the brute in handcuffs. Barry went to his side and took his hand.

'Come with me and I'll explain.' He took the old man into the living room and sat him down on the big armchair by the fire. They listened as McGarry read the doctor his rights and he was man-handled out of the kitchen and out into the street.

The gentle old man stared into Barry's eyes, lost in confusion and no longer in control. Barry hugged him, sensing it was what he needed right now. McGarry came in and waited as Barry comforted the old man.

'Mr Winslock. I realise this is a difficult time for you but I need to speak to you about Dr. Collins.' He indicated towards the chair opposite and Barry nodded. He sat and flipped open his notebook.

'Mr Winslock. The man we have just arrested is a criminal we have been trying to catch for a long time. He is a murderer and con-man.' The old man's expression changed to one of disbelief.

'Dr. Collins?'

'Yes. I'm afraid so, sir. He and his accomplice,' He referred to his note book, 'A Mr. Greg Wilkes, have been running a con where they lure wealthy elderly gay men and rob them of their money and homes.'

'Greg? Not my Greg?' The inspector nodded and Barry held the old man's hand. 'Oh dear. How awful!' The inspector pointed towards Barry and said,

'If it wasn't for this clever young man and his family, they would have got away with it and that injection the doctor was about to give you would have killed you, as it was poison, not insulin!' The old man's jaw dropped and he pointed towards Barry, who had become quite flushed.

'Barry did this? He helped you catch him?' The inspector nodded. Barry squeezed the old man's hand and said,

'It wasn't just me. Peter, my uncle. Beth and my aunty Bill -- We all helped.'

'Beth -- the writer girl with the big hair?' Barry nodded and smiled. The old man was still very confused and Barry suggested that the inspector leave his questions until tomorrow and that he will take care of the old man. The inspector agreed and said he'd arranged for the professor to get his insulin from the local nurse, who will be here soon.

Barry placed a cushion behind the old man and lowered him back into the deep seat. 'You take it easy. I'll make you some hot tea.' The old professor just stared into space and let Barry slip from his grip.

Justin was standing at the door and welcomed Barry into the kitchen. "Poor old bugger,' said Justin. 'He's not the first I've seen this happen to.'

'What's going to happen to him tonight?' asked Barry. 'I can't leave him all alone after this.' Justin sensed Barry was getting worked up again and he pulled him into his arms and hugged him, resting his chin on his shoulder.

'Does he have any family we can call?' asked Justin. Barry wasn't sure and pulled himself away from Justin's embrace.

'I'll stay with him tonight!'

'Are you sure? I'd stay with you and help but as you have just seen, we have three criminals to interrogate. If we interview them tonight, there's more chance of getting more out of them before they call in their lawyers.'

'Three criminals?' quizzed Barry.

'Yeah! We also picked up Greg and the bent solicitor at the same time, before they warn each other.' Barry grinned.

'Nice!'

'I'll have to go. I probably won't be around for a while. These interviews can take a couple of days sometimes.' Barry smiled and kissed him goodbye. He headed off towards the front door. He remembered something just as Barry was pouring out the hot water. He popped his head around the door. 'And good luck for tomorrow night. With any luck I'll be there but if not, here's my congratulatory peck on the cheek for now.'

He pulled Barry towards him and kissed him passionately on the lips, lingering a little too much. Barry felt his jeans begin to tighten, so he pushed him off and told him he'd see him later.

Barry made a quick call to his uncle and told him he'd be staying with the professor for the night and he'd be back in the morning.

Twenty Five

The wind was getting up. The tall trees of the, normally sheltered, avenue were swaying and rustling. There was litter flying up and down the road and people's wheelie bins were being tossed around like skittles.

Peter looked out of the living room window and gasped at the strength of mother nature. 'You should see this,' he said, calling out to Bill in the kitchen. 'Mrs Titmarsh... you know... her who works at the butchers? Well her wheelie bin has just landed in her greenhouse. Oh dear! Poor cow. That'll teach her to short-change me again!'

Bill came in with a basket of washing. 'I was going to put this on the line but its just too windy. Get me the clothes horse from under the stairs dear and I'll put them by the fire.' Peter quickly did as he was instructed and stretched out the zig-zag airer in front of the fire and turned it on.

'The forecast says we are in for a storm,' said Bill as he laid out the clothes on the airer. 'Have you heard anything from Barry yet?'

Peter shook his head as he watched a man walking his dog, struggling to keep upright in the wind, which he battled against in earnest. He eventually gave up and picked up his little dog and tucked it into his heavy coat.

'No. He told me last night that he would try and get back for around ten this morning.' Peter dropped the net curtain and turned to Bill. 'I do hope the old man is okay. It must have been very distressing for him.' He looked at Bill for a response and both of their eyes widened as they heard a slow creaking noise and then a sudden whoosh and crash. They both felt the floor vibrate and the sound came from the back of the house. They rushed through into the kitchen and looked out of the window into the back garden.

The old oak tree that had stood in the corner of the garden ever since they had bought the house was lying on its side. Its branches buried in the side of the garden shed. Peter's jaw dropped and Bill's expression changed as he noticed the tree had also brought down the telephone wires that stretched across from the telegraph pole opposite.

Bill went into the hall and checked the phone. 'Yes!' he said. 'It's dead. Damn!' Peter came through and sat on the sofa.

'What are we going to do?' asked Peter as he rummaged around in his Bag for his mobile phone. He looked at the screen and said, 'It's okay. I've still got a signal. Do you want me to ring the phone company about the phone not working?'

Bill took Peter's phone. 'No. I'll do that. You've got a lot to get ready for this evening.' Peter agreed and got out his spiral-topped notebook and looked at the long list of things he had still to do in preparation for Barry's big night. Bill sat at the dining room table and rang the number on top of the phone bill.

'I'm in a queue,' said bill as he tapped the top of his biro against his forehead. Peter noticed something on the list he needed and he went upstairs to find it. He walked past Beth's room and he could hear her snoring. It was almost nine thirty but Beth was still fast asleep. Peter peaked his head through the gap of her door and glanced around at the chaos. Clothes hung from every piece of furniture and there were open books on the floor and makeup scattered on every surface.

Beth shuffled and her eye opened, noticing Peter at the doorway. 'Morning,' she said in a half-asleep yawn. Peter said good morning and asked her if she wanted a bacon sandwich for her breakfast. 'Umh! That sounds nice,' she said, stretching her arms out wide and swinging her legs over the edge of the bed. 'Is Barry back yet?'

Peter said no and told her he said he'd be back about ten. Beth opened the door and pushed past Peter, heading for the bathroom. 'Sorry. I need a pee!'

Peter retrieved the clips he needed for Barry's wig and returned to the kitchen, where he put the grill on for Beth's bacon. Bill joined him. He didn't like other people in his kitchen, so he nudged Peter out of the way and took over preparing Beth's breakfast.

'They say they have been inundated with calls today. Apparently, the storm has brought down lots of trees and telegraph poles all over the north east and they are working as quickly as they can to get the phone lines up and running. They said they have a team of engineers in the area and they should be able to get to us sometime today. They said, it could be anytime up till ten pm.

Peter's face froze. 'Ten pm? They can't expect us to wait in for them all night!' Peter then realised something more important. 'Oh my god!.. Barry's debut. We can't miss that...'

Bill held Peter's arm, the way he did when he knew Peter was about to go into a panic attack. 'Shhh!' He rubbed his forearms and calmed Peter down. 'Don't you worry about that. I'll stay in and wait for the engineers. You just focus on Barry's big night.' Peter looked at Bill's gentle and kind face.

'But you'll miss it. You've been looking forward to this as much as I have?' Bill nodded.

'Yes, I have. But I can see him on Tuesday can't I? Tonight might be his debut but we have bookings for him to perform twice a week right up till Christmas.' Peter looked surprised.

'Really?' Bill nodded and smiled.

'Yes, apparently the words already spreading. I've had calls from some of the local venues and they've all wanted to book Barry. Some have said they got good reviews from the Eric.'

Peter thought for a moment. 'Ah! Eric. But he only saw Barry doing his practice session at the club last week.'

'Apparently that must have been enough. He's been telling everybody on the scene about him and all the clubs want to book him now!'

'Wow! A star before he's even done his first show!' Peter grinned, proud of his protégée. 'Do you think we should tell him? Or should we leave it until after the show... It might make him more nervous.'

Bill agreed. 'Tell him after the show. It will make it an even bigger reward for all of his... and your, hard work.' Peter smiled and nodded. Bill, heading back to the kitchen, noticed the pile of Christmas cards still to do on the sideboard and said, 'Anyway, it'll give me a chance to get the last of the cards done.'

Beth, drawn by the smell of bacon fat sizzling under the grill, came down stairs and plopped herself on the sofa. Bill immediately placed a mug of tea in front of her. 'Thanks Bill,' she said, scratching her head. She looked over at Peter, still making lists. 'I had this really strange dream last night. At least, I think it was a dream... I heard this big bang and I think it woke me up...

Then I must have went back to sleep again.' She looked confused, not quite awake yet.

'That will have been the storm,' said Peter pointing out of the window. 'That big old tree in the garden came down and crashed into the shed!'

Beth's panda eyes widened. 'No!' Peter nodded.

'And it's brought down the phone lines with it!' said Peter as he took a sip of his tea.

Just as he was about to tell her about the phone company they heard the front door slam and in came Barry, wrapped up like an Eskimo. Peter got up to help him off with his things and walked him over to the fire to defrost.

'It's mad out there. The metros were off, so I had to walk most of the way.' Peter began to panic. He rubbed Barry's shoulders, as if trying to thaw him with friction.

'Oh. You poor boy! Here. Sit down and I'll get you a bacon sandwich.' Beth looked up at the thought of hot food.

'So, how's the old man,' asked Beth as she was handed a small plate of bacon sandwiches by Bill.

'He's surprisingly okay,' said Barry as he gratefully accepted a plate from his aunty. 'We sat up and chatted until late evening. I think he was pleased to have some company.' Barry bit into his sandwich and wiped a small droplet of tomato ketchup from his chin with his finger.

'He's got his cousin staying with him for the day, so that's a relief. Justin called me and said they would need to ask him a few questions but he promised to keep it brief and not upset him.' Barry sat back in his chair, warming by the fire. 'Justin's good with people. He's promised to look after the old professor and keep me informed about Collins and Greg.'

Beth sat up, already having cleared her plate. 'I hope they are both put away for life.'

'Justin told me that, as expected, Collins is waiting for his lawyer to arrive but Greg is terrified of going to prison, so he's being very cooperative and they hope to get him to shop Collins for a deal.' Peter butted in,

'Deal?' Barry nodded and continued. 'Well... We all know what happens to pretty boys in prison?' He looked around the room and

Beth grinned and Peter held his handkerchief to his mouth and smirked.

'Exactly! So, apparently Greg is wanting to do a deal with the police. Justin says, he's agreed to tell them everything to put Collins away, if they will promise that he won't get a custodial sentence himself.'

'Can they do that?' asked Beth, mesmerised by the whole idea. Barry nodded.

'Apparently so. Justin says it quite common. Anyway... He says, they're going to ask Greg about Jo's case and see what they can find out about that as well. He said he'd ring me later.

Peter sat up and said, 'Oh! It would be wonderful if we could find out exactly what did happen to Jo. It would be brilliant to be able to put Agnes's mind to rest.' They all nodded in unison.

Twenty Six

The club was already busy when they arrived. Peter managed to get the small car parked in his usual spot at the back, under the fire escape and he looked over at Barry, sitting in the passenger seat next to him. He saw the sparkle in his eyes and Peter said, "Ready?'

Barry grinned and nodded. They collected all of their bags, dresses and carrier bags and struggled through the strong, gusty wind to the stage door. Peter kicked it a couple of times and it was answered by an old, wrinkled man in a warehouse coat. He held the door as Peter and Barry man-handled their luggage in and down the corridor to their dressing room.

Peter waited and watched Barry as he approached the door. He knew Barry had been in the room many times before but tonight was different. Tonight was Barry's night and Peter had laid on a little surprise for him.

Barry noticed it as soon as he approached the door. On the grubby surface of the door was a golden star, about six inches wide, with the name "Barry Sidewick", professionally printed below it. Barry grinned and looked over his shoulder to his uncle.

'Aw! Uncle Peter!.. Did you?..' He dropped his baggage and swung his arms around Peter and hugged him tightly. 'Thank you.'

Peter shrugged him off. 'Come on, we have people waiting to see us on stage!'

Peter was due on first. It was seven thirty and Barry started to unpack Peter's dress and prosthetic bosom. He knew he would have to get himself dressed during Peter's performance but he knew there was plenty of time, as Peter's show lasted an hour.

He helped Peter on with his bosom and did up the straps on the back. 'At lease you don't have to wear one of these for your act,' said Peter as he ran his finger under each of the straps that held the prosthetic in place. Barry giggled and nodded.

'Yes. If I had to wear this thing, I'd fall flat on my face with the weight.'

There was a knock on the door and Peter said, 'Come in!' It was Eric, the manager. He glanced at the half-dressed Peter but then quickly returned his gaze to Barry, where it lingered as he spoke to Peter.

'Just checking we are all present and correct.' He smiled at Barry and continued. 'We have almost a full house this evening.' Barry's face showed signs of distress and Eric touched his arm. 'And they've all come to see you,' he said. Barry didn't like the feel of Eric's greasy hand on his arm and he pulled it away gracefully, not wanting to encourage such intimacy.

Peter turned, about to begin his makeup. 'A full house! That's nice.' He too noticed the worried look on Barry's face and he told Eric to leave them to get ready.

'Don't worry, my dear. You'll be great!' Barry looked at him directly in the eye.

'Are you sure?'

Peter pulled out his purse and told Barry to go to the bar and get them both a drink -- to steady their nerves, he added. Barry wasn't sure if he should be drinking before a performance but he realised there may not be a performance if he can't learn to relax. He took the note being wafted in front of him and Peter said, 'And don't forget the change.'

Barry pushed his way through the crowds to the bar. He was nodded at by a few of the regulars and one man asked him if he could buy him a drink. Barry ignored them. He was in professional mode now and he had to focus.

He ordered two tall Martini's and waited patiently. The act on stage was a young man doing Madonna. Barry watched for a while but he could see the young man had no idea about style or performance. Just another amateur, he thought. He was handed the two drinks and made his way through the swinging crowds of young men. His phone buzzed in his pocket but he couldn't get to it. He let it ring and by the time he got back to the dressing room, it had stopped.

Peter's eyes widened as Barry passed him his drink. 'Ah! Just what I need!' Barry put his drink down and looked at the screen of his phone. He read the text: "One Missed Call from Justin."

Peter noticed and asked if it was anything important. 'No. Just a call from Justin. Probably wanting to wish me the best for tonight. I'll put it on silent while we are working and I'll call him later.'

'So. How's it going with Justin. He seems a nice lad?'

Barry blushed. 'Yes he is... For a policeman, I mean.' Peter smiled and sipped his drink.

'Beth says it's getting serious,' said Peter lifting his big wig in place and fastening it with clips. Barry became brightened and replied,

'Oh! Don't listen to her. She knows nothing.' Barry stood up and put on his professional face. 'Business comes first!' he said, coming around behind Peter and attaching his fake diamond necklace. Peter frowned and put his hand on Barry's hand.

'No. My dear. You are wrong.' Barry looked at him in the mirror, surprised at the statement. 'Business is very important... But love must always come first. Love is the only real purpose to life. It doesn't matter how successful you become in life or how much money you make, it is all pointless if you have nobody to share your life with.'

Barry looked at his uncle and smiled. 'Thanks uncle.'

Peter looked the clock on the wall. He was due on in five minutes. Barry cleared the way, so his big dress could get through the door and he stood back holding it open for him. 'Now try and get yourself ready while I'm on. I'll give you a hand during my mid show break but I won't have a lot of time. Barry nodded and let Peter pass him and he headed down towards the back of the stage. He could hear the manager warming up the crowd and preparing them for Peter's show. Barry suddenly felt nervous. He was on next.

Twenty Seven

Beth held onto Gerald's arm tightly as they entered the bustling and noisy bar. They giggled like a couple of schoolgirls and Beth cleared the way to the side table Peter had reserved for them. Gerald sat down, his eyes staring at all of the young men around him in their ripped jeans and white T-shirts. He seemed entranced.

'I'll get us some drinks,' said Beth. The old man just nodded and watched the act on stage. 'That's Peter up there!' she shouted over the noise. 'Barry's uncle!' The old man's eyebrows raised and he smiled.

'Really? Wow!'

She looked up at the stage and Peter noticed her and pointed to her as he sang the words, 'Hungry Again!' She blushed and headed for the bar. When she returned the old man was swaying in his seat, obviously enjoying himself.

'What do you think?' asked Beth as she placed a colourful cocktail in front of the old man. 'Isn't he great?' The professor nodded and added,

'And such style, as well.' He sipped his cocktail through its long curly straw and winced at it's strong taste. 'I can't wait to see Barry up there.'

'Yes. I haven't seen his act yet either. I've watched him prancing around in his Y-fronts, singing into his hair brush but it's not the same, is it?'

The old man, obviously trying to picture the image in his mind said,' I'd like to see that too.' Beth slapped him jokingly on the arm and told him to behave.

Peter's show was reaching its halfway point and he thanked his audience and said he would be back after a short break. Beth spotted the nod from Peter and she left the professor surveying his onlookers and joined Peter at the back of the stage.

'Brilliant Peter, brilliant!' she said as she held open the door for him and watched as Barry, wearing only his underwear and slippers, stood aside to let him into the seat in front of the mirror.

Peter was perspiring and Barry did his usual role of wafting him with a sheet of stiff card while Peter mopped himself with a small towel and re-applied some makeup. Peter looked at Barry and he could see he was really nervous.

'How you feeling?' Barry looked in shock. 'It's a great crowd, so they're going to love you.' Beth butted in,

'The professor's here.' Barry looked up and smiled. 'He's having a rave of a time. Eyeing all the young totty -- he's in his element.'

Barry laughed and relaxed a little. Peter looked at the clock and drunk from the glass of iced water, Barry had got ready for his break.

'I wasn't expecting it to be this busy... On my first night,' said Barry holding his hand to his chin. He realised that he was beginning to mimic his uncle and wondered whether that was a good thing or not.

Peter, conscious of the time and realising there was little he could do now to reassure Barry asked Beth if she would mind helping Barry prepare for his turn. He was due on in half an hour.

Beth nodded and opened the door for Peter to return to the stage. 'Good luck, darlin'. You knock 'em dead!' Barry smiled and watched as Peter walked the short walk to the back of the stage. Within seconds he heard the manager announce his name again and the crowd roared.

It was the roar that frightened Barry. He had worked for months getting ready for this day and now he wasn't sure if he was ready. Was he making a big mistake. Should he just get a job in a chemist, like Beth, he wondered.

'Wow! Did you hear that? They love him.'

'Yes. They do... But will they love me?' said Barry as he looked in the mirror. Beth put her arm around him and squeezed him close.

'Of course they will. You're the north east's biggest new attraction -- according to Peter, that is.'

'Yes but I've never even performed in front of an audience. So... How will I know for sure?' Beth turned Barry's skinny body towards the mirror and looked at him straight in the eye.

'By getting your frock on and putting on your makeup and that wig and then getting out there and bloody doing it!' Barry smiled and he knew she was right. Beth glanced down at Barry's Y-fronts. She sucked in a short breath and held herself back from giggling.

'You seem to be missing something,' she said nodding down towards Barry's crotch. 'Oh my god! You haven't had the operation and not told anyone, have you?'

Barry nudged her away and told her to shut up. 'It's a trade secret,' he said, covering his crotch with his dress and telling her to fetch his shoes from the bag.

Within a few minutes, Barry was ready. His dress was on, his wig clipped in place and his shoes fastened. Beth stood Barry in front of the mirror again and straightened his dress. She stood back and said, 'Are you ready?'

'Ready as I'll ever be.'

Beth looked at the clock and new Peter's act was about to end and she knew the old man would be wondering where she was. 'Come on then. This is it.' She held out her hand and Barry grasped it tight.

They walked to the back of the stage and stood next to the manager, Eric. He glanced at Barry up and down and said, 'Nice. You're on next.'

Peter finished his last song and thanked his audience. Eric pulled back the curtain and let Peter out, before heading on stage himself.

Peter was sweating and he looked at Barry, all ready to go. He couldn't think of anything to say, so he just opened his arms and Barry nuzzled into his shoulder. Beth slapped him on the back as they all heard Eric say, 'Please welcome on to the stage a marvellous new talent. A bright new star in the northern sky. Barry Sidewick!'

The curtain was pulled back and Eric welcomed Barry onto the stage. He glanced at Peter and then at Beth and he entered the stage, with its bright lights and the music began. Beth and Peter stood behind the curtain and listened as Barry began his first number. 'All That Jazz...' The crowd roared and Peter knew he was going to be fine.

'Give me five minutes to get out of this and I'll join you front of stage,' said Peter as he darted down the corridor.

When Beth returned to the table she saw the old professor chatting to a camp young man and she decided not to interfere, in case he'd pulled, she joked to herself.

She found a space at the bar and ordered a couple of drinks. Barry danced around the stage like he owned it and Beth could see he was loving every minute of it. She was relieved after his earlier nerves.

The crowd were loving it to. Shouts of, 'We love you Barry' and 'Another one, ' rebounded around the audience. Peter joined her, grinning from ear to ear.

'They seem to like him, then?'

'Yeah! They love him!' she shouted over the roars of appreciation. Barry started his next number. A much quieter, calmer piece and he gripped the microphone stand and swayed to the music. The change in style moved the audience and they whistled and shouted out, 'Yes!' At Barry's obvious skill at pleasing them.

Peter was in a buzz of his own. Barry was great and the atmosphere was amazing. He sipped on his drink and leant against the bar. Out of the corner of his eye he saw a face he recognised. Pushing their way through the crowd was inspector McGarry and young Justin.

He waved and nodded towards them, assuming it was Barry they had come to see. The expression on both of their faces didn't look good. It looked like they had both been running and when McGarry saw Peter, he quickly pulled him to his mouth so he could make himself heard.

'We need to speak to you urgently,' he said and Peter, puzzled, told him to follow him. He led the way back to the dressing room and Beth followed behind, taking note of Justin's cute bottom.

The din of the stage was muffled as Peter closed the door behind him. Peter was quite high with Barry's success and wasn't in the mood to discus police matters right now.

'We've been trying to ring you all evening but we haven't been able to get you on your home number.' Peter butted in,

'Yes. Sorry about that. The storm...' McGarry butted in again,

'Yes we know about the telephone line being down -- we checked with the phone company. We also tried your mobile and,' he looked at Justin, 'Finkle also tried to ring Barry but we couldn't get in touch with either of you.'

Peter was about to explain that they turn there phones off when working when Justin butted in. 'This is very important!'

Peter looked startled. McGarry took a deep breath and explained.

'We have managed to get a full confession from Greg Wilkes for all of the murders the con men have committed.' Peter's face glowed with excitement.

'Wow! That's brilliant!' McGarry butted in again.

'Yes, yes but the point is Greg has told us how they killed Joe Trolley!' Peter's jaw dropped.

'He says that Collins doctored some postage stamps with poison, knowing that Jo liked to write letters and would lick the stamps -- and that is what killed him! The problem is, we can't find the stamps anywhere in Joe's house. The scenes of crime report said there were some stamps in Joe's desk draw but when we checked they were missing.'

Peter screamed and the others stood back in shock. He started to shake violently, not sure what to do. He fumbled for his phone and flipped up its cover and pressed the speed dial for home. The phone was dead, then he remembered.

'Oh my god...Oh my god!' repeated Peter. He paced back and forth around the dressing room and the others watched him.

'What's up Peter?' asked Beth as she held him by the elbow.

'The stamps... The stamps... They are sitting on top of a pile of Christmas cards on my sideboard!' McGarry stood up and Justin held on to Peter, who was becoming hysterical.

'Calm down,' said McGarry. 'What do you mean?'

'I took the stamps from Joe's desk when I was there last. I didn't think he'd be needing them anymore.' He held his hands to the side of his head and screamed again.

'What's wrong,' asked Beth.

'Bill said he would catch up with the last of the Christmas cards tonight and get them all stamped up, ready for the post tomorrow!'

The door swung open and in walked Barry, sweating and grinning.

'What's up?' he said as he surveyed the group and noticed his uncle Peter in a bit of a state.

Peter took Barry's hand and dragged him out of the door. 'Come on... We have to get home NOW!'

McGarry pushed in front. 'Come on. We'll go in the squad car.' He held open the fire exit door and everybody piled out past him into the car park.

Barry said, 'But I'm due back on stage in five minutes.' Beth pulled him by the arm and whispered in his ear what had happened and he immediately hitched up his dress and got into the back of the squad car.

Justin was at the wheel and he turned on the flashing lights and the siren. The car sped through the streets, ignoring traffic lights and pedestrians. He spun the fast car around the corner and headed up the high street towards Peter's house. Barry felt exhilarated and watched as cars and people moved out of the way to allow them through.

They turned off the high street and into Peter's road. The car was brought to a sudden stop when Justin slammed on his brakes. The road was totally blocked by a fallen tree. Peter panicked and pushed open the car door. The others followed as he hitched up his Dolly Parton dress and ran with all his might along the street, followed by Barry in his Liza dress and Beth.

They approached the house and Peter could see Bill through the living room window, sitting at the dining room table. The light of the room illuminated the foot path as they bounded towards him. Beth got her key out ready, realising that neither Peter or Barry would likely have theirs.

She pushed ahead of Peter and stuck her key in the lock, twisted it and pushed the door open. She stood to one side, letting Peter burst in. Barry and Peter watched as Bill held a stamp in his hand.

They both yelled, 'NO!' and they leaped onto Bill, pulling his hand away from his mouth. Bill's chair fell to one side and he didn't know what was going on.

'What the...' he said as Peter gripped his wrist firmly and Barry held his skinny hand over his mouth.

Peter shouted at Bill, 'How many stamps have you licked?' Bill looked at him, confused as to what all the commotion was about and he thought for a moment.

'None.'

Peter looked at the pile of cards and envelopes on the table top, several with stamps already fixed to their envelopes.

'None?'

Bill nodded. 'These are self-adhesive stamps. I got them from the post office this morning.' Peter released his grip and stood up. He went back into the hall and pulled out his jacket. He felt in the inside pocket and pulled out the sheet of stamps he'd got from Joe's house. Bill noticed them and said,

'Oh good. I'll need a few more.'

Read the next book in the series:

Cruising For Beginners
The Second Book In The Drag Queen Detective Series

ISBN: 978-1-907900-03-7

30594852R00117

Printed in Poland
by Amazon Fulfillment
Poland Sp. z o.o., Wrocław